A Harlequin

JANET DAILEY

Collector's Edition

Harlequin

JANET DAILEY

Collector's Editions

A Harlequin

JANET DAILEY

Collector's Edition

Harlequin Books

TORONTO • NEW YORK • LOS ANGELES • LONDON
AMSTERDAM • PARIS • SYDNEY • HAMBURG
STOCKHOLM • ATHENS • TOKYO • MILAN

These books by Janet Dailey were originally published as
follows:

HEART OF STONE
Copyright © 1980 by Janet Dailey
First published by Mills & Boon Limited in 1980
Harlequin Presents edition (#391) published
November 1980

BIG SKY COUNTRY
Copyright © 1977 by Janet Dailey
First published by Mills & Boon Limited in 1977
Harlequin Presents edition (#244) published July 1978

ISBN 0-373-80604-3
First edition October 1982

CONTENTS

HEART OF STONE

"ANY WOMAN WOULD SATISFY YOU, BROCK."

And Stephanie knew that the words she spoke were true.

"But you're the one in my arms. Why don't you satisfy me?" Brock challenged softly.

Stephanie's heart ran away with itself at the thought. Both his arms were around her, his fingers spread as they roamed over her shoulders, her back, slowly caressing and molding her to him, his virility a potent force that left her weak. Her head was tipped back, enabling her to look into his eyes. They were smiling at her, with an inner satisfaction and supreme confidence, the certainty of his ability to seduce her.

Stephanie supposed she was transparent; her pride was injured that she was such an easy conquest for him. But was there a woman born who could deny his attraction for long?

CHAPTER ONE

THERE WAS a sudden flurry of activity outside Stephanie's office. Located in the heart of the luxurious New Hampshire inn, it gave her ready access to all phases of the operation. Through the open doorway Stephanie had a partial view of the front desk, which gave her a feeling of the comings and goings of the guests. Across the hall was the housekeeping department. The office next to hers belonged to her brother, Perry Hall, the manager of the inn, and her boss.

When Mrs. Adamson, the dining-room hostess, went hurrying past Stephanie's door, her curiosity was throughly aroused. Something unusual was going on. Even though she had actually worked in the White Boar Inn a short three months,

Stephanie felt the accelerated tempo of the inn's pulse, a tense quickening of interest.

The unbalanced ledger sheet on her desk was forgotten as she speared the lead pencil through the chestnut hair above her ear and rose from her chair. Bookkeeping was invariably the last department to know anything if she allowed routine to run its normal course. Since Perry was her brother, she didn't choose to sit back and wait to be informed. She had been isolated from the mainstream of life for too many years to let it continue now that she had rejoined it.

In the hallway, she glanced toward the front desk. Her blue eyes noted the expressions of harried excitement in the faces of the usually unflappable pair manning the registration counter. It was rare indeed for the arrival of an important personage to create such a disturbance, since the inn catered to the wealthy and the notable. Besides, every room was already taken, occupied by guests on hand to view the autumn splendor of the White Mountains, and there were reservations all the way through the winter season to spring.

Puzzled by the unknown cause of all this barely subdued commotion, Stephanie absently fingered the scarab pendant suspended by a gold chain to nestle in the valley between her breasts, the loose weave of her white rollneck sweater providing a backdrop for the jewelry. The slight frown remained in her expression as she walked the few feet to her brother's office. The door was standing open and she paused within its frame, not wanting to interrupt her brother's consultation with Mrs. Adamson.

"Get a bottle on ice right away," he was instructing the woman, who was hastily making notes on a pad. Perry, too, was consulting the papers in front of him, not glancing up to see Stephanie in the doorway. His brown hair was rumpled as if he had run his fingers through it many times. "Fix a tray with a selection of cheeses and fresh fruits to go with it. You'd better recheck the wine cellar and make sure you have an ample supply of his favorite wines in stock, too. Alert your staff. I want them on their toes in case he decides to dine in the restaurant this evening. I don't want—Flowers!" Perry interrupted himself to exclaim. "I nearly forgot the damn flowers." He punched the buzzer to summon his secretary.

For once the young girl appeared within seconds. She looked pale and anxious, more timid than usual. Despite her youth, Connie York was highly skilled and competent. Her chief flaw was a marked lack of self-confidence, which was blatantly in evidence at the moment.

"Yes, Mr. Hall?" She made a question of her response to his summons, her small face pinched into tense lines of unease and framed with dark hair.

His upward glance took note of Stephanie in the doorway, but he didn't acknowledge her presence in his office beyond that. "Call the florist. If they can't have a bouquet of roses delivered here within ninety minutes, I want you to pick them up."

"Yes, sir." Her head bobbed in quick agreement, but she didn't make any move to follow through with the order.

Perry, who was usually extraordinarily patient with his self-effacing secretary, sent her an irritated look. "You aren't going to get it done standing there, Connie. Go on!"

"I know, but . . . ." She wavered uncertainly.

"What is it?" he demanded in short temper. "I haven't got time to coax it out of you."

Stephanie's gaze wandered over her brother's face in surprise. Six years older than herself, he rarely allowed stressful situations to shake him. He had been more than just her big brother: he had been her idol for as long as she could remember. Life hadn't been easy for him . . . or for her, either. Their mother had died when Stephanie was only four. Perry had played surrogate mother to her, fixing meals and keeping house while their father worked long hours, skilled only as a ski instructor and bartender, to make ends meet.

Five years ago, when Stephanie was seventeen, it had seemed the world would become their oyster. Perry had obtained a scholarship to attend a prestigious postgraduate law school and Stephanie had been accepted by a prominent women's college. Then a freak skiing accident had left their father a paraplegic, and Perry had given up his scholarship to take the position of assistant manager of this inn, while Stephanie stayed home to take care of their father. A virulent pneumonia virus had claimed their father four months ago. In many ways, his death had been a blessing— for him and for them.

Stephanie hadn't completely adjusted to the freedom from responsibility that had matured both of them beyond their years, while it deprived them of the pleasures of youth. The night course she had taken in accounting, to supplement their income by doing bookkeeping at home for small businesses, had provided her with the experience to take the post as bookkeeper at the inn when her predecessor had retired with a few grumblings about nepotism, because her brother had become the manager in the last year.

She liked working at the inn, being with people and being part of things. Most of all, she liked working with her brother. She had come to respect his competency in a position the duties of which were far ranging and varied. Perry always appeared to be totally in control whether dealing with a crisis in the restaurant kitchen or organizing the staff. Which was why Stephanie was surprised by his harried attitude at the moment. It didn't seem in character.

"It's just that . . . I was wondering . . . ." Connie was stumbling over the reason for her hesitation.

"I don't have all day. Please get to the point," Perry ordered.

"It's your appointment," his secretary began, intimidated by his abruptness.

"I told you to cancel them." His mouth thinned with impatience.

"Yes, but . . . ." She bit her lower lip.

Perry appeared to mentally count to ten in an effort to control his temper. "But what, Connie?" he asked with forced evenness.

"You're supposed to speak at a luncheon this noon." She rushed the explanation. "It's been on the agenda for two months. They couldn't possibly get anyone to take your place at such late notice."

Perry groaned. "Is that today?"

"Yes, sir." Anxiety tortured Connie's expression. "What should I do?"

"Do? There's nothing you can do," he sighed. "I'll have to attend the luncheon, but cancel everything else. And get those flowers."

"Yes, sir." With a nod of her head, the girl disappeared inside her adjoining office.

Returning his attention to the woman in front of his desk, Perry raked a hand through his dark hair again, adding to its disorder. "You know the routine, Mrs. Adamson. I trust you to handle it." He cast a glance at his wristwatch, in effect dismissing the hostess.

Stephanie stepped to one side so the woman could exit through the open door. From the conversation she had overheard, she had a general idea what was happening. With the exception of the private suite, the inn was fully booked. And the suite was reserved exclusively for the owner or his personal guests. Before she had a chance to ask whose arrival was anticipated, Perry was addressing her.

"Whatever your problem is, Stephanie, it will have to wait—unless someone has absconded with the receipts. In that case, I don't want to know about it for three days," he declared with a tired shake of his head.

"I don't have any problem," she assured him. "I'm just trying to figure out what's going on. Who's coming? The place is in a quiet uproar— if there is such a thing."

Sighing, Perry rocked back in his swivel chair. Eyes the same blue as her own, skimmed her slender figure in its white sweater and green tartan skirt. A faint smile touched his mouth when his gaze returned to her face with its soft frame of sleek chestnut hair.

"Brock is making another one of his impromptu visits. He called a half an hour ago to say he'd be here by two this afternoon. He's driving up from Boston," he explained, as tension etched lines in his strong face.

"Aha!" Stephanie mocked him to ease his concern. "Now I understand why everyone is jumping at the slightest sound. The big man himself is coming to inspect his property."

"It's all right for you to joke about it. Canfield expects the best and I am the one who has to explain why, if he doesn't get it." Perry rubbed his fingers against a spot in the center of his forehead.

"I don't know what you're worrying about." Stephanie walked to the back of his chair and let her hands knead the taut cords between his neck and shoulders. "Don't forget I've been keeping

16

the books for the past three months. I know how very well the inn has been doing. Brock Canfield can't possibly have any complaints about your work or how you run the inn."

"We have done well," he admitted, relaxing under the massage of her hands. "If that trend continues through the winter ski season, we should have our best year ever."

"That proves my point, doesn't it?" she reasoned.

"The point will be proved only when it's accomplished," Perry reminded her. "In the meantime, Brock is going to judge by what he sees on this trip."

"He won't have any complaints." Stephanie was certain of that. The service at the inn was flawless. Even the hard-to-please guests found little to grumble about. "Do you know this will be my first opportunity to meet this paragon of all manhood, Brock Canfield?" she realized. "You have worked here what? Five years? Everybody talks about him as if he was God. Depending on their sex, they either tremble or quiver when they hear his name." She laughed. "I've heard him alternately described as a ruthless tycoon or a gorgeous hunk of man. Now I'll be able to find out for myself which is the real Brock Canfield!"

"He's both, plus a few other things." Her

17

brother took hold of one of her hands to end the rubdown and pull her around to the side of his chair. Handsome in an attractive kind of way, he studied her for a quiet second. "I have this luncheon to attend, so I'll have to deputize you to stand in for me in case I'm not back when Brock arrives."

"Me?" Stephanie frowned her surprise.

"Somebody has to be on hand to welcome him. Connie practically cringes every time he looks at her," Perry explained with a wry grimace. "And Vic is home sleeping after being on duty all night," he added, referring to the night manager. "I can't think of anyone else. Do you mind?"

"Of course not. What do I have to do, besides being on hand to greet him?" Despite her willing agreement, Stephanie experienced a shiver of unease at some of the more formidable descriptions she'd heard applied to the inn's owner.

"Show him to his suite and make certain everything is in order. Connie is getting the flowers and Mrs. Adamson will have a bottle of champagne on ice, along with some cheese and fruit. In general, just see that he has everything he wants."

"That sounds simple enough," she shrugged.

"Watch your step, Stephanie," her brother advised, suddenly serious.

She was confused by the warning. "I'm not likely to say anything that would offend him." She wasn't the outspoken type. Most of the time she was very tactful—able to curb her tongue despite the provocation.

"I know you wouldn't." He dismissed that possibility with a wave of his hand. "I was trying to say that you should stay clear of Brock Canfield. He goes through women the way a gambler goes through a deck of cards. He's rich, good-looking in a way, and can be both persuasive and forceful. I'm told that can be an irresistible combination."

"I've heard a few stories about him," Stephanie admitted.

"I wouldn't like to see you get mixed up with him, because I know you'd be hurt. Honestly, Steph, I'm not trying to play the heavy-handed big brother." Perry seemed to smile at himself. "It's just that I know he's going to take one look at you and get ideas. You haven't had all that much experience with men—especially his kind."

"Experienced or not, I think I can take care of myself." She didn't mind that Perry was worried about her. In fact, she liked the idea that he cared enough about her to try to protect her. A smile hovered around the corners of her mouth. "Is that why you never brought him home to dinner when I suggested it during his other visits?"

"Partly," her brother admitted. "But mostly it was because Brock isn't your home-cooked meal type. He's smooth and finished, like a diamond that's been cut into the perfect stone, hard and unfeeling."

"And diamonds don't sit down at a table set with ironstone flatware," Stephanie concluded in understanding.

"Something like that," Perry agreed. "Now, off with you," he ordered in a mock threat. "I have to find my notes for the luncheon speech."

She started for the door and hesitated short of her goal. "When will you be back—in case Brock asks?"

"Between half-past one and two."

"Maybe he'll be late," she suggested and walked to the door.

Forty-five minutes later, Perry stuck his head inside her office to let her know he was leaving to keep his luncheon engagement. "Take care of Brock if he arrives before I get back," he reminded her, unnecessarily.

"I will," she promised. "Good luck with the speech."

He waved and left. A few minutes later Stephanie closed her office to have lunch. Her appetite was all but nonexistent, so she chose a salad plate and picked at it for twenty minutes before giving up. A few minutes before one, she obtained the key to the private suite from Mary at the front desk and checked to be certain all was in readiness for Brock Canfield's arrival.

There had been no occasion for Stephanie to enter the private suite before. It consisted of a spacious sitting room, an equally large bedroom with a king-sized bed and an enormous bath. Stephanie explored it with unashamed curiosity.

Bronze-tipped, double-paned windows offered an unparalleled view of the White Mountains cloaked in their rust and gold autumn colors. Sunlight streaming through the glass laid a pattern of gold on the stark white floor of Italian ceramic, set in a herringbone design. There was nothing about the sitting room that resembled New England except for the scene outside its windows.

The furnishings included a white leather armchair and ottoman. A pair of short sofas were upholstered in natural Haitian cotton with coffee tables of antique white. The walls were covered with grass cloth in an ivory shade. A floor-to-ceiling cabinet, which included a shelf for a television to be rolled out, had been built into one

21

wall. A glass-topped rattan table and four chairs were the only natural wood pieces in the room, besides an eight-foot-high secretary, hand carved in walnut. A gold-leaf, coromandel screen opened to reveal a bar. In total, it was an eclectic blend of periods and designs.

Stephanie took note of the bouquet of long-stemmed roses on the coffee table. The arrangement had an oriental touch with bare branches rising above the blood-red blooms. A vintage bottle of champagne was on ice in a silver bucket supported by a stud. A tray of cheese as well as an attractive bowl of fresh fruit was on the rattan table.

When Stephanie ventured into the bedroom, she stepped onto thick, shrimp-colored carpeting. The same color was repeated but dominated by black in the patterned bedspread and matching drapes. An ornate ebony headboard adorned the king-sized bed and was flanked by carved night-stands of the same dark hardwood. A hunting scene was depicted on an elephant tusk and a second was repeated in a massive collage. They gave the room the masculine accent.

The bathroom was a bit overwhelming in its luxury, with the shrimp carpeting extending into it. A white Jacuzzi bathtub was set in a platform faced with Italian marble that continued all the way up to the ceiling: The wall area not covered with marble was hung with black silk, a collection of framed South American butterflies making use of its backdrop. The bath towels were all a very sensual black velour material, thick and rich looking.

Leaving the suite was like stepping into another world. The inn was luxurious, but it attempted to give its guests the flavor of New England. It was obvious that Brock Canfield had decorated the suite to please himself. Stephanie wasn't certain if she liked the result or whether she was indulging in a little inverted snobbery.

As she entered the lobby, she thought she preferred the wide spaciousness of the white-painted woodwork and its massive stone fireplace with the welcoming warmth of the flames emitting the pungent aroma of woodsmoke. Expensive Currier and Ives lithographs adorned the white walls and added the flavor of New England to the lobby. The brass chandelier suspended from the ceiling was a nuisance to clean, Stephanie knew, but the hurricane globes were attractive and homey.

She stopped at the front desk to return the key. "Any sign of Mr. Canfield yet, Mary?"

The mere mention of the owner's name seemed to unnerve the usually calm woman. "Mr. Canfield? No, not that I know of. Ben, have you seen him?'' She suddenly didn't trust her own answer and sought the confirmation of the bellboy.

"No. He hasn't arrived yet.'' He was much more positive.

"I'll be in my office,'' Stephanie replied. "Let me know as soon as he comes.''

Circling behind the registration counter, she walked down the short hallway to her office. She left the door open so she could be aware of the activity going on outside her four walls. The excited buzzing and whispering hadn't lessened since the news had circulated through the inn's grapevine of the imminent arrival of its owner. There was electricity in the air, and Stephanie wasn't immune to its volatile charge.

Before she put her bag away, she paused in front of the small mirror on a side wall to freshen her lipstick. But the new coat of bronzed pink on her mouth only accented the faint pallor in her cheeks. She stroked on a hint of blusher, then retouched her long lashes with mascara. By the time she was finished, she had completely redone her makeup.

Studying her reflection, she decided she was attractive but definitely not a raving beauty. The combination of thick chestnut hair and Corinthian-blue eyes was pleasing, but not startling. Her figure was slender with all the proper curves,

but not eye-popping. There was a certain fresh-
ness about her, although she looked twenty-two.

All the while, she assured herself that this assessment had nothing to do with Brock Canfield
or the warning Perry had given. Still, there was
a little part of her that was wondering what it
would be like if someone like Brock Canfield
made a pass at her—a passing curiosity, no more
than that, she insisted, just a flattering thought.

"Stephanie!" Mary hissed from the doorway.
"*He* just drove up out front. Ben's going out to
get his luggage now. And he has a woman with
him."

Initially Stephanie smiled at the woman passing the information in such a frantic whisper.
Who would hear? And what would it matter? But
the last sentence wiped the smile from her face.
Too late she remembered that in the past, Perry
had mentioned that Brock Canfield often brought
his current girl friend with him.

But what was the procedure? Did the woman
stay in his suite? There wasn't any choice, was
there? There wasn't a single other empty room
in the entire inn. But she was attacked by the
same uncertainty that Mary had suffered earlier,
and the need to have someone back up her conclusion.

"Was Perry informed that Mr. Canfield was bringing a guest?" she asked the desk clerk.

"He didn't say anything to me about it," Mary replied with a negative shake of her head.

"Mr. Canfield wouldn't expect us to . . . have a separate room for her, would he?" There was no longer any need for the blusher on her cheeks. Mother Nature was doing an excellent job of providing color for Stephanie. "I mean, he didn't give us any warning."

"I seriously doubt if he wants her in a separate room." Mary's voice was both dry and suggestive. She glanced toward the lobby and quickly hissed, "He's coming through the door now!"

Stephanie took a deep breath to calm her suddenly jumping nerves and mentally crossed her fingers. Be calm, cool and collected, she told herself as she started toward the lobby. What did she have to be nervous about? Brock Canfield was only a man.

CHAPTER TWO

ONLY A MAN. That phrase Stephanie instantly revised the minute she saw the tall, dark-haired man in the lobby. Lean and virile, he was completely finished masculinity. The planes and contours of his tanned face had been chiseled into the final product of total manliness. An expensive topcoat hung from a set of broad shoulders and tapered slightly to indicate narrow hips before falling the length of his thighs to stop below the knees. Its dark color was contrasted by the white silk scarf around his neck.

Yet not for one minute did Stephanie believe that the elegant male attire covered a body that was other than superbly fit and muscled. It was evident in his ease of stride and natural coordination. Perry's description became very clear—

a hard, finished diamond. Brock Canfield was all that and all male.

Stephanie felt the awesome power of his attraction before she ever walked in front of the counter to greet him. It was even more potent when she came under the observation of his metallic gray eyes. Their lightness was compelling, at odds with the darkness of his brown hair.

His gaze made a thorough appraisal of her feminine assets as she crossed half the width of the lobby. His study was so openly one of male interest that she would have been offended if it had come from another man. But, no matter how hard she searched, she couldn't come up with any sense of indignation. Almost the exact opposite happened. Her pulse quickened with the inner excitement his look had generated.

Seeking a balance, she switched her attention to the blonde clinging to his arm. There was a surface impression of class and sophistication. Yet beneath it, Stephanie noticed the blue cashmere sweater was a size too small. The fine wool was stretched to emphasize the full roundness of the girl's breasts. So was the material in the complementing shade of darker blue pants that was forced to hug her hips and thighs.

Brock Canfield might regard the result as sexy and alluring, but Stephanie thought it was disgusting. Then she wondered if she was being bitchy. She didn't have time to decide as she reached the point where she had to speak.

"Hello, Mr. Canfield. I'm Stephanie Hall," she introduced herself, and offered her hand. "I hope you had a pleasant trip."

"An uneventful one." The grip of his hand was firm, its warmth seeming to spread up her arm and through her system. His gaze had narrowed in sharp curiosity. "Stephanie Hall," he repeated her name, his smooth voice giving it an unusual texture to the sound of her spoken name. "I wasn't aware Perry had got married. When did this happen?"

"Perry isn't married," she replied in quick surprise, then tried to explain. "At least not to me. I mean, he isn't married to anyone." She regained control of her wayward tongue and managed a more controlled, "I'm his sister."

"Ah, yes." He seemed to step back, to withdraw somehow, yet he didn't move except to release her hand. "I remember now that he mentioned he had a younger sister. Somehow I had the impression you were much younger."

Stephanie decided it was best if she didn't comment on that. "I'm sorry Perry isn't here to meet you himself, but he's a speaker at a club luncheon today. He should be back within the hour."

"Fine." His faint nod was indifferent. The blonde arched closer to him as if to remind him of her presence. It earned her a glance that was amused and tolerant, yet Stephanie detected no affection in his look. "Helen, I'd like you to meet Stephanie Hall, her brother manages the inn for me. This is Helen Collins."

But he deliberately omitted identifying the blonde's relationship to him. What could he have said? That she was his current mistress, his current lover? Stephanie wasn't certain if she could have handled such frankness. The glint in his eye made her suspect that Brock Canfield had guessed that. She didn't like the idea that he might find it—and her—amusing.

"May I show you to your suite?" Her stilted suggestion sounded as stiff and defensive as she felt.

"I think it would be an excellent idea." The line of his mouth was slanted in faint mockery.

The action pulled her gaze to his mouth. The firm set of male lips seemed to hint at worldly experience, their line strong and clean. Stephanie's curiosity ran rampant, wondering how expert they were.

Forcing a smile onto her mouth, she turned and walked to the desk to obtain the key from Mary. The woman slipped two keys into her outstretched palm. Out of the corner of her eye, Stephanie noticed Ben struggling with the luggage and knew he would be following them to the suite.

When she rejoined Brock Canfield and his female companion, the couple had already started in the general direction of the hall leading to the private suite. Stephanie would have preferred simply to give the man the keys, since he obviously knew the way, but she remembered Perry's instructions—take him to the suite and make sure he has everything he needs.

"Do you work here, Miss Hall? Or are you just helping your brother out?" The question came from Helen Collins, her tone on the acid side.

"I work here," she replied smoothly, and tried not to let her instinctive dislike of the blonde become obvious.

"In what capacity?" The masculine thickness of an eyebrow was arched in her direction, again assessing and appraising, but from an intellectual level.

"I take care of the books." Her answer was cool, prompted by an uncertainty whether Brock Canfield hadn't actually known or merely forgotten.

"So you're the reason the monthly reports have

suddenly become legible these last few months," he concluded.

Something in the remark had been faintly taunting. Stephanie was spared from replying as they reached the suite. She unlocked the door and quickly led the way inside, anxious to bring the task to an end and regroup her scattered senses.

"It's stunning, Brock!" Helen exclaimed, betraying that it was her first visit to the suite. She released his arm when she saw the roses on the coffee table. "And roses! They're gorgeous. You knew they were my favorite." She bent to inhale the fragrance of one of the large blooms, and Stephnie worried about the seam of her pants and whether the thread could stand the strain.

"There's a bottle of champagne on ice for you," Stephanie murmured and made a small gesture with her hand in the general direction of the silver bucket.

Brock Canfield's gray eyes skimmed her face, their look mocking and amused, as if he sensed her discomfort. There wasn't any need for him to comment on the information, since Helen discovered the bottle of champagne seconds afterward.

"Darling, you think of everything," she declared, and plucked the bottle out of the ice. She wrapped it in the towel and brought it to him. "Open it, Brock."

As he shrugged out of his topcoat, Stephanie saw her opening to be excused. "If there's anything else, Mr. Canfield—" she began.

"Don't leave yet, Miss Hall." His smooth order stopped the backward step Stephanie had taken to begin her retreat. But he offered no more explanation than the simple command that she remain.

She stood silently by, trying to appear as composed and calm as her jittery nerves would permit, while he tossed his coat and scarf over the white leather chair. A minute later his suit jacket joined them. Then he was expertly popping the cork out of the champagne bottle and filling the two glasses Helen had in her hands.

"Would you care to join us, Miss Hall?" he inquired. "There are more glasses in the bar."

"No, thank you," she refused with stiff politeness. "I have work to do this afternoon."

"One glass of champagne would interfere with your ability to function?" he mocked her, but returned the bottle to the ice bucket without reissuing his offer.

There was a knock at the door. Since Stephanie was closest, she answered it. It was Ben with the luggage. She motioned him inside the room.

"Put it in the bedroom," Helen instructed, and followed him to supervise.

"I think you'll find everything in order, Mr. Canfield." Stephanie tried again to make her exit. "I checked the suite myself before you arrived."

"I'm sure I will," he agreed.

Her opportunity was lost a second time as Ben came out of the bedroom. She was rather surprised when Brock gave him a tip for bringing the luggage. After all, he was the owner, so it wouldn't have been necessary. Ben thanked him and left.

"Here are your keys, Mr. Canfield." Stephanie crossed the front half of the room to give them to him.

He didn't immediately reach out to take them. Instead he turned to set the champagne glass on an antique white table. The white of his shirt complemented his supply muscled torso without emphasizing it. He looked lean and rangy like a wild animal on the prowl.

Minus the suit jacket, he appeared more casual, more approachable. Her unsteady pulse revealed the danger of such thinking, as she dropped the keys in his outstretched hand. The glitter of his gray eyes seemed to mock the action that avoided physical contact.

When Helen Collins appeared in the bedroom

doorway, his gaze slid from Stephanie. He didn't wait for the blonde to speak as he issued his instructions. "Unpack the suitcases, Helen, and make yourself comfortable. I'm going to be tied up for the afternoon."

He was politely but firmly telling his companion to get lost, dismissing her from his presence until he had time for the toy he had brought along to play with. Stephanie watched the curvaceous blonde smother the flash of resentment to smile and blow him a kiss before shutting the bedroom door.

"You don't approve of the arrangement, do you?" Amusement was threaded thickly through his question.

Stephanie worked to school her expression into one of indifference. "I wouldn't presume to pass judgment on your personal affairs, Mr. Canfield. They have nothing to do with me."

"Spoken with the true discretion of an employee to her indiscreet boss," he mocked her reply.

When he absently moved a step closer, Stephanie had to discipline her feet not to move back in an effort to keep a safe distance from him. Her nerve ends tingled with the sexual force of his attraction at such close quarters. The not unpleasant sensation triggered off a whole series of alarm bells in head.

"Will there be anything else, Mr. Canfield?" She made a show of glancing at her watch as if she was running late. "I really should be getting back to my office."

For a long second he held her gaze. Then his glance slid downward as he turned away and slipped the keys into his pocket. "You probably should." He picked up the glass of champagne.

Taking his agreement as permission to leave, Stephanie started toward the door. Relief was sweeping through her, the tension disintegrating with a rush. She could fully understand how curiosity killed the cat.

She was still five feet from the door when Brock Canfield stopped her with a low question. "Did your brother warn you about me?"

The plaid swirled around her knees as she pivoted to face him. "I beg your pardon?"

She felt cornered, trapped like a little brown mouse that almost escaped before a set of claws gently forced it back into the mouth of danger. A faintly wicked smile was deepening the corners of the firm male lips.

"Perry is very conscientious and thorough. That's why I made him manager," Brock stated and let his eyes run over her slender figure. "Surely he told you that I eat little girls like you for breakfast." He sipped at the champagne and gave Stephanie the impression he was drinking the essence of her.

Her throat worked convulsively for a second before she could get an answer out. "Actually, I think Perry said you go through women like a gambler goes through decks of cards." She matched his frankness, but she was shaking inside.

"Very aptly put." His glass was lifted in a mock salute. "Because generally I discard them after very little use—sometimes for no greater reason than that I want something new." Again, he took a drink of champagne and studied her with unnerving steadiness over the rim of the crystal glass. "After all these years of keeping you hidden away, your brother took quite a risk sending you in his place. Why did he do it? Are you supposed to provide me with a distraction so I won't uncover some current problem?"

"There aren't any problems. Everything is running smoothly." She denied the suggestion that it was otherwise. "Perry asked me to meet you because there wasn't anyone else. The night manager is at home sleeping and Perry's secretary is . . . terrified of you. That only left me to represent the managing staff, unless you throw out protocol. Then anyone would do."

"She's a timid soul. Her name's Connie, isn't it?" Brock Canfield mused and wandered toward Stephanie. "Do you suppose she's afraid of sex?"

"She's naturally shy," Stephanie defended her brother's secretary, and fought the warmth that was trying to color her own cheeks.

When he reached her, Brock didn't stop but went on past her. She heard him set the glass on a table and started to turn. "Perry must have told you that if you become involved with me, I would hurt you."

His constant changing from directly personal to impersonal was keeping her off balance. Stephanie tried to adjust to this current reversal of tactics. He made a leisurely circle to stop on the opposite side of her. Her head turned slightly to bring him into the focus of her side vision. He didn't seem to expect a reply from her, and she didn't make one.

"It's true," he went on. "I know your kind. You eat Yankee pot roast on Sunday while I have Chateaubriand. I live out of hotel suites and you want a house with four bedrooms."

He reached out to lift the scarab pendant from her sweater and study it. His hand made no contact with her body, but the sensation was left, anyway. When he replaced it, his fingertips trailed down, tensing her stomach muscles.

"You want children, a boy and girl to mother, but I have no desire for an heir. It's time the Canfield name died." His gaze roamed to her breasts. The shallowness of her breathing had them barely moving beneath the ribbed knit of her sweater. "More than likely, you're the type that would want to nurse your babies yourself."

Stephanie didn't dispute any of his statements. She couldn't, because she guessed there was a fragment of truth in all of them. Her silence was ruled mostly by the knowledge that she was being seduced.

Brock Canfield was stating all the reasons why an affair with him would never last at the same time that he was persuading her to surrender to his desire, anyway. She couldn't raise a single objection when he was saying them all. It was crazy how helpless she felt.

When he moved to stand in front of her with only a hand's width separating their bodies, she was conscious of his maleness. Eye level with the lean breadth of his shoulders, she lifted her chin to study the strength of his masculine features, the darkness of his hair and the burnished silver of his eyes. He threaded his hands through the sides of her hair to frame her face.

"You want a man you can snuggle up to in bed and warm your cold feet," he said. "And

I want to enjoy a woman's body, then sleep alone on my side of the bed. We're oil and water. The combination doesn't mix.''

His gaze shifted to her lips. Her heartbeat faltered, then shifted into high gear, but she managed to control the downward drift of her eyelashes and kept them open, offering no silent invitation. Brock Canfield didn't need any. Her nerves tensed as his mouth descended toward hers with excruciating slowness.

First, the fanning warmth of his breath caressed her sensitive lips. Then she was assailed by the stimulating fragrance of some masculine cologne, the scent tinged with dry champagne. The hint of intoxication swirled through her senses an instant before his mouth moved expertly onto hers.

With persuasive ease, he sampled and tasted the soft curve of her lips, not attempting to eliminate the distance between them. Stephanie didn't relax nor resist the exploring kiss. Of their own accord, her lips clung to his for a split second as he casually ended the contact to brush his mouth against her cheek.

''You're a delectable morsel.'' His voice was deliberately pitched to a caressing level of huskiness. ''Maybe I'll save you for dessert.'' A light kiss tantalized the sensitive skin near her ear before he lifted his head to regard her with lazy gray eyes. "If you're smart, you'll slap my face, Stephanie."

"I'm smarter than that, Mr. Canfield." She was surprised she had a voice—and that it sounded so steady. "I'm not going to fight you—or in any way heighten your interest in the chase."

A smile of admiration spread across his face. It gentled the overwhelming virility of his tanned features. Stephanie's heart stopped beating for a full second, stunned by the potent charm the smile contained. He untangled his hands from her hair and stepped away to reclaim his champagne glass.

"Now you've intrigued me, Stephanie," he murmured, and downed the swallow of champagne.

"Believe me, that wasn't my intention." Agitation stirred her voice.

"Wasn't it?" Brock challenged with a knowing lift of a dark eyebrow.

"No." But she couldn't hold his gaze so she looked away, lifting her chin a fraction of an inch higher.

The phone rang and Brock walked away from it, ordering over his shoulder, "Answer it."

Stephanie hesitated, then stepped to pick up the white receiver. "Yes? Mr. Canfield's suite."

"Stephanie?" It was her brother calling. He

sounded surprised that she had answered. "Connie said Brock arrived fifteen minutes ago. Why are you still there? Any problems?"

"No, I was just leaving." She was glad her voice sounded normal and not as emotionally charged as she felt. "Mr. Canfield is right here. Would you like to speak to him?"

"Yes, put him on," Perry agreed to her suggestion a little thoughtfully.

She held out the receiver to Brock. "It's Perry."

He walked over to take the phone from her hand, without attempting to touch her. His hand covered the mouthpiece. "It's a pity we have to postpone our discussion just when it was becoming interesting."

She refused to rise to his bait. "I hope you enjoy your stay with us," she offered, as if she was addressing a hotel guest instead of the owner.

As she turned to walk to the door, his voice followed her. "That remains to be seen, Stephanie."

His remark held the hint of a promise that their discussion would be resumed at a later time. The part of her that wasn't ruled by common sense was looking forward to it.

Crossing the threshold into the hallway, Stephanie half turned to close the door. Her gaze was drawn to the leanly muscled man on the phone, but he had already forgotten her. His dark head bent in concentration as he listened to what Perry was saying. Very quietly she shut the door and walked swiftly down the carpeted hallway.

When she reached her office, she closed its door. It was a defense mechanism to prevent her from watching for Brock Canfield. She paused long enough at the mirror to smooth the hair his hands had rumpled, then spread the daily entry sheet on her desk and started to work.

Once she heard Perry and Brock's voice in the hall outside her office. Unconsciously she held her breath, but they didn't stop. She guessed her brother was taking Brock on a brief tour of the inner workings of the inn. It sounded logical although Brock was probably very familiar with all that went on.

Late in the afternoon, Perry knocked on her door and walked in. "Stephanie, do you have those cost projections on renovating the pool house into a sauna and exercise club?"

Her gaze ricocheted off her brother to be stopped by the masked gleam of Brock's gray eyes. A charcoal pullover had taken the place of his tie, the white collar of his shirt extending over the neckline of the sweater. The casual attire didn't diminish the air of male authority that draped him like a second skin.

"I have a copy." She dragged her gaze from Brock to open a side desk drawer. "I believe I saw yours at home."

"That's right," Perry remembered. "It's in the library on the desk." He took the portfolio Stephanie handed him and passed it to Brock. "As you can see on page two, the cost of equipping it is within range of the estimate. The main stumbling block is this bearing wall." He unrolled the architect's drawing on Stephanie's desk to show Brock where the difficulty had arisen in revamping the pool house.

Stephanie leaned back in her chair, unable to work while the two men discussed the problem. The inaction gave her too much freedom to study Brock Canfield. Sitting sideways on the edge of her desk, he listened attentively to Perry's explanations and counterproposals.

His position pulled the material of his slacks tautly over his thigh as his muscles bunched beneath it. She liked the clean, strong lines of his profile, the vibrant thickness of his dark brown hair and his lean, well-muscled build.

What bothered her was his innate sex appeal that didn't rely on good looks. He was handsome in a hard kind of way, but it was much more than that. She couldn't look at him without being aware that he was a man.

All the warnings didn't mean a damn, Stephanie realized—not coming from Perry or Brock. It was like being warned against the dangers of getting too close to a fire when she was shivering. She'd take the risk for the chance to be warmed by the flames. Glancing away from the compelling figure half-seated on her desk, she nervously moistened her lips as she realized what she was admitting.

When she looked back at Brock, he was watching her, a smile in the gray depths of his eyes as if he knew what she was thinking and the decision she had reached. It was totally impossible. But she didn't draw an easy breath until he returned his attention to the green portfolio.

"Let me make a suggestion, Perry," he said. "I'll study these blueprints and the cost projections and we'll discuss it this evening. You and your sister can join me for dinner." He straightened from her desk, his glance barely touching her as he bent to roll the blueprints. "Have you made other plans for dinner?" The question was an afterthought, addressed to her brother, not Stephanie.

"I'm free this evening, but I can't speak for Stephanie." There was a silent warning in the look Perry gave her, that said he would back up any excuse she chose to give.

"You'll come to keep the numbers even, won't you?" The statement was issued in the guise of a question as Brock studied her with knowing certainty. "You and Helen can gossip while Perry and I discuss business."

"We could always postpone it until morning," Perry suggested.

"Business before pleasure," Brock insisted with a glance in the general direction of her brother before his gaze returned to lock with hers. "Shall we meet at eight o'clock in the restaurant? That will give you time to go home and change."

"Eight o'clock will be fine," Stephanie agreed as she had known she would all along.

Perry gave her a look that said she had taken leave of her senses—but that was precisely what had happened. It didn't matter how foolish or futile it seemed. She was way out of her league with Brock Canfield, and there was no future in pursuing a relationship with him.

But she wasn't ruled by logic. A more powerful force was directing her actions.

CHAPTER THREE

"DID HE make a pass at you?" Perry slipped the curly jacket over her shoulders, his hands lingering for a second.

"Of course." At his muffled curse Stephanie laughed. "That shouldn't come as a surprise to you. You did warn me that he would."

The laughter eased the tension gnawing at her nerve ends. Dining out was a luxury that they had rarely been able to afford. It was rarer still when her occasional dates had taken her out to dinner. Therefore her wardrobe was sadly lacking in dressy clothes.

The simple lines of the rust-colored dress came the closest to being what Stephanie deemed appropriate to wear. To it she added a plain gold belt and two strands of gold chain to overlap the jewel neckline. She tried to consider her choice as understated elegance as opposed to underdressed.

Luckily, Perry hadn't arrived at the house until twenty minutes ago, so he didn't know how she had agonized over what to wear. He had barely had time to shower and change into a fresh suit and tie. His brown hair still glistened from the shower spray. She could feel him eyeing her with brotherly concern while she buttoned the short jacket.

"What happened, Stephanie?" he questioned with less anger.

Turning to face him, she made a pretense of straightening his tie. "I didn't swoon at his feet, if that's what's worrying you," she joked.

"Will you be serious?" Perry insisted, acting every inch the wise older brother. "I can assure you that Brock isn't regarding it so lightly."

"Probably not," Stephanie conceded, sobering a little.

"Listen, if you want to change your mind, I'll make an excuse for you. One of your friends drove up for the weekend or something," he suggested.

"And fix something to eat when I can dine out? No, thanks." She shook her head in definite refusal. "Besides, you're going to be there to chaperon me. Not to mention the fact that his girl friend will be with us, too.'' The thought left a bad taste in her mouth. She moved to the front door. ''We only have ten minutes to make it to the inn.''

''I forgot about the girl he brought along.'' Perry followed her out of the house to the station wagon that belonged to the inn. There was a frown in his expression when he opened the car door for her. ''Are you attracted to him, Stephanie?''

''I wouldn't be normal if I wasn't,'' she admitted. ''Don't look so worried, Perry. It's better that I know it and admit it than have it hit me all of a sudden one day when it's too late.''

''I suppose there's some logic in that thinking.'' But he didn't sound convinced.

When her door was shut, he walked around the front of the car to slide in the driver's side. Stephanie studied his grim profile as he started the motor. Impulsively, she reached out to touch his arm.

''Try not to worry about me too much, Perry,'' she said. ''I know you'd like to fight all my battles, big brother, but some of them I have to face alone.''

''I'm being overprotective,'' he admitted. ''But

it's become a habit to look after you. It's hard to remember that you're an adult.''

''I know.'' And Stephanie did understand. She didn't resent the concern Perry voiced, because she knew his intentions were the best.

Tactfully, he switched the subject to the renovations of the pool house, which had been his idea. He was certain it would enhance the overall appeal of the inn and ensure their ability to compete with the newer, more modern ski lodges in the area. So far, Brock hadn't vetoed the plan, which made tonight very important.

The inn possessed two restaurants, but the formal dining room was only open during the evening dinner hour. It was one of the few dining rooms in the area that required proper attire, yet it was rarely empty. After spending the day hiking, skiing or cycling, guests seemed to welcome the excuse to dress up. Local residents often dined there as well, making reservations almost a necessity. This Friday was no exception.

After leaving her jacket at the coat check, Stephanie let Perry escort her to the table where Brock and his blond companion were waiting. Brock rose at their approach, his dark elegance reaching out to ensnare Stephanie. A ghost of a smile touched his mouth as he met her look. She felt oddly breathless, but her reflection in the mirrored wall didn't show this inner disturbance.

"Have you been waiting long?" Perry asked, more out of politeness than concern that they were late.

"No, Helen and I have just arrived. I don't believe you've met Helen Collins," Brock introduced. "My manager, Perry Hall. Of course, you member his sister Stephanie."

Stephanie received no more than a cursory glance from the blonde, who did manage to smile at Perry. It was obvious by the forced pleasure in her expression that Helen resented their presence. She had probably looked forward to having Brock all to herself that evening, Stephanie realized.

That little trill of gladness that sang in her veins was the result of suppressed jealousy. The discovery brought Stephanie briefly to her senses. She wasn't going to spend the entire evening being envious of the slightest attention Brock paid to Helen.

"Sit here, Perry." Brock indicated the empty chair to his left. "That way we'll be able to talk without having to shout across the table."

Which left the chair opposite him for Stephanie. She wouldn't be sitting beside him, but she would be facing him through dinner. She knew she would have to guard against staring at him. Something told her Helen Collins wouldn't be very talkative.

It proved to be a very accurate prediction. Courtesy insisted that Stephanie make some initial attempts to start a conversation by inquiring where Helen was from, etcetera. When the other girl made no attempt to keep the conversation going, Stephanie didn't, either.

In consequence, she sat through dinner listening to the two men discuss the proposed renovations. She didn't find it boring. On the contrary, she was fascinated by the quickness of Brock's mind—shrewd and astute. And she was rather proud of Perry's ability to keep up with his fast-thinking employer.

But it became increasingly obvious that Helen didn't share Stephanie's appreciation of the conversation. She began smoking incessantly, since it gave her an excuse to interrupt the talk to have Brock light her cigarette. Stephanie was more embarrassed than envious of the way Helen gazed so limpidly into Brock's eyes and bent closer as if inviting his embrace. Brock's reaction was a mixture of aloofness, tolerance and amusement.

Occasionally his glance did stray to Stephanie, but he made no attempt to flirt with her. She was glad, because it would have made a mockery of the business discussion with her brother if he had.

After the dinner plates were removed, the waiter wheeled the dessert cart to the table. "Aren't you going to have something, Brock?" Helen protested when everyone ordered something except him.

"No." He gave her a lazy smile that remained in his expression when he glanced around the table. "I'll have my dessert later." His gaze lingered for a fraction of a second on Stephanie.

Her recall was instant and vivid, remembering that he had mentioned saving her for dessert. There was a wild fluttering in her stomach as she quickly dropped her gaze to the bowl of sweetened fresh fruit in front of her.

She was constantly off-balance with him. Just when she had become used to being ignored, he had reminded her of that intimate remark. Somehow she had to learn to keep both feet solidly on the ground whenever she was around him. It was the only way she would survive this tumultuous interlude.

"The dining room closes at ten, Mr. Canfield," Stephanie remarked. "If you want dessert, perhaps you should have it now."

"Now?" His mouth twitched with a smile as his gaze dared her to repeat that challenge. "I'd rather have it later. If it happens to be after ten, and the craving is too great, I'll simply raid the refrigerator.''

"If you'd like, I can arrange to have a selection sent up to your suite," Perry suggested, and Stephanie nearly choked on a strawberry.

"Can you?" There was a wealth of understated meaning to Brock's droll response. "I'll try to remember that." The waiter was at his elbow with the silver coffee pot. "Yes, black, please."

While they finished their coffee and dessert, it was decided that Perry would contact the architect and arrange a meeting early on Saturday morning. Brock had changes he wanted made in the plans before he gave his final approval. Stephanie knew her brother's sense of achievement at Brock's acceptance of his idea and felt proud for him.

"I'm beginning to get the feeling your talents are not being fully utilized at the inn," Brock remarked, studying Perry with a narrowed look. "Is this your ambition? To be in charge of a place like this?"

Perry hesitated, darting Stephanie a quick look. His uncertainty was obvious. "I wouldn't say it's my sole ambition, but I find it challenging, always different."

"That's a diplomatic answer. Now, what's the truth?" Brock challenged.

"That's the truth," Perry laughed, but insincerely.

"The truth is, Mr. Canfield, that Perry has always wanted to be a lawyer," Stephanie inserted, disregarding the silencing look her brother sent.

"What stopped you? I've seen your college transcripts."

"My father had a skiing accident. I was needed at home," her brother explained simply and immediately changed the subject. "The long-range forecast for the winter calls for a lot of snow. It's predicted the area will have its best ski season to date."

"The reservations show it." Stephanie followed his lead, her way of apologizing for bringing up the education he had been forced to abandon. "We're booked solid all the way to March."

"I noticed." Brock went along with the new topic.

"Excuse me." The brittle words were issued by Helen as she pushed away from the table to stand. "I'm going to the powder room to freshen my lipstick."

Brock caught at her hand. "We'll meet you in the lounge. Don't be long."

The sullen look was immediately replaced by a bright smile. "I won't," the blonde promised and hurried away with a provocative sway of her hips.

"We should be going home," Stephanie murmured to her brother.

"Yes, it is late," he agreed, with a glance at his watch.

"Have one drink with us," Brock insisted. "We haven't toasted your new plan. It was a brilliant idea of yours, Perry, to utilize an existing building for the sauna, especially since it's virtually unused. It makes an already attractive package both practical and economical."

"I'm glad you think so, Brock," her brother replied modestly. "But I'm certain you would have come up with the plan if I'd suggested building an entirely new building."

"I hope so." Again there was that wide smile, all lazy charm. "How about that drink? Will you join us?"

After exchanging a glance with Stephanie, Perry agreed. "Just one. We don't want to intrude any further on your evening."

"Just one," Brock nodded.

He was at her chair when Stephanie rose. His hand seemed to find its way to her waist to guide her to the side door leading to the lounge. His touch was lightly possessive, impersonal yet warm. She could feel the imprint of his fingers through the material of her dress. The sensation seemed to brand her as his property.

The lounge was crowded, as it generally was on the weekends. A dance combo was playing, sprayed by a rotating rainbow of lights in the otherwise dark room. During the off-season, the inn only had live entertainment on the weekends. In the winter, when the White Mountains were filled with skiers, they had a group seven nights a week.

Brock found an empty booth in a far corner of the room. By the time they had ordered a round of drinks, Helen arrived. She ignored his invitation to join them and instead coaxed Brock onto the dance floor. Stephanie watched the blonde become the sultry enchantress, weaving her web around Brock, and knew she could never compete with such tactics.

"Would you like to dance?" Perry suggested.

Stephanie glanced up to refuse, but one look at the challenging gleam in his eyes made her realize how dispirited she had become in the span of a few minutes. A faintly chagrined smile curved her mouth as she nodded acceptance of his invitation.

Once on the dance floor, the swinging music

soon made its upbeat rhythm felt. Concentrating on the dance steps distracted her from the sight of Helen with Brock. Also there was the knowledge that she and Perry danced well together, their steps always matching, but he had also been the one who taught her how.

When the song ended, she was breathless and laughing. "Feel better?" Perry smiled as he guided her off the dance floor.

"Much better," she agreed, glancing over her shoulders to smile at him. "Thanks."

The lights were dimmed to a single blue color for a slow number. Her eyes didn't adjust immediately to the change of light, and she had to stop for a minute to keep from running into a table or chair in the semidarkness.

Her gaze saw Brock and Helen on a course parallel with theirs. He bent his head to murmur something to the blonde, who didn't look pleased by his statement. Then he was leaving Helen to make her way back to the booth alone, and crossing to intercept Stephanie.

"You don't object if I have this dance with your sister before you leave, do you, Perry?" Brock asked, although Stephanie didn't know why. He had already taken hold of her arm to direct her back to the dance floor.

She was certain Perry answered him, but she

didn't hear what was said. Almost the instant they reached the cleared area, Brock was turning her into his arms. As usual, there were more couples on the floor to dance to the slow tunes, so it became less a matter of dancing and more a matter of avoiding others. They were soon swallowed into the center of the group.

He folded her arm against his chest while his hand slid up her spine to force her closer. Stephanie could feel her heart thudding against her ribs as they swayed together, moving their feet without going anywhere. Ultimately she became conscious of the hard wall of his chest, the flatness of his stomach and the leg shifting between hers in rhythm with the music.

When he released her hand to leave it against the lapel of his jacket, Brock seemed to give up all pretense of dancing. Both arms were around her, his fingers spread as they roamed over her shoulders, ribs and spine, slowly caressing and molding her to him.

Stephanie could barely breathe. This was what she had wanted all evening, yet she couldn't relax. She felt like a child who had been given a giant lollipop and was afraid to enjoy it too much, because she knew it was going to be taken away from her.

His chin rubbed against her temple, his breath

stirring her hair. A silent whimper of suppressed delight sighed through her when he turned his mouth against her, investigating the corner of her eye and the curve of her cheekbone.

"I could develop a sweet tooth for dessert." Finding her ear, he nuzzled aside the silken chestnut hair covering it to let his moist lips nibble at the lobe, shattering her equilibrium.

In another second she was going to melt like a piece of sugar on his tongue. "You already have." Her voice wasn't all that strong, the words coming out in a thin, taut whisper.

"Is that right?" His mouth curved against the skin of her cheek.

All she had to do was lift her head and Brock would find her lips, but she lowered her chin a fraction of an inch. Her eyes were closed by the feathery brush of his mouth across her lashes.

"Any member of the opposite sex would satisfy you when you're in an amorous mood," she insisted, because she knew it was true. Brock was pursuing her because she was new, not because he thought she was special. It was a fact she acknowledged without bitterness. "You have such a healthy appetite that you bring your nighttime treats along with you."

"But you're the one in my arms. Why don't you satisfy me?" he challenged softly.

Her heart ran away with itself at the thought of satisfying him and being satisfied by him. His virility was a potent force that left her weak. She could imagine the devastation his practiced skill could wreak if she let herself become carried away by it. Someone jostled her shoulder in the melee of dancing couples and her head lifted in faint surprise.

In the next second, she was immobilized by the touch of his mouth against the corner of her lips. Then she was turning to seek the completeness of it, mindless of the others around them. It was a devouring kiss, hard and demanding, ending within seconds after it had begun. It hadn't seemed to help that she had both feet on the floor. Discretion had been swept aside so easily.

"Do you do this with all your women? Make love to them on the dance floor? First Helen, now me." She found the strength to mock him, although her voice was a little shaky.

Her head was still tipped back, enabling her to look into his eyes. The dim interior of the lounge had enlarged the black pupils, leaving a thin silver ring around them. They were smiling at her, with an inner satisfaction and supreme confidence, certain of his ability to seduce her.

Stephanie supposed she was transparent. Her pride was injured that she was such an easy conquest for him. But was there a woman born who could deny his attraction for long?

"I've aroused you, despite that cool and composed expression you're wearing," Brock stated. Cool? Composed? Her? It seemed impossible. His hand moved to caress her neck, stopping when it found her pulse point. She could feel it and hear it hammering against his fingertip. "Your pulse is racing. Feel what you're doing to me."

Taking her fingers, he carried them to his neck and pressed them to the throbbing vein. She felt its wild beat, not so far behind the swift tempo of her own. Had she disturbed him? Or was it only desire? She had felt safer with the jacket beneath her fingers rather than the vital warmth of his skin.

"Your hand feels cool," he murmured.

That seemed impossible when she felt hot all over. When she tried to withdraw her fingers from his grasp, it tightened. He lifted her hand to his mouth and sensually kissed the center of her palm.

"I want you, Stephanie," he said as the last note of the song faded and the rainbow of lights came on.

The sudden murmur of voices shattered the intimacy of the moment. Stephanie didn't have to find an answer to that heady comment as the exiting dancers forced them apart. He retained his hold of her hand while she let the crowd lead her off the floor.

Fixing her gaze on Perry in the far booth, she weaved her way through the tables. Before she reached it, she gave a little tug to free her hand from Brock's grip. He let it go without protest. She didn't squarely meet the look her brother gave her when she slid onto the booth seat beside him. Her glance darted across the table to Helen, whose bored and impatient expression spoke volumes.

"I hope you've finally fulfilled all your obligations for the evening, Brock," Helen voiced her irritation at being left to her own devices for so much of the evening.

"Stop bitching, Helen." As he sat down, he stretched his arm across the backrest behind the blonde and picked up his drink. "I warned you this would be a business trip." It was a lazy reminder, a steel edge cloaked in velvet tones.

Over the rim of his glass, his gaze locked with Stephanie's. She read his message of dissatisfaction and desire, schooled with patience. She took a sip of her own drink, but the ice had melted, diluting it and leaving it flat and tasteless. She set it down and pushed it aside to glance at her brother.

63

"It's getting late, Perry. We should be going." Knowing he would agree, she rose and moved aside so he could slide out.

"I'll see you in the morning, Brock." He shook hands with Brock, who was also standing.

"It was a pleasure meeting you, Miss Collins." Stephanie nodded at the blonde, not caring that it was only a polite phrase she offered. Her only response was an indifferent glance. Then she addressed Brock. "You're leaving on Sunday, aren't you?"

"Yes, late in the afternoon," he acknowledged with a slight narrowing of his gaze.

"I doubt if I'll see you again before you leave, so I hope you have a safe trip." She placed her hand in his.

Brock held on to it when she would have withdrawn it. "Aren't you working tomorrow?"

"No." Conscious of Perry at her side, she sent him a sideways glance, smiling. "I have a great boss. He gives me the weekends off so I can do his laundry and clean the house."

He released her hand somewhat absently and smiled at her brother. "Good night. I'll meet you in the morning around eight."

Before they had taken a step away from the booth, Brock was sitting down and turning his attention to Helen, who was suddenly all smiles.

Stephanie tried desperately not to remember that only moments before he had been holding her in his arms. Now someone else was going to satisfy him. She didn't do a very good job of convincing herself that she was the lucky one to be walking away relatively unscathed.

They stopped at the coat check for Stephanie's jacket and Perry's overcoat. Both were silent as they walked outside into the crisp autumn night to the station wagon.

The only thing that was said during the drive home came when Perry remarked, "I hope you know what you're doing, Stephanie."

"So do I," she sighed.

CHAPTER FOUR

THE DIRTY breakfast dishes were stacked in the sink. Stephanie paused at the counter to drink the last swallow of coffee from her cup. Her gaze automatically wandered out of the window above the sink to the foothills emblazoned with the reds and golds of autumn.

In the back of the old farmhouse, a brook rushed through the rolling acreage, complete with a romantic stone bridge crossing it. Cords of firewood were stacked near the back door of the house—fuel for the cold New England winter.

Sighing, she turned away from the beauty of the clear autumn morning and set her cup with the rest of the dishes. She'd wash them later. Right now she wanted the hot water for the first load of clothes.

The back porch doubled as the washroom; a washer and dryer were ensconced in one corner. The small floor space was littered with baskets and piles of dirty clothes that Stephanie set about separating into individual loads, tossing the white clothes directly into the washing machine.

It was a nice enough day that she could hang the clothes on the line to dry. Besides, the clothes always smelled so much cleaner and fresher that way.

She pushed the sleeves of the old gray sweat shirt up to her elbows. It was one of Perry's, which meant it was several sizes too large for her, but it was comfortable to work in and it didn't matter if she spilled bleach on it. Her blue jeans were faded and shrunk from numerous washings and snugly hugged her slender hips and thighs, but the denim material was soft like a second skin.

Her hair was pulled away from her face into a ridiculously short ponytail, secured with a piece of blue yarn. She hadn't bothered with makeup. By the time she washed the clothes, dusted the furniture and swept the floors of the two-story farmhouse, there wouldn't be any trace of it left, anyway. Besides, the only one who came on Saturday mornings was Mrs. Hammermill with fresh eggs for the week.

When there was a knock at the front door, Stephanie didn't hesitate over who it might be. "Come in!" she shouted, and continued separating the clothes. At the sound of the door opening, then closing, she added, "I'm in the kitchen, Mrs. Hammermill," which was close enough to her location. "You can put the eggs on the counter. If you have an extra dozen, I'll take them. Perry mentioned he'd like an angel food cake. I thought I'd try my hand at making one from scratch this afternoon."

There was a movement in the doorway to the porch, but Stephanie didn't glance up. She was busy examining the white shirt in her hand that Perry had somehow managed to mark up the front of with ball-point ink.

"You don't happen to know what I can use to get this ink out of Perry's shirt, do you?" she frowned. "I've tried just about everything at one time or another and . . . . When she looked up, she saw Brock leaning a shoulder against the doorjamb, his arms crossed. She froze at the sight of him. "Brock!" His name was startled from her.

"Try hairspray. My secretary swears by it," he suggested with a trace of teasing amusement in his droll voice. His corduroy pants were desert brown, the same shade as the heavy sweater with the stag's head design on the chest.

Her gaze flew past him to the cat clock on the kitchen wall with its switching tail for a pendulum. It was a few minutes before half-past eight.

"What are you doing here?" she asked in confusion, still clutching the shirt and standing amid the piles of dirty clothes. "I thought you were—"

"The egg lady? Yes, I know." He finished the sentence for her and uncrossed his arms to stand up straight. "The answer to your question should be obvious. I came to see you."

"Yes, but . . . you were supposed to meet Perry this morning," Stephanie said in vague protest.

"I did . . . for a few minutes. Are you going to come here? Or am I going to have to wade through all those clothes to get to you?" He both challenged and mocked her.

Stephanie laid the shirt over the side of the washing machine. In doing so, she became conscious of her appearance. Her gaze slid down the front of her sloppy sweat shirt and faded jeans. She felt the nakedness of her face, minus even lipstick.

"You should have called before coming over." Raising a hand to the hair tied back, she stepped over the pile of clothes blocking her path to the doorway and Brock.

"If I had, I wouldn't have got the chance to see this domestic scene." Brock reached out to take the hand she was balancing with and pulled her into his arms, locking his hands behind her back while he studied her upturned face. "And you know you look like a sexy little girl in that outfit."

It wasn't exactly the compliment she wanted to hear as she turned her head away to let his kiss land on her cheek and pushed her way past him into the kitchen. The floor seemed to roll under her feet, but she knew it was only her knees quaking.

"I don't want to look like a little girl," she declared, and lifted both her hands to untie the knotted yarn around her hair. But she had tied it tight and the knot defied the attempts of her trembling fingers to loosen it.

When she felt Brock's push hers out of the way, she tried to move away, but he clamped a hand on her shoulder to keep her in place. "Hold still," he ordered, and Stephanie stood quietly while he worked the yarn free of the knot. When it was untied, he turned her around and combed her hair into place with his fingers. "Now you just look sexy. Are you happy?" he asked with a lazy glint in his gray eyes.

But he didn't wait for her to answer, he bent

his head to cover her lips with his mouth, skillfully parting them as he curved her into his arms. Her fingers curled into the wool of his sweater, clinging to the only solid thing she could find in the deepening intensity of his kiss. She was exposed to a whole set of raw, new emotions that had her straining toward him in trembling need. He dragged his mouth roughly across her cheek to her ear.

"Did you really think you wouldn't see me again before I left?" He sounded almost angry.

"I'm not sure if I believed it or not," Stephanie admitted with her eyes closed as he nibbled his way down her neck to her shoulder.

"Where are your parents? Who else are you expecting besides the egg lady?" he demanded.

"My parents are dead," she whispered, and wondered why he didn't know that. "There's only Mrs. Hammermill. She usually comes before nine."

She felt as well as heard the deep shuddering breath Brock took before he lifted his head to smile tightly at her. "In that case, why don't you fix me some breakfast? I didn't bother to eat before I came over. I thought you might do your shopping in the morning and I didn't want to miss you."

Not knowing how much she dared into that

statement, Stephanie decided not to comment on it. "Do you want bacon and eggs?" she asked instead.

"What I want, I can't have at the moment." His hands slid up her back, suggestively pressing her closer to him before he released her and stepped away. "Bacon and eggs will do."

"How do you like your eggs?" She walked to the refrigerator, glad to have something to do. She took out the package of bacon and the last two eggs from the shelf.

"Sunny-side up, and crisp bacon."

She spied the pitcher of orange juice on the refrigerator shelf. "Juice?"

"No, thanks." Brock came to stand beside her while she laid the bacon strips in the skillet.

When it began to sizzle, she walked to the cupboard on the other side of him and took down a place setting. She glanced uncertainly at the kitchen table, then at him. "Would you like to eat in the dining room?" she suggested.

"No," he said with a decisive shake of his head. "I have no intention of letting you out of my sight."

His look, as well as his answer, was disturbing, but it also gave her such much-needed confidence. She was smiling as she arranged the plate and cutlery on the gingham-clothed kitchen table. She walked back to the stove to turn the bacon.

"When was the last time you had breakfast in somebody's kitchen?" she asked curiously, eyeing him with a sidelong glance.

"Probably not since I was a child," he admitted what Stephanie had suspected. "Are you a good cook?"

"Not as good as Perry, but he's had a lot more practice than I have." The bacon was beginning to brown nicely, so Stephanie kept turning it.

Brock took up a position behind her, his hands caressing the curve of her shoulders, while his thumbs rubbed the hollows of her neck. "Why did he have more practice?" He didn't really sound interested in the subject.

"Our mother died when I was only four. Since our father had to work at two jobs to support us, Perry had to do the cooking and look after me."

It was difficult to concentrate on what she was doing under the caress of his hands. She managed to rescue the bacon before it was burned and set it aside to drain on a paper towel.

"What did your father do?"

"He considered himself a ski instructor, but mostly he earned money as a bartender and cutting firewood . . . until his accident." She cracked the eggs and slipped them into the hot bacon fat.

"The accident that forced your brother to give up his law career," Brock guessed.

"Yes, he was crippled in a skiing accident." She looked over her shoulder, a curious frown knitting her forehead. "Perry has worked for you for over five years. Surely you knew that."

"No. I don't bother to inquire about the personal lives of my employees unless it affects their work. There's never been any reason to fault your brother's work." There was an indifferent and dismissing shrug of his shoulders.

"But surely you want to know something about their backgrounds," Stephanie insisted.

"Only their qualifications for their particular position. As long as I get the results I want, I couldn't care less who or what they are as individuals." There was a curve to his mouth, but it wasn't a smile. "You think that's a very callous attitude, don't you?"

She concentrated her gaze on the eggs in the skillet, the bright yellow yolks staring back at her. "Yes, I do."

"White Boar Inn represents half of one percent of the gross business Canfield Enterprises earns annually. Maybe that will give you an idea of how many Perry Halls I have working for me," he suggested. "I couldn't possibly become involved or have knowledge of their personal lives without losing perspective of my overall responsibility. By rights, I should sell the inn.''

''Why don't you?'' She could see the logic in his argument, but she mentally recoiled from this evidence of his lack of feeling. The eggs were done, so she moved away to fetch his plate from the table and scoop them onto it with the spatula.

''For personal reasons,'' Brock answered. Stephanie didn't think he intended to explain what they were, but she was wrong. ''My parents spent their honeymoon at the White Boar when they eloped. He bought it for her on their sixth anniversary. He was the one who decreed that the honeymoon suite would be reserved only for Canfields.''

''No wonder you're reluctant to sell it.'' Her smile was soft and radiant when she gazed at him, touched by this unexpected display of sentiment.

''Six months after he bought it, they went through a messy divorce that lasted two years. My mother has since remarried several times. My father, wisely, contented himself with a stream of mistresses.'' Brock watched her smile fade almost with satisfaction.

''Is . . . is he living?'' Averting her gaze, Stephanie walked past him, carrying the plate of eggs and bacon to the table.

"Yes. He's retired to the south of France. I believe his current lover is a twenty-year-old model." Brock followed her. "Of course, he refers to her as his protégée."

"Coffee?" When she set his plate down, she searched for an excuse to find something else to do.

"Black with no sugar."

Stephanie moved away from the table as he sat down to eat. "You must not have had a very happy childhood," she guessed.

"That depends on your definition of happy. My grandfather raised me even before my parents were divorced. They were always vacationing in some exotic resort in a far-off corner of the world. The divorce had little effect on me. Most of the time I was away at school or else with my grandfather. From the day I was born I was groomed to take over the company, and when my grandfather died a few years ago, that's exactly what I did."

Stephanie poured two cups and carried them to the table. "And the last time you ate in somebody's kitchen, that was with your grandfather?"

"Hardly." Brock laughed shortly. "He had all his meals at his desk unless it was a business dinner. No, I spent a week at the home of one of my classmates."

"Why don't you sell the inn?" Stephanie watched him, half-afraid to hear his answer. "It's obvious that you feel no sentimental attachment to it."

Brock was slow to answer, but it wasn't due to any hesitancy. "It reminds me that intimate relationships don't necessarily last forever no matter how strong the attachment appears on the surface."

"You make the trip here on an average of four times a year. Yet I've never heard of you bringing the same woman twice. Is that why?" But that question simply prompted another. "Why did you come this morning when Helen is back in the suite?"

"Because I didn't want to be with her. I wanted to be with you." His sharpness dissolved into a chuckle. "You are having a hard time trying to understand me, aren't you? The Helens of this world go in and out of my life all the time. I have the sex drive of any normal male. There's no pretense, on either side, that we're together for any reason other than the purely physical—or sexual—if you prefer. She understood the ground rules going in—no emotional claims on me or my time. In return, I treat her with respect and courtesy. I'm not attempting to brag or shock you: I'm only trying to explain the circumstances that dictate my life-style."

Stephanie was trying but it all sounded very cold-blooded. "I am sure you can rationalize any behavior," she replied stiffly.

Leaning forward in his chair, Brock reached for her hand and gripped it firmly in his. The intensity of his gaze was piercing. "What I'm not making clear to you, Stephanie, is how difficult it is for me to have the kind of relationship you regard as normal—with any woman. I don't have time to carry out a courtship." A muscle was working convulsively along his jaw. "Tomorrow I'm driving to New York. When I arrive, there might be a phone call that will take me to the West Coast. I could be there a month, maybe two. Or I might be there a day and leave for Zurich—I have hotel suites in a dozen cities. I'm with you today, but it might be six months before I can see you again. How can I build a relationship on that? How can I ask a woman to wait for me without being able to tell her when I'll see her again?"

"It's really quite hopeless, isn't it?" Her voice was choked, the futility swamping her.

He released her hand with controlled irritation, pausing a second before he resumed eating the rest of his breakfast. "Sometimes I forget that it is, but the inn reminds me . . . every month when I see the name on the report."

"That's why you said you didn't want an heir—that it was time the Canfield name died," she said, suddenly understanding.

"No one should have this responsibility unless he wants it," Brock stated.

"You. . . you could sell?" Stephanie suggested hesitantly.

"This is what I was trained for—what I'm good at." His mouth slanted in a half smile. "I doubt if I can make you understand that. I wouldn't change my life and what I do, even if I had the choice." He wiped at his mouth with a napkin. "That was a very good breakfast. Is there more coffee?"

"Yes, of course." A little numb, Stephanie stood up to take his cup. After all he had explained, she was still trying to figure out where she might fit into his life.

Brock must have read the bewilderment in her eyes, because he reached out to stop her when she started to pass his chair, his hand resting lightly on her forearm. "When I find something I want, I reach out and grab it, Stephanie, because it might not be there the next time I come back. I live hard and fast—and I love the same way. If I forget to say you're beautiful or that your eyes are the color of the morning sky, it isn't because I don't think of it. I just don't waste precious time."

"Yes, I—" Her reply was interrupted by a knock at the front door. It startled her until she realized who it was. "It's Mrs. Hammermill."

"The egg lady," Brock nodded, and dropped his hands to leave Stephanie free to answer the door.

Setting his cup down, she walked toward the living room. "Yes! Come in, Mrs. Hammermill!" she called, and the front door opened to admit a short, stout woman in a dark pillbox hat. Two dozen eggs were balanced under one short arm.

"I'm sorry I'm late, but the mister's been sick with the flu. I've been doin' his chores as well as my own."

"I hope he's feeling better soon," Stephanie murmured and led the way into the kitchen. The woman stopped short at the sight of a strange man and eyed him suspiciously. Stephanie quickly introduced them.

Mrs. Hammermill was instantly all smiles. "Maybe you can talk to Perry about letting me supply the eggs for the restaurant. I would have to buy some more layers, but—"

"I'll talk to him about it," Brock assured her.

Taking the egg money out of the jar on the

counter, Stephanie paid the woman and tactfully hurried her on her way. She almost regretted identifying Brock, but the gossip about a strange man would have been worse.

After she had shown the woman out, Stephanie returned to the kitchen. "I'm sorry Mrs. Hammermill tried to persuade you to let her have the egg account at the restaurant inn," she apologized to Brock with a wry smile. "What she really wants Perry to do is finance it. She would have to buy more laying hens, which means she'd need to build a new coop, as well as the initial cost of more grain. She's a marvelous, dependable woman, but I don't think you want to go into partnership in the egg business." At the table she stopped to stack the dishes and add them to those in the sink waiting to be washed.

"You're right, I'm not interested in the chicken business—or the dishes. In fact—" Brock took hold of her hand and pulled her to his chair and onto his lap—I only have one merger on my mind—the one with you."

Off-balance by the move, Stephanie was dependent on the supporting steel of his arms. There was a wild flutter of her pulse as he made a sound under his breath, almost like a groan. Her hands encircled his neck, fingers seeking the vibrant thickness of his dark hair.

The kiss was sensual and exploring, their mouths mating in delighted discovery; the slow, heady joy of it insulating Stephanie from all thought. In the hard cradle of his lap, she felt the burning imprint of his thighs beneath her, the flatness of his stomach and muscled breadth of his chest and shoulders. So male, so virile! It stirred her already disturbed senses.

As he kissed her, Brock mouthed her lips and cheek, the angle of her jaw and the hollow under her ear, setting afire the urgent yearning of her body. Arousing as his kisses were, she was stimulated by the chance to let her lips wander intimately over his smooth jaw and cheek, tangy with the astringent flavor of after-shave. It was a wildly novel experience to have this freedom to reciprocate the sensuous exploration.

His caressing hands became impatient with the thick, loose folds of the large sweat shirt she was wearing. When he lifted the hem to expose her bare midriff, Stephanie drew in a breath of startled surprise that was never quite completed. Her flesh tensed under the initial touch of his hand, then melted at its firm caress.

He seemed intent on personally exploring every naked inch of her ribs and shoulders. She was quivering, her white breasts straining against the lacy material of the confining bra. When he covered one with his palm, there was a rushing release of tension that was wildly gratifying.

Yet, as his fingers sought the back fastener of her bra, sanity returned a fragment at a time. She had let herself be carried away without knowing for certain it was what she wanted. She drew away from him, pressing her hands against his chest for breathing space while she tried to clear her head of this heart-pounding passion.

"Stephanie." His voice both coaxed and commanded as he planted a kiss on an exposed shoulder bone.

"No." She gulped in the negative and swung off his lap, taking a couple of quick steps away from his chair while she pulled her sweat shirt down to her hips. "The first time I saw you, I knew I had to keep both feet on the ground or you'd knock me right off of them. I should have meant that literally." Stephanie laughed, shakily, trying to make a joke out of it even though she knew it was the absolute truth.

"I want you, Stephanie. I told you that last night," Brock reminded her. And Stephanie walked to the kitchen counter, keeping her back to him, in a weak attempt to escape the heady seduction of his voice. "If anything, it's more true at this moment."

At the scrape of the chair leg indicating he had

risen, she grabbed hold of the edge of the counter, needing to hang on to something. "It's all happening too fast for me," she tried to explain without sounding as desperate as she felt. "You don't understand, Brock. I can't be as casual about sex as you are."

"How much do you know about sex, Stephanie?" When he spoke, she realized he was directly behind her, his tone steady with patience and confidence.

Her knuckles were white from gripping the counter edge in an effort to keep from turning around. If she did, she knew she would be lost.

To counter his sureness, she became sharp and defensive. "I'm sure I don't know as much as you do, Mr. Canfield."

"Mr. Canfield?" His voice was dangerously low. His fingers gripped her shoulders and forced her to turn around. She was rigid in his hold, but she didn't resist him. Under the narrowed regard of his gray eyes, her head was thrown warily back. "Hey, what is this?" Brock demanded.

"Sex is just a physical act to you, like kissing. I don't treat it that lightly," she defended her hesitation and uncertainty.

He studied every particle of her expression for such a long time that she felt herself growing hot.

"Are you a virgin, Stephanie?" He seemed to doubt the accuracy of his conclusion.

Her gaze fell to the neckline of his sweater. "Should I apologize for my inexperience?" The challenge was a little angry, a little hurt and a little defiant.

"How old are you?" His fingers dug into the flesh of her shoulders.

"Twenty-two," she answered stiffly.

"My God, where have you been all your life? In a convent?" Brock was dryly incredulous and mocking. "Twenty-year-old virgins went out with hula hoops."

His remark ignited her temper. "It's too bad if you think I'm an oddity. My father's skiing accident left him almost completely paralyzed. I had to feed him, bathe him, dress him, read to him, do everything for him, for five years. Daddy never complained for himself, but he used to cry because I didn't go out and have fun. Perry took care of him whenever he was home, but he never knew when an emergency would come up and he'd have to go to the inn. I dated now and then." She was angry and didn't attempt to conceal it. "But who wants to get serious about someone with a sick father? We couldn't afford to hire anyone to take care of him full time. I'm not complaining about those five years. I don't regret a single one of them, because they brought me closer to my father than I'd ever been. So you can make fun of me if you want—''

He covered her mouth with two fingers to check the indignant tirade. His chiseled male features were etched in sober lines. ''I'm not making fun of you.'' He traced the outline of her mouth and became absorbed with the shape of it. Her anger vanished as if it had never been. ''It's simply rare to meet someone with your passionate nature who hasn't been around. It doesn't change anything.'' His gaze lifted to catch her look and hold it. The dark silver glitter of his eyes dazzled her. ''I'm going to keep trying to get you into bed. Knowing I would be the first just makes you a prize I'm more determined to have.''

Very slightly, his fingers tilted her chin. Then his mouth closed onto hers in consummation of his promise. A fluttering surge of desire rose within her, like a slow-burning flame fanned to burn hotter.

Brock gathered her into his arms, unhurriedly, arching her backward, his hips pinning her to the counter. The wayward caress of his hands was keenly pleasurable. He shifted his attention to the pulse quivering so wildly in her throat.

''Whose sweat shirt is this?'' he muttered when a hand became tangled in the loose folds.

"Perry's." It was a husky admission, shattered by her vivid awareness of his stark masculinity.

"*This* has got to go." He pulled at a shoulder inseam, saying the words against her neck, punctuating them with kisses. "From now on, if you wear a man's clothes, they're going to be mine."

"Whatever you say," she whispered with a throbbing ache in her voice, boneless and pliant in his arms, her forehead resting weakly against his shoulder while he rained havoc on the sensitive skin of her neck and throat.

"You know what I say." Brock seized on the submissive response, his tone fiercely low and urgent. "I've been saying it every time I looked at you or touched you. I want to make love to you—here and now. You have both feet on the floor. What do you want?"

But it wasn't that simple. Not for Stephanie. Not even with the twisting, churning rawness knotting her insides. The awful confusion kept her from answering him, but he must have felt her stillness and chose not to press the point. Instead he loosened his arms, letting his hands move in a series of restless caresses over her shoulders.

"I've postponed everything until after lunch so we could spend the morning together," he informed her in a slightly thick voice. "But there isn't any way I'm going to be able to stay in this house alone with you and not . . . ." He took a deep breath and released her entirely. "We'd better go for a drive somewhere. At least with my hands on the steering wheel, I'll be able to keep them off you. Go and change, fix yourself up—whatever you want to do. I'll wait for you down here."

Stephanie looked at him, reluctant to agree to his suggestion, but his gray eyes warned her not to protest unless she was willing to accept the alternative. That was something that still confused her.

"I'll only be a few moments," she promised.

CHAPTER FIVE

THE ROADS were crowded with the cars of tourists, eager to see the spectacle of the autumn foliage and catch a glimpse of the lore that personified Yankee New England—wooden covered bridges, white church steeples, antique shops and village squares. The route Brock took became less a planned drive and more a matter of choosing a path with the least resistance.

Stephanie relaxed in the contours of velour-covered seats, enveloped in the luxury of the blue Mercedes. The radio was turned low, its four speakers surrounding her with the serene sounds of the music. A riot of color exploded outside the window: reds and yellows against the backdrop of dark green pine forests climbing the slopes of the White Mountains, and a crisp blue sky.

Traffic thinned in the lane ahead of them as

Brock made the turn that would take them on the road south through Franconia Notch. An outcropping of granite loomed into view, and a contented smile curved Stephanie's mouth when she saw it.

"There's my friend," she murmured, unconsciously breaking the companionable silence.

"Which one?" Brock's gaze narrowed on the rear view mirror, trying to identify which of the cars they had passed that had contained her friend.

"Not that kind of friend." Her smile broadened as she pointed. "Him. The old man of the mountains." She gazed at the jagged profile Mother Nature had carved into the granite millennia ago. "I used to make up stories about him when I was a child—the way some kids do about the man in the moon, I suppose."

"If he's my only competition, I've got it made." Brock sent her a sidelong glance that was warm and desiring, beneath its teasing glitter.

"At least your heart isn't made of stone like his." They had passed the granite profile, immortalized so long ago by Nathaniel Hawthorne in his classic "The Great Stone Face." Stephanie settled back into her seat again, letting her gaze roam to Brock's profile, much more virilely alive and vigorous. Just to look at him made her feel warm. "When I was little, I was certain there was a way that I could make him come to life, some magic I could perform the way the fairy godmothers did with their enchanted wands. And he would tell me all the secrets of the world." She laughed softly at her whimsy.

"Now?" Brock sounded curious, speculative.

Stephanie shrugged. "I grew up, I guess."

"No. All you have to do is touch me and I come to life." His low delivery was heavy with its sexy intonation, repeated by the languid yet serious gleam of his look. "I can prove it whenever you want."

Swallowing, Stephanie glanced away, feeling the feverish rise of heat in her veins. Her gaze made a restless sweep outside the window at the passing scenery, seeking escape without wanting to find it. The interior of the luxury car seemed suddenly very small and intimate. The click of the turning signals startled her, pulling her gaze to Brock.

"I think we could both use some air," he offered by way of explanation.

Before they reached the end of the mountain pass, he turned off and parked at the visitors' lot to the flume. When he switched off the motor, Stephanie opened the passenger door, not waiting for him to walk around the car to do it for her. The invigorating briskness of the autumn air immediately cleared her head, freeing her senses to notice other things around her.

As she waited for Brock to join her, she zipped the front of her Eisenhower jacket—a combination of dyed white and gray rabbit fur and tan leather. The legs of her deep burgundy corduroys were tucked into her high boots. The short jacket added to her clean-limbed look. The air was cool enough to turn her breath into a frosty vapor.

When Brock reached automatically for her bare hand, she automatically placed it in his, the warmth and firmness of his grip filling her with a pleasant sensation of belonging. He crooked her a faint smile before setting off to join the band of tourists lining up to get on the bus that would take them to the flume.

The endless chatter of the tourists negated the need for them to talk. Stephanie didn't mind. It left her free to savor the sensation of being squeezed close to Brock on the bus seat so a third passenger would have a place to sit.

His arm was around her, her shoulder resting against the unbuttoned front of his parka; the muscled length of his thigh and hip imprinted on her own. There was safety in the knowledge that she was surrounded by people, allowing her to simply enjoy the closeness with the temptation removed to take it to a more intimate degree.

As the bus slowed in approach of their destination, Brock murmured in her ear, "If you turn out to be a damned tease, I'm going to wring your lovely neck—after I take a bite of it.''

Her head pivoted sharply in alarm. She looked up, relieved to see he was smiling. The remark had been aimed to let her know he was deriving his own kind of pleasure from having her body crushed to his side. He lightly brushed his lips across the wing of her eyebrow in a fleeting kiss.

An older woman behind them twittered in a whisper to her companion. ''Isn't it wonderful— a pair of lovers!'' Which deepened the corners of Brock's mouth without curving them. Stephanie glanced to the front, feeling a little self-conscious.

When the bus stopped to let them out, neither of them rushed to join the mass exodus. They let the other tourists hurry on ahead of them while they followed more slowly. Stephanie wasn't as comfortable with the silence between them as she had been. When Brock removed his hand from the back of her waist to button the middle buttons of his coat, she paused with him. Ahead was the railed boardwalk winding through the cool shadows of the gorge.

''It's really better to come here in the summer when it's hot,'' she said to fill the silence. ''Then you can appreciate the coolness and the shade.''

''If you want to get warm, just let me know. I'll only be too happy to oblige.'' When her gaze fell under the lazily suggestive regard of his, he reached out to lace his fingers through her chestnut hair, pulling her toward him and lightly stroking her cheek and his other hand. He smiled gently. "You don't know how to handle all this sexual bantering, do you?"

"I've never been with anyone . . . who alludes to it as constantly as you do," she admitted, trying not to be embarrassed.

"I'm just saying what's on my mind," Brock stated, gazing deep into her blue eyes. "On my mind every time I'm near you." The vibrancy of his low voice caught at her breath, cutting it off in her throat. "Does that disturb you?"

"Yes."

"I'm glad." It was said gently, his mouth swooping down to feel the coolness of her lips against his own. Straightening, Brock took his hand away and wrapped an arm around her shoulders to turn her toward the boardwalk.

They entered the deep ravine in silence, walking side by side until the boardwalk narrowed and Stephanie moved ahead. On both sides of them, a sheer rock wall towered upward to seventy feet in the air. Moss grew thickly on the moist rock, hugging the striated crevices. In the spring and summer, delicate and rare mountain flowers blossomed in the shadowy darkness of the gorge.

A laughing stream tumbled over the rock bed running alongside and below the boardwalk. The long chasm was carved by nature and the swift waters of the Pemigewasset River, centuries before the glaciers of the Ice Age moved across the land.

The cool temperature and the high humidity combined to pierce the bones with a chilling dampness. Stephanie shoved her hands deep into the pockets of her jacket to protect them from the numbing cold. They strolled along the boardwalk that twisted and curved with the ravine. Red and gold leaves swirled downward from the trees high overhead to float in the little stream like colorful toy boats.

Stephanie paused near the end of the flume where the boardwalk made a right angle turn with the gorge. Leaning against the railing, she gazed down at the stream. A sodden group of leaves had formed a miniature dam, but the rushing water had found a spillway at one end and was fast eroding the fragile blockage.

"It's peaceful here, isn't it?" She glanced at Brock, standing beside her, leaning a hand on the railing, but it was she who had his undivided attention.

"Have dinner with me tonight, Stephanie," he said. "Just the two of us. In my suite—with wine, candlelight and soft music. I'll hire a car and send Helen wherever the hell she wants to go—Boston, New York, Rome. We'll have the whole night and top it off with breakfast in bed tomorrow morning.''

Stephanie made to move away from him, but Brock blocked the attempt, shifting his position to trap her to the rail, a hand on either side of her. ''I met you less than twenty-four hours ago,'' she reasoned helplessly.

When he began brushing kisses over her neck and cheek, Stephanie didn't resist this persuasive tactic of a master. She was conscious of the warmth of his breath and coolness of his mouth against her skin, making her tingle with awareness.

''Pretend that when we met yesterday afternoon, it was two weeks ago. Dinner was a week ago and this morning was yesterday. Time is something I don't have in quantity. We have to make the most of what's available, not waste it on all these needless preliminaries,'' Brock murmured. ''Stay with me. We'll have all night to get to know each other—in every way there is.''

She shuddered with exquisite longing and drew back, tossing her head in a wary kind of defiance. ''You don't understand, Brock.'' Her voice was tight and soft. ''I want to be more than a virgin you slept with one October in New Hampshire.''

His look became stony as he straightened from

the railing. "All right," he said grimly. "Forget about tonight." His balled fists sought the pockets of his jacket, facing her with nearly a foot between them. "I have to leave shortly after noon tomorrow. What are you doing in the morning?"

The question caught Stephanie off guard. "I . . I usually go to church."

The muscles along his jawline tautened, flexing in suppressed anger. There was a bleakness in his gray eyes that chilled her with its wintry blast. "I suppose you're going to ask me to come with you. My God, Stephanie, I'd be sitting in that pew lusting after you," he expelled the words in a rush of hot anger. "Please, spare me the hypocrisy of that!"

Her mouth opened but she couldn't find anything to say. His hand snaked out to grab her elbow and propel her along the boardwalk. The serenely quiet and peaceful ravine suddenly became rife with raw tension.

Not a word was exchanged until they had returned to the car and Brock started the motor. "Will I see you before you leave?" Stephanie risked a glance at his forbidding profile as she asked the subdued question.

"Not tonight. I haven't got that kind of control."

He didn't even look at her as he reversed out of the parking space. Before he turned onto the road, he let the car idle and glanced at her. There was a softening in the hardness of his expression—a surfacing patience that was reluctant.

"We'll get together in the morning . . . before church. In the meantime—" he pushed back the sleeve of his parka to see his watch "—it's time I was back at the inn. Perry and I have an appointment to meet the architect at one."

At the farmhouse, Brock didn't bother to get out of the car. When he looked at her, not moving, Stephanie leaned across the seat to kiss him. His hands didn't touch her and his response to the contact of her lips was severely checked, barely warm.

Vaguely dejected, Stephanie walked to the house and paused at the door of the two-story brick structure to watch Brock drive away. She didn't really blame him for his attitude, but she knew that hers was not without justification, too.

ON SUNDAY morning, Stephanie awakened earlier than usual. Since Brock hadn't given her any indication when he might call or come, she didn't take the chance of being caught unaware. She was dressed complete with makeup when she went downstairs to make coffee and get the Sunday newspaper the paperboy had delivered to their doorstep.

Before she drank her second cup of coffee, she

was on pins and needles waiting for the phone to ring or the sound of a car driving up the lane. All the while the knowledge that Brock would be leaving at noon and she didn't have any idea when he would come back kept preying on her mind. A noise in the living room sent her rushing out of the kitchen, certain she had missed hearing Brock's car, but it was a bleary-eyed Perry who had caused the sound.

"Brrr, it's cold in here! Why haven't you started the fire?" he grumbled, and shivered in his corduroy robe. His hair was mussed from the night's sleep and a pair of old slippers covered his large feet as he moved tiredly toward the Count Rumford fireplace. "You're up and dressed very early this morning. How come?" He waved aside the question, kneeling to set dried logs on the grate. "I remember. You told me at supper that Brock was supposed to come over this morning."

"Yes, he is." While her brother got the fire going, Stephanie walked to the front window to look out. "You were late coming home last night."

"I know. I hope you have the coffee made," he sighed. "Is the Sunday paper here yet?" The fire was crackling merrily in the fireplace, already chasing out the chill in the room.

"Yes, to both. I'll bring them to you," she volunteered, and retraced her steps to the kitchen

99

to pour a cup of coffee for her brother and bring him the newspaper.

When she returned, he was stretched out in his favorite armchair, his feet on the footstool, his eyes closed. She set his coffee on the lampstand beside him and dropped the paper on his lap. Perry stirred, slowly opening one eye and yawning.

"Why didn't you sleep longer?" Stephanie chided. "There wasn't any reason for you to get up this early." Sundays were, theoretically, his days off, except in the winter, but he usually stopped by the inn in the afternoons.

"I'm really bushed," he admitted. "But I woke up and couldn't go back to sleep."

While he sipped at the steaming hot coffee, Stephanie wandered to the hooked rug covering the wide floorboards in front of the fireplace. The living room was large and open, with exposed beams and hand-planed wainscoting. The sliding glass doors were decorated with October frost, partially concealing the hills rising behind the house.

"I always think I'm doing well until I come away from a meeting with Brock." Which was where Perry had been the night before until well after midnight. "Now, I feel drained and empty. He's like a sponge, absorbing everything I know out of my brain and asking endless questions," he sighed.

"About what?" Stephanie turned to study her brother, wondering if Brock had asked about her.

Perry started to answer, then interrupted her look. "No, he didn't ask about you. Obviously you told him that I gave up graduate school in law when dad had his accident."

"Why? What did he say?"

"A lot of nonsense about night school and summer courses." His mouth tightened grimly. "Which would take me forever, plus there's the problem of commuting back and forth and keeping the inn operating the way it should. No, it just isn't possible."

"What else did you talk about?" They had discussed the possibility of Perry resuming his education many times, always with the same conclusion, so Stephanie didn't argue with him now. She was too eager for any snippet of information about Brock.

"Everything from the difficulty of getting and keeping good help to renovating the whole place and turning it into the most famous ski lodge on the continent." Her brother paused, appearing to consider something. "You know, Stephanie, most of the time I feel like I'm a pretty experienced guy, but last night, in his suite, he was getting calls from half the world. My whole life

101

is centered around that inn, yet I doubt very seriously if the inn earns enough money to pay his travel expenses for a year. I represent pretty small potatoes to his organization. The place could burn down and he'd never miss it.''

"Why are you thinking like that?" It didn't sound like her brother: his attitude was defeated and inferior.

"I don't know." She shrugged and sighed. "Maybe I'm jealous. Hell, I know I am," he laughed shortly. "There I am sitting in his suite last night, trying desperately to concentrate on the discussion, and this chick of his keeps waltzing in and out of the bedroom dressed in this sheer lacy peignoir. I spent more time imagining . . . ." Perry stopped at the sight of the ashen color that spread over Stephanie's face. "I'm sorry. Stephanie, don't be a fool."

"Please, don't say anything," she protested softly. "There isn't anything you can say that I haven't told myself already." She turned, needing a few minutes by herself. "Excuse me. I'm going to get some coffee."

When she returned to the living room, Perry was buried in the front page of the newspaper, and the conversation wasn't resumed. Stephanie sat on the sofa to drink her coffee. The minute it was gone she was up, walking to the window to look at the empty scene. Back and forth she went—too nervous to stay seated, while the grandfather clock ticked away the minutes.

"A watched pot never boils," Perry remarked on her tenth trip to the window.

"I know it." She walked to the fireplace to add another log to the waning fire.

"It's getting late," he observed. "I'd better get dressed for church. Are you coming?"

Rising, she glanced toward the window. "I . . . ." Then Stephanie saw the blue Mercedes coming up the drive. "He's here!"

She dashed to the door and was outside by the time Brock stepped from the car. Her smile froze into place when she spied the blonde sitting in the passenger seat. Her gaze swung in hurt confusion back to Brock as he approached, his features grimly drawn.

"I have to leave. With luck, I'll make it to New York in time to catch the afternoon flight to Geneva," he said.

Stephanie couldn't speak, her throat paralyzed. She could only stare at him with her rounded blue eyes. The frosty chill of the October morning wasn't nearly as cold as she felt. He was leaving, and they wouldn't even have the morning together.

"I came to say goodbye," Brock continued. "I should have called, but . . . ." His jaw hardened. "I told you this could happen. Dammit,

I warned you!'' He grabbed her by the shoulders as if to shake her.

The physical pain was almost welcome. In the next second, he was yanking her into his arms and bruising her lips with a hard, angry kiss, relentless in its punishment. But his savagery aroused an emotion stronger than pain. It engulfed her, leaving her weak and breathless when he broke the contact.

He pushed her away and had already turned to walk to the car before he muttered a rather final sounding, ''Goodbye, Stephanie.''

But she couldn't get that one word out—not even his name. The car had been started and was turning around. Still Stephanie hadn't moved from where he'd left her at the door.

There was no last glance from Brock—no wave, nothing. Tears misted over her eyes, blinding her vision. She didn't see the exact moment when his car disappeared from view down the long lane.

Entering the house, she was aware of Perry's blurred outline near the stairwell. ''He had to leave . . . for Geneva.'' Her voice was choked and very small. Her brother looked at her for a long minute, but didn't say anything as he turned to climb the stairs. Stephanie walked blindly into the kitchen where she cried slow, silent tears.

THE NORTH WINDS came to strip the leaves from the trees, exposing the dark skeletons of the trunks and leaving piles of brown leaves to carpet the ground. The first snow flurry of the season came the last weekend in October. November arrived.

Stephanie had written Brock two letters, short ones with news of the inn and the area, minus any personal messages. The only address she had was the one the monthly reports were sent to. She couldn't be sure if they would reach him. Last week, she had sent merely a postcard.

There hadn't been a single reply of any kind, and she was gradually becoming convinced he had forgotten her. She couldn't shake the feeling that she had been on the brink of discovering something wonderful, only to lose it.

The ring of her office extension drew a sigh. Unclipping an earring, she answered the phone. "Miss Hall speaking. May I help you?"

"How are you?" a familiar male voice inquired.

Incredulous, Stephanie tightened her grip on the receiver, the blood singing in her veins. "Brock?" She could feel her voice choking. "Where are you?" In the background she could hear a hum of voices.

"Can you believe it?" His short laugh was a quietly harsh sound. "I'm in the middle of a board meeting. I don't know who the hell they think I'm talking to, but I had to call you."

"I'm glad." Her answer was hardly above a whisper.

"The mail packet caught up with me this morning. I got the letter and postcard you sent," he said.

"I . . . I wasn't sure if I should write," she admitted.

"These are liberated times, but I'm not surprised that you're behind them," he mocked, but not unkindly.

A voice intruded from the background. "Mr. Canfield, here's the breakdown report you wanted on the foreign currency exchange this quarter."

"Good, Frank," was Brock's partially muffled response, then clearer, "Are you still there?"

"Yes, I'm here," Stephanie assured him, her voice regaining its strength.

Brock started to say something, then changed his mind. "This is the most frustrating means of communication." His tone was low and charged with irritation. "I can't see you or touch you."

"I know." There was a certain torment in hearing his voice.

"Mr. Canfield?" The same voice interrupted Brock again.

"Dammit, Frank, can't you see I'm on the phone?" he demanded. He came back on the

about breakfast this morning. I'm going out to put the snow chains on the wagon. We'll eat when we get to the inn."

"When the weatherman said snow last night, he meant it, didn't he?" She glanced out of the frosty window at the large flakes veiling the gray white hills.

"We're in for a storm," Perry prophesied. "It wouldn't hurt if you grabbed a clean shirt and my shaving kit, and something for yourself. If this keeps up, we'll just sleep at the inn tonight. Our road is always the last one the snowplows hit." He grimaced and ducked out the back door amid a whirl of snowflakes and cold air.

The drive from the farmhouse to the inn usually took ten minutes, but the limited visibility and the slippery roads caused by the falling snow increased it to twenty-five. The car radio forecast worsening conditions.

Before breakfast was over the area slopes were closed to skiers. The inn suddenly seemed more crowded than usual because all the guests were virtually confined to the inn. They congregated in the lobby around the fireplace, the games room, the lounge and the restaurants. There was even a line to use the recently completed sauna and exercise room. Almost any flat surface was commandeered for a game of cards. Impromptu chess and checkers tournaments were held.

Shortly after twelve noon there was a mild panic when it was discovered that two cross-country skiers hadn't reported in from an overnight trip. Perry and Stephanie had just sat down to the restaurant's turkey dinner. The adventurers were finally located at another lodge, but their dinners were cold when they returned to them.

Then the deluge of stranded motorists began. Although they were full, Stephanie temporarily doubled up rooms where she could, shifting all the members of one family into a room, helped housekeeping figure out how many spare blankets, sheets, cots and pillows were on hand and how many motorists they could handle, and filled in wherever else she was needed.

"Don't forget to save us a place to sleep," Perry reminded her at one point when she was working out the capacity of the sofas in the lobby.

"There's always the floor," she retorted with a laugh.

It was almost a relief when the storm knocked the telephone lines out late in the afternoon and the switchboard finally stopped buzzing. The dinner hour didn't bring a letup in the frantic pace. With all the extra people, both Perry and Stephanie lent a hand in the restaurant kitchen, doing everything from helping to fix the food to running the dishwasher.

At nine-thirty Perry laid a hand on her shoulder.

"You've done enough, Steph. Why don't you call it a night?"

"Yessir, boss," she agreed readily. "What about you?"

"I'm going to the lounge. Freddie needs some help behind the bar. And—" he breathed in tiredly "—I'd better be around in case someone gets rowdy."

Stephanie was tempted to insist he let someone else do it, but Perry took his responsibility as manager too seriously to shrug it onto someone else. "Okay, I'll see you in the morning."

"Wait a minute!" He called her back when she started to turn away. "Where do I sleep tonight?"

"On the couch in your office . . . unless it's already occupied," she joked. "In that event, you're on your own."

"Thanks a lot, sis," he retorted in a mock growl.

Stopping at her office, Stephanie picked up the small overnight bag she had packed and started down the hallway. She didn't know which sounded more divine—a shower or sleep? With luck, she would be able to have both.

Before she knocked at the door of the suite, she heard the childish giggles coming from in

111

side. Her knocks produced some shrieks and more giggles. The door was opened by a young woman, barely a year older than Stephanie. She looked tired, harassed and exasperated, her smile growing thin.

"Hi. It's me, your roommate for the night." Stephanie struggled to sound cheerful.

"Of course, come in, Miss Hall." But she was diverted by the impish little five-year-old girl who appeared in the connecting doorway to the bedroom. "Amy Sue, you get back in that bed before I spank you!" the woman threatened, and the little nightgowned figure fled in laughter. "I'm sorry. I've been trying to get the girls asleep for the last hour. They think this is some kind of a party."

"It's all new. They're just excited, Mrs. Foster. And please, call me Stephanie," she insisted.

"I'm Madge." She walked to the bedroom. "And these are my daughters, Amy, five, and Marsha, four."

Amy, the oldest, quickly scurried under the covers. The king-sized bed seemed to swallow up the two small girls with their dark hair. The pair eyed Stephanie with bold curiosity.

"Hello, Amy and Marsha," she smiled. The two looked anything but sleepy with their bright brown eyes.

"Hello. Who are you?" The youngest asked,

exhibiting no shyness because Stephanie was a stranger.

"My name is Stephanie," she replied.

"My friend in day care has that same name," Amy piped.

"Will you read us a story?" Marsha dived for the storybooks on the nightstand beside the bed. "Read mine."

"No, mine!" Amy protested.

"Girls!" Madge Foster attempted to intervene with some measure of authority.

"I don't mind," Stephanie murmured. "I'll read to them while you relax in the tub." When the woman hesitated, obviously tempted, Stephanie repeated, "Really, I don't mind."

"Thank you. I don't know what to say," the woman faltered. "All day long, trying to drive in that storm, with those girls bouncing all over, then being stranded here . . . my nerves could use a rest. But I won't leave them with you for long, I promise."

"Read my story, please?" Amy pleaded.

"I'll read them both," Stephanie promised. "But we'll start with Marsha's first."

She set her overnight case on the floor by the bed and walked over to sit on the edge where the bedside lamp was lit. Marsha immediately pressed her book into Stephanie's hands. They grumbled when she insisted that they had to crawl under

113

the covers and lie down before she would read to them. They didn't give in until she had agreed to show them the pictures on each page.

Her ploy worked. By the time she had read the first story for the third time, both girls had fallen asleep. When the bathroom door opened Stephanie held a silencing finger to her lips. Madge Foster smiled and shook her head in disbelief.

"You must have my husband Ted's kind of voice. I can read until I'm hoarse, but they go right to sleep for him," she whispered. "I don't think my head is even going to have a chance to touch the pillow before I'm asleep. The bathroom is all yours, and it's like heaven."

"Good." Stephanie flexed her shoulders as the fatigue began to set in. She picked up her night case and started toward the marble bathroom.

"Oh, Miss H . . . Stephanie, do you mind if I leave the lamp burning on my side of the bed? The girls don't like to sleep in the dark. I've been trying to break them of it, but this is a strange place and . . . if it wouldn't bother you. . .?"

"No, it won't bother me. I'm like you," Stephanie explained. "I'll probably be asleep before my head's on the pillow."

"The girls don't toss and turn very much, so I don't think they'll disturb you."

"I'm sorry we weren't able to provide you with a room of your own," Stephanie apologized.

"Listen, I'm just grateful for a bed to sleep in. And heaven knows, this one is big enough to hold two more," Madge smiled. "Go and take your bath. And good night."

"Yes, good night."

The hot bath water made Stephanie realize how mentally and physically exhausted she was. It was an effort to towel dry and pull on her nightdress. All three were asleep when she reentered the bedroom. She moved quietly to the far side of the bed on the fringe of the pool of light cast by the lamp. She, too, drifted into sleep within minutes.

A coolness roused her, a vague sensation of a draft. Stephanie tried to pull the covers tighter around her neck, but something held them down. She started to turn onto her side, only to become conscious of something heavy weighing the edge of the mattress down.

Her lashes opened to a narrow slit, then widened at the outline of a person sitting on the bed beside her. It was a full second before she realized who the man in the white shirt was.

"Brock!" Was she dreaming? She said his name softly in case she scared his image away.

But his hand touched her face in a light, cool caress and she knew it wasn't a dream. "Hello."

"What are you doing here?" she breathed, keeping her voice low.

He looked tried and drawn: she could see that in the half-light from the lamp. But the glint in his gray eyes was anything but weary.

"Here you are finally in my bed, and there isn't room for me." His gaze danced to the sleeping children in the center of the bed, their faces illuminated by the soft glow spilling from the lamp.

"The storm—" Stephanie started to explain in a whisper.

"Yes, I know. I stepped over bodies in the lobby." Without warning, Brock straightened to fold back the covers and slide his arms beneath her, picking her up.

Stephanie clutched at his neck, too stunned and sleepy to struggle and too conscious of the possibility of waking the children or their mother. "What are you doing, Brock?" The question was issued in confused excitement, her pulse accelerating at this contact with his leanly muscled frame.

"I'm taking you into the other room with me," he stated, and carried her through the connecting door to the sitting room. "We have an hour of Thanksgiving left and I mean to spend it with you."

Brock didn't put her down until they were inside the room and the door was shut. A single light burned in the far corner. Outside the window the snow was still falling, but slower and not as thickly as it had been earlier.

Not quite able to believe he was really there in the flesh, Stephanie gazed at his manly features, the darkness of his hair and the melting grayness of his eyes. His hands encircled her waist, gliding over the silken material of her nightgown to bring her slowly closer as if he enjoyed the feel of her.

When his mouth began a downward movement toward her, Stephanie went on tiptoes to meet it. He took possession of the yielding softness of her lips with a gentle sensuality. It was so different from any other kiss that she could hardly understand what was happening to her.

His hands were at the small of her back, caressing but firm against her silk-covered skin and holding her close to the hardening contours of his thighs. Her blood ran with fire as he practiced the subtle art of seduction so expertly and so effortlessly. Stephanie was lost to his skill and she didn't care. When at last he released her lips to seek the bareness of a shoulder, she sighed her enchanted contentment. It gradually dawned on her that the coolness she was feeling against her scantily clad body did not come from any draft in the room. It was Brock who was chilled.

"You're cold," she murmured in concern.

"So?" His mouth was against her ear, his tongue circling its sensitive hollows. "Warm me up."

Taking him literally at his word, Stephanie pressed closer to him in an effort to warm him with her body heat. "How did you get here in this storm?" she asked, her mouth brushing the coolness of his shirt at his shoulder. "I still can't believe you're really here," she sighed at the miracle of being in his arms.

"Neither can I!" His arms tightened fiercely for an instant. "There were times when I wondered whether I would make it," he admitted in a tired and rueful sigh.

"Why did you come? With this storm and all. . .?" Stephanie lifted her head, shuddering when she thought of him out there in that blizzard. She was frightened by what might have happened. Her hand glided along the smoothness of his jaw and he rubbed his cheek into her palm.

"Why did you take such a risk?" Her voice was choked by the dangerous chance he had taken.

"I wanted to be with you." He gazed deep into her eyes, letting his look add a heady force to his statement. "I didn't want to spend the holiday without you."

"You should have called. You should have let me know you were coming," Stephanie admonished, but she knew she would have been worried sick about him.

"I wanted to surprise you." His mouth twisted in a wry line. "It's been an eighteen-hour obstacle course—closed airports, diverted flights, trains not running, highways closed. When I finally admitted there was a distinct possibility I wouldn't make it, the telephone lines were down. I couldn't get through to tell you I wanted to be here."

"Brock. . . ." The frustration he had suffered was very real to her.

"I know." The circle of his arms tightened as he pressed a kiss to her temple.

"How did you get here?" She still marveled that he had actually made it.

"I rented a car and bribed a maintenance crew to let me follow their snowplow," he explained.

"How did you guess I'd be here at the inn?"

"I didn't. I went to your home first," Brock told her.

"But the lane—" Stephanie's eyes widened in alarmed protest.

"Was blocked," he finished the sentence for her. "I had to leave the car on the road and walk back to the house. It's a good thing you and Perry are the trusting sort and left the back door unlocked. When I discovered the house was empty, I guessed you'd decided to spend the night at the inn, so I came here. Of course, I never expected

119

to find you sleeping in my bed. Lucky for me, the night clerk knew where you were bunking and I didn't have to go around knocking on doors in the middle of the night trying to find you. Perry would have had some irate guests on his hands come morning.''

She was shaken by his single-minded determination to find her, to be with her. Surely it had to mean something? Mere sexual attraction couldn't be all it was that they shared. The thought left her feeling slightly euphoric and dazed by the fiery surge of emotion rushing through her system.

"Come." Moving, Brock took hold of her hand and led her to the side of the room. "I took the seat cushions off the sofa and the spare pillows and blankets from the closet to make us a bed on the floor in here.''

Stephanie stared at the blanket-covered cushions on the floor and the two pillows lying side by side at the top. Brock was studying her, waiting for her reaction. But there was none—at least, not a negative one.

"I'll turn out the light.'' Releasing her hand, Brock moved to the opposite side of the room where the lamp burned.

Stephanie watched him. There wasn't any conscious decision on her part. She was only aware of how very close she had come to losing him to the winter storm. All arguments for and against going to bed with him paled in comparison to that unshakable fact. It was truly the only thought in her mind.

When the click of a light switch buried the room in darkness, she sank onto the hard foam cushions. A sublime calmness settled through her as she folded back the blanket to slide beneath it.

She loved Brock. The quiet knowledge wasn't a rationale for her action, but the simple truth. Implausible as it seemed, as short a time as she had known him, she loved him. The unshakable strength of emotion made her feel mellow and warm, ripe with the fullness of it.

Brock was a dark shadow as he approached the makeshift bed. Not until he had joined her under the covers did he take form and substance. Lying on his side, he reached for her to draw her into his embrace.

Her hands encountered the muscled bareness of his chest, its dark hair sensually rough beneath her palms, his legs shifting to tangle with hers. The sweet intimacy twisted its knife-sharp blade into her stomach, a heady desire building.

His mouth sought and found hers, covering it with a softly bruising force and demanding a response that she had no wish to suppress. He mastered her with a fiery hunger, possessing her

121

heart and soul, which she was only too willing to give into his keeping. With a surrendering sigh, she slid her arms around the smooth skin covering his hard shoulders to bring more of his weight onto her.

The blanket slipped to a position over their hips as Brock pushed the silken strap of her nightgown off a shoulder. His mouth explored the rose-crested top of a breast that had been exposed to his dark gray eyes. It heightened the taut desire curling her toes and knotting her insides. Then his mouth returned to crush her lips while the sensually abrasive hair on his chest brushed across the sensitive skin of her naked breast.

A moaning sound came from his throat, his warm breath filling her mouth with suffocating sweetness. The thin barrier of her nightgown didn't keep out the sensation of the growing limpness of his body.

Reluctantly, Brock drew away from her to roll onto his back, an arm flung above his head onto the pillow. Stephanie was confused and aching by this withdrawal. Turning onto her side, she levered herself onto an elbow to gaze at him.

His gaze slid to her, the vibrant glitter fading from his eyes. He reached out to slide the strap of her gown onto her shoulder, his hand remaining to silently caress her. A half smile was lifting one corner of his mouth. Even that seemed to require a lot of effort.

"What's wrong, Brock?" Stephanie asked uncertainly, wanting to curl herself into his arms, but refraining to obey the impulse because of the lack of an invitation.

"I've been working some long hours the last few days, trying to clear up any business that might come up at the last minute and kept me from coming here to be with you." His hand moved to rest on the curve of her neck beneath the curtain of chestnut hair. "I've had six hours of sleep in the last fifty-two. That's what's wrong."

She heard the weariness in his voice, but in the dimness of the darkened room she could only guess at the strain of fatigue etched in his features. When he chuckled softly, she frowned in confusion.

"Don't you see the irony of this, Stephanie?" Brock murmured. "After all this time you're finally beside me—here in this bed, just the way I imagined it. And now I'm too damned tired to do anything about it," he sighed in irritation.

Her personal dissatisfaction was forgotten in a rush of loving concern for him. Leaning forward, she kissed his lips with infinite tenderness. A loving smile curved her mouth when she straightened.

"You'd better get some sleep before you collapse," she advised, and turned to sweep back the covers to return to her own bed.

"No." Brock waylaid her action with an outstretched hand. "Stay with me tonight."

Her hesitation was fractional. Accepting his invitation, she lay down once more beside him. Brock turned her onto her side with her back to him and curled her against his length. His arm was around her waist, a hand possessively cupping a breast.

Stephanie was warmed by the memory that Brock had once insisted that he preferred to sleep alone. He shared this need to be close—a need that transcended every thought and feeling that might have been true in the past. What they had was unique. Stephanie knew it, and she suspected Brock did, too.

Hugged close to him, she heard his breathing grow deep and heavy as tiredness carried him quickly to sleep. She closed her eyes, not certain that she would drift off so quickly, but the utter contentment soon whisked her away. Thus they slept spoon fashion, enfolded in an embrace of passive desire.

Morning light infiltrated the room through the large windows, pricking at Stephanie's eyelids. She became conscious of a heavy weight across her legs and stomach. A delicious heat was radiating from something and she snuggled closer to it. When she realized the heartbeat she was hearing did not belong to her, she opened her eyes.

A pair of broad shoulders were in front of her, tanned skin stretched across sinewy muscles and darkened with rough, curling hairs. The weight across her stomach was Brock's arm, his hand cupped to her hipbone in firm possession, while a leg was hooked across her knees. Peering through the top of her lashes, she studied the unrelenting strength of his face in sleep. Lean and powerful, he stirred her senses.

There was a very strong impulse to kiss him awake, but the amount of sunlight streaming through the windows and the muffled voices of others in the outer hall warned Stephanie of the lateness of the hour.

Reluctantly she slid out of his hold and out of the makeshift bed on the floor. Her bare feet made no sound as she entered the bedroom where the young woman and her two children were still sleeping. With her overnight bag in hand, she slipped into the bathroom to wash and dress.

There wasn't a sound from anyone when she came out. She hesitated in the sitting room, but Brock was still sound asleep. He had left the key to his suite lying on an end table. Stephanie slipped it into her pocket and quietly left the room through the hall door.

. She went directly to the restaurant kitchen. The inn was already astir with early morning breakfasters. Outside, the sky was clear—almost too blue against the pure snow white of the ground. She laid a tray with china cups and a pot of coffee to take to the suite.

As she was passing through the lobby, her brother appeared. "Stephanie!" he called out to stop her. "Brock's here," he said when he reached her side. "He arrived last night."

"Yes, I know," she nodded. "I'm taking him some coffee now. He's still sleeping. He made a bed on the floor of the sitting room." She didn't mention that she had shared it with him. It wasn't an attempt to conceal the knowledge from Perry. Rather, she preferred to choose her own time to tell him when there weren't others around who might overhear and misinterpret her action.

Perry glanced at the tray, then at her, studying her closely. "Why is he here? Did he say?" he questioned.

"He wanted to have Thanksgiving here." She hesitated over carrying the explanation further, but she needn't have.

Her brother did it for her. "With you," he identified the reason specifically.

"Yes," Stephanie nodded, unable to keep the radiance from shining in her eyes.

Perry shook his head in absent amazement.

"In that blizzard . . ." he murmured. He bit at his lip in a second of pensive silence. "Maybe I was wrong about him . . . and his interest in you," he offered. Whatever else he was about to add, he changed his mind and flashed her a wry smile. "You'd better take that coffee to him before it gets cold."

"I'll be back shortly," she promised.

"No rush," Perry insisted. "After the long day you put in yesterday, you can be as late as you want this morning."

Her smile was full of affection for her brother. "Thanks, boss."

At the door to the suite, Stephanie had to set the tray on the floor to have her hands free to unlock the door. The cups rattled on their china saucers as she entered the sitting room, but the delicate noise didn't waken Brock, who was still sleeping soundly on the floor. Only silence came from the bedroom where the young woman and her two little girls were.

Stephanie carried the tray to the rattan table and set it there. Knowing how little sleep Brock had in the last few days, she didn't pour him any coffee yet, only a cup for herself. The thermal pot would keep the coffee hot for a long time. She walked to a chair, unconsciously choosing one that would permit her to watch Brock in sleep.

The blanket was down around his hips, exposing his lean, untanned torso to her inspection. Briefly she was fascinated by the button roundness of his navel, a dark hollow in his flat stomach. He was lying on his side, facing her.

Stephanie let her gaze wander upward to his strongly defined mouth and the thickness of dark lashes resting against his cheekbone. His brows were thick and malely arched. Across his forehead was a thatch of rumpled dark hair. Even in sleep, Brock exuded an incredible virility. She wanted to touch him so much, it was almost a physical pain.

When he stirred, she unconsciously held her breath. His hand moved across the empty cushion beside him, as if instinctively seeking something. Was he in search of her? What a wondrous thought! His hand froze for a full second, then instantly he was awake, turning onto his back and alarm flashed in his expression.

"Stephanie!" He called out for her in an impatient voice a fraction of a second before he saw her seated in the chair. His expression changed immediately to one of satisfaction.

"Good morning." Her voice was husky with the knowledge that he had missed having her sleeping form beside him.

"Not so good," Brock denied her adjective

in describing the morning. "You should have awakened me when you awoke."

"Would you like some coffee?" Stephanie rose, conscious of his gaze taking in her fully dressed appearance, detail by detail. Without waiting for his acceptance, she walked to the table and poured a cup for him.

"Why did you get dressed right away?" he questioned before his gaze flickered past her to the sunlight that drenched the room. "What time is it?"

"Nearly nine o'clock." She carried the cup to him.

The blanket had slipped a little farther downward, giving her a tantalizing glimpse of the elastic waistband of his white jockey shorts. It was crazy the way her pulse reacted to the sight, yet she had entered her brother's bedroom many times to waken him when he slept through his alarm, and found him similarly clad. She hadn't even blinked an eye then.

"I suppose you have to work this morning." His mouth was grim as he looked up when she stood beside the crude bed. He was still supported by his elbows and forearms in a half-reclining position.

"No. Perry said it was okay if I was late," she assured him, and knelt down to give him his coffee.

But Brock didn't reach for it. "In that case, come back to bed." His gaze became obsessively attached to her lips, sending her heart knocking against her ribs.

Stephanie couldn't find her voice. She recovered it after he had sat up and circled one arm around her waist while his hand curved itself to the back of her neck, pulling her toward him.

"I'm going to spill the coffee," she warned a breath before his mouth covered her lips to hungrily remind her of the volatile attraction they shared.

Her hand gripped his hard shoulder for balance while the cup of coffee jiggled in its saucer in the opposite hand, the steaming liquid sloshing over the china rim. But she offered no resistance to his kiss, melting under his heady domination.

"Ged rid of that coffee and those clothes, and come back to bed with me," Brock ordered against her mouth, and proceeded to outline her lips with his tongue.

He kissed her thoroughly and sensually before drawing away. Stephanie was drugged in a euphoric state, barely capable of thought when she met the gray darkness of his eyes. A sound intruded, a mere irritation until a movement entered her vision, drawing her glance.

Five-year-old Amy was standing in the doorway wearing her flannel nightgown, one bare foot on top of the other, eyeing the pair of them curiously. Stephanie was brought sharply to her senses. Brock turned to look behind him and barely stifled a curse of frustration rather than anger. There was a glitter of ironic amusement and profound regret when he glanced back to Stephanie.

"Who's that man?" Amy wanted to know. "Is he your husband?"

Brock rescued the cup of coffee from her shaking hand and arched a mocking brow in her direction. "No, he's a friend," Stephanie explained a little self-consciously.

The little girl padded quickly across the room as if invited. "Why are you sleeping on the floor?" she asked Brock, and bounced onto the cushions to sit on a pillow with her legs under her.

"Because there wasn't any place else for me to sleep," he replied, regarding the little girl's intrusion with a patience and tolerance that faintly surprised Stephanie.

"There was lots of room in the bed," Amy insisted.

"It looked a little more crowded than I wanted." His glance darted to Stephanie, heavy with secret meaning.

A drowsy Marsha entered the room, rubbing her sleep-filled eyes and hugging her storybook in front of her. She pattered quickly to her older sister's side and curled onto the edge of the pillow, sitting cross-legged and yawning.

Brock took a sip of his coffee and murmured to Stephanie, "This bed is nearly as full as mine was last night."

"Were you going to wrestle?" the oldest brunette girl inquired innocently.

His look was amused, yet narrowed. "Why do you ask?"

"Because mommy and daddy do that sometimes in the mornings," she explained. "Daddy tickles and tickles her. It makes mommy laugh so hard she cries. Then daddy kisses her like you were doing."

"I see." The corners of his mouth deepened with the containment of a smile. "Then what happens?"

Stephanie gasped in sharp embarrassment, drawing the wicked glint of his gaze.

"Then mommy's cheeks get pink like Stephanie's are," Amy admitted with guileless charm. "She shoos us to our own rooms and helps us get dressed so we can go outside and play."

The answer didn't put Stephanie any more at ease under Brock's disturbing and mocking look. "Is your mother awake?" she asked, hoping to change the subject.

"Not yet." It was obvious it didn't matter much to either of the girls. "Do you have any children?'' Amy directed the question to Brock. Like any female, she was drawn to the male of the species.

"No," he replied as his gaze roamed over the two little girls.

"Wouldn't you like to have a little girl of your own?" Amy seemed puzzled. "Daddy says it's wonderful, especially when you have two."

"He does, does he?" Brock was deliberately noncommittal although he glanced almost automatically at Stephanie.

"Yes. You can have little boys, too," Amy hastened to add.

"But they can be mean sometimes," Marsha piped in for the first time. "Jimmy Joe Barnes stepped on my doll and broke its head on purpose."

"But daddy fixed it," Amy reminded her, before turning back to Brock. "Which do you think you'd rather have?"

"I don't know. Do little boys crawl in bed with their parents in the morning, too?" he asked with his tongue in his cheek.

"I think so." Amy's frown revealed she didn't understand the relevancy of that question.

"Which would you rather have, Stephanie?" Brock eyed her with deliberate suggestiveness, stealing her breath. "Boys or girls? Or one of each?"

133

"I—" She was spared from answering that provocative question by the interruption of Madge Foster's voice coming from the bedroom.

"Amy? Marsha? Where are you?" she called in sleepy alarm.

"We're in here, mommy," Amy answered immediately.

"What are you . . . ." the question was never finished as the young woman appeared in the doorway.

The sight of Brock sitting half-naked with Stephanie and her daughters made the woman suddenly and embarrassingly conscious of the revealing nightgown she was wearing. Quickly she stepped behind the door, using it as a shield.

"You girls come here right now," she ordered. "You haven't brushed your teeth yet," she added, as if that was the reason.

The pair hopped blithely to their feet and dashed into the bedroom. Madge sent Stephanie a grimacing look of apology before closing the door.

"Now—" Brock caught at Stephanie's hand to pull her off-balance and into his arms "—where were we before we were so rudely interrupted?" His mouth had barely touched her lips when there was a knock at the hall door. Releasing her, he muttered, "This place is turning into Grand Central Station. You'd better hand me my

134

pants, there's likely to be a parade through here any minute."

Before she answered the door, Stephanie handed him the trousers draped over a nearby chair. It was one of the housekeepers doing a room check. When Stephanie turned around after closing the door, Brock was on his feet, semidecently clad in the dark pants.

"More coffee?" she suggested.

"Since circumstances don't allow anything else, why not?" he shrugged with a wry smile. She had just started to fill his cup when the telephone rang. Brock motioned her to stay where she was. "I'll get it." He answered it, then hesitated, glancing at Stephanie as he responded to the caller, "Just a minute, please." He held the mouthpiece slightly away. "The young woman occupying the bedroom—is her last name Foster?"

"Yes, it is," Stephanie nodded.

"It's her husband on the phone," he explained. "Evidently the telephones are back in service. There's an extension by the bed she can use."

"I'll tell her." She handed Brock his cup before she walked over to knock on the connecting door. "Madge, your husband is on the phone."

The delighted shrieks of the two young girls came first from the bedroom, then echoed into the sitting room through the phone in Brock's hand. He set the receiver on its cradle and let a glance slide at Stephanie.

"How do you suppose she's going to explain that a man answered?" he mocked.

"With the storm and all, I'm sure her husband will understand." She dismissed it as a problem and retrieved her coffee cup from the side table to refill it.

As he was pouring the coffee from the thermal pot, Brock came up behind her, sliding an arm around the front of her waist and bending to kiss the side of her neck. "Believe me, if I called you and a man other than your brother answered the phone, you'd have a lot of explaining to do."

A delicious tingle danced over her skin at his nibbling kisses. "I'll remember to always answer the phone myself from now on," she mocked, "especially when I'm entertaining male friends."

His arm tightened with a sudden fierceness. "I'm not joking, Stephanie. Just thinking of someone else touching you—"

Someone rapped very softly on the hall door. Brock cursed savagely as he broke away from her and crossed the room with long, impatient strides to jerk the door open.

Perry stood outside, briefly startled. "I wasn't sure if you were up yet."

Brock's laugh was a harsh sound. "I'm awake, all right. Thanks to two little girls, then their mother, then a telephone call from their father, and a housekeeper fits in the order of things somewhere. Come in—everybody else does.'' Irritation negated the attempt at humor. ''I suppose you need Stephanie.''

''Indirectly.'' Perry's gaze was ruefully apologetic when it met hers. ''I need the revised rate schedule we made yesterday afternoon. I looked on your desk, but I couldn't find it.''

''It's in the folder in the top, right-hand drawer of my desk,'' she quickly supplied its location.

''What's it like getting out of here?'' Brock demanded unexpectedly. She stared at him, not wanting to believe the implication of that question. Brock didn't even glance her way.

''The airport is closed still, but the highways are open. The snow is drifting in places, but otherwise it's in good shape, according to the highway-patrol report we got this morning,'' her brother replied.

''You aren't leaving?'' Stephanie almost accused.

''I have to.'' Then he flashed her an angry look, noting the sharp hurt in her expression. ''Dammit! I don't like it any more than you do!''

Very quietly, Perry slipped out of the room, leaving them alone. Stephanie turned away from Brock, trying to hide her bitter disappointment. She heard him set his cup down and walk up

137

behind her. His hands settled hesitantly on her shoulders.

"Twenty-four hours was all I could spare, Stephanie," he explained grimly. "I've already used more than that, most of it trying to get here."

"I understand that." She turned and was confronted by the naked wall of his chest. Lifting her gaze she looked into his face. "Honestly, I'm glad you came . . . for however long or short it has to be."

His gray eyes no longer smoldered with a resenting anger, but burned with a sultry fire as they lingered for a long, disruptive moment on her parted lips. There was no longer any hesitation in the touch of his hands as he drew her up to meet his descending mouth.

His kiss seared her with the rawness of his hunger, arousing her to the full awareness of his need and making her ache for male aggression of his wants. Her arms wound around his neck as she was crushed willingly against his chest. Before the embrace erupted out of control, Brock set her from him with a groan.

"You'd better go now," he advised tightly. "We aren't going to have any more time alone. And I'd rather say goodbye now."

"Brock!" It was a silent protest.

"Believe me, it's better this way," he insisted. "I'll see you when I can, you know that, don't you?"

"Yes," she nodded, and tried not to think about how long that might be.

He walked her to the hall door, brushing her lips with a kiss before she left the room. Her throat was raw and her eyes burned, but she didn't cry. An inner voice warned her that these farewells were something she had better accept. They would be very numerous in any prolonged relationship with Brock Canfield.

Perry didn't say anything when she walked into her office to find him going over the schedule he had removed from her desk drawer. There was gentle sympathy in his look and a suppressed concern.

For nearly two hours she waited, clinging to the hope that Brock would stop by to see her one last time before he left. But he went without seeing her again. Squaring her shoulders, she began concentrating on her work.

Keeping busy was the one sure way to make the time pass faster until she saw him again. The feeling that he cared as deeply about her as she did for him made it seem easier somehow. There was strength to be drawn from that.

CHAPTER SEVEN

"MISTLETOE?" PERRY HELD UP the sprig by its red bow and cocked an eyebrow at Stephanie, kneeling in front of the fireplace to arrange the Nativity scene on its snowy blanket. "What on earth do we need mistletoe for in this house?"

"That's a good question." She sent him a teasing glance over her shoulder. "Maybe for that new schoolteacher, Miss Henderson. I understand she came into the restaurant for dinner again last night. I also understand that you just 'happened' to take your break at the same time."

"The restaurant was crowded," he defended himself, a redness spreading upward from his neck. "It seemed logical to ask her to sit at my table."

"But twice in half a week?" she mocked. "I didn't realize schoolteachers were paid the kind of wages that would allow them to eat at an expensive restaurant on Monday night and again on Wednesday. Or did she pay for her own meal both times?''

''Pattie really has a big mouth,'' Perry sighed in disgust.

And Stephanie laughed at the reference to the cashier, her source of information that had betrayed the fact that Perry had bought the young, attractive teacher's dinner the night before. ''Pattie is just worried about your single status.''

''It's none of her business.''

''Maybe not,'' she conceded. ''But in case you decide to invite Miss Henderson over for a glass of holiday cheer, why don't you hang the mistletoe from that center beam? It looks like a strategic location to me.''

''Who said I was going to invite her over?'' Perry bristled.

''Not me,'' Stephanie countered with wide-eyed innocence. ''But if you do, let me know. I can always spend the night at the inn.''

''Hang up your own mistletoe.'' Perry tossed it aside in ill humor and reached into the box of Christmas decorations to take out the wreath for the door.

''Get me the ladder and I will,'' she agreed, realizing that the new schoolteacher was an unusually touchy subject.

A sigh slipped from her lips as Perry stalked out of the room to fetch the ladder. She regretted ribbing him. It must be more than a casual flirtation for Perry to be so sensitive about it.

She certainly wasn't in any position to make light of someone else's relationship. She hadn't heard from Brock since Thanksgiving, which was two weeks ago. And two weeks could seem an eternity.

Perry returned with the ladder, not saying a word as he set it up beneath the beam where Stephanie had suggested that the mistletoe be hung. Leaving behind the smaller hammer, he took the heavier one and a couple of tacks, as well as the Christmas wreath of evergreen garlands, pinecones and red bows, and flipped on the outside light. He stepped outside and closed the door to keep the cold night air from chilling the living room.

Finished with the Nativity scene, Stephanie took the sprig of mistletoe, the hammer and a tack and climbed the ladder. One step short of the top she stopped and stretched to reach the hardwood beam.

Even though there was only the two of them, they traditionally hung their Christmas decorations after the tenth of December. The Christmas tree wasn't put up until the week before Christmas. Stephanie realized, a little ruefully, that

142

neither of them was in the Christmas spirit on this night.

The phone started ringing before she had the mistletoe tacked into place. Stephanie hesitated, then continued to tap with the hammer, ignoring the commanding ring of the phone. The front door opened and Perry glared at her.

"Can't you hear the phone?" he snapped.

"That's only the third ring," she retorted just as impatiently.

"Fourth," he corrected, and walked briskly over to pick up the receiver and silence the irritating sound. "Hall residence," he answered with ill-tempered shortness, then paused. "Just a minute." He laid the receiver on the table with a thump. "It's for you."

The tack bent on the last strike of her hammer, which meant she had to start all over again with a new one. "Find out who it is and tell them I'll call back."

"I already know who it is—Brock." Just for a moment his expression softened. "Do you really want me to tell him you're too busy to talk right now?"

The mention of Brock's name sent her scrambling down the ladder, nearly upsetting it in her haste to get to the telephone. When she grabbed for the receiver, it slipped out of her fingers and crashed to the floor. Terrified she had broken it, Stephanie clutched it to her ear.

"Brock? Are you there?" Her voice was a thin thread of panic.

"My God, Stephanie! What did you do?" he demanded.

"I dropped the phone. I was on the ladder hanging the mistletoe when Perry answered the phone." She hurried her explanation. "I didn't realize you were the one who was calling until he told me. Then I was . . . ." It was too revealing to admit how excited she had been, so she changed her sentence. "I was in such a hurry to get to the phone that I became all thumbs."

"Are you glad I called?" His voice changed its texture, becoming warm and searching.

"You know I am," Stephanie murmured, and noticed her brother slipping out of the room so she could have some privacy. "It seems so long since I've heard your voice. I . . . ." She stopped, unable to actually admit the rest.

"You what, Stephanie? What were you going to say?" Brock insisted that she complete it. "Have you missed me?" He guessed her words.

"Yes, I've missed you." Her voice vibrated with the force of it.

"Why didn't you tell me that in your letters?" he demanded. "I couldn't stand it any longer, not knowing whether you were going through the same torment I've been suffering. The way you write, I get the feeling that everything is white and wonderful back there.''

"Have you really missed me, too?'' She hardly dared to believe it was true.

"I've been out of my mind.'' An urgency entered his tone. "Stephanie, I have to see you. I can't wait any longer.''

"I want to see you, too.'' Her hand tightened on the telephone, trying to hold on to this moment. "C-can you come here?''

"No.'' He dismissed it as out of the question. "I'm in Palm Springs. I don't have a chance of getting away, not until around the holidays, *maybe*.'' He stressed the questionable status of that time. "I want you to come here, honey. I'll make all the arrangements. You can leave tomorrow morning and be here by noon. I'll only be able to spare a few hours in the afternoons to be with you over the weekend, but we'll have the nights—all of the nights.''

"Brock!'' She was overwhelmed by the invitation and his determination to see her, whatever the cost.

"Don't worry about packing much or digging out your summer clothes. We'll go on a pre-Christmas shopping spree—just you and me.''

"You don't need to buy me anything,'' she interjected swiftly.

"I want to," he replied. "I wake up nights, thinking you're going to be lying beside me. I can't describe the hell I go through when you aren't there. Stephanie, will you come?"

A positive answer was on the tip of her tongue when she realized, "Brock, I can't." Disappointment throbbed in her voice, acute and painful.

"Why? What do you want me to do—beg?" He was angry and vaguely incredulous that she was refusing. "Why can't you come?"

"I have the payroll to finish. Tomorrow is payday for the employees at the inn," Stephanie explained.

"To hell with that! I want you here with me. Isn't that more important?" Brock argued. "Let someone else finish it."

"But there isn't anyone else who's qualified?"

"Your brother can do it. And don't tell me he doesn't know how," he retorted.

"He's overworked as it is, with the inn booked solid and temporary winter help. I couldn't do that." What Brock was asking was unreasonable and Stephanie tried to make him understand. "It isn't that I don't want to come, Brock. I can't."

"You can if you want to badly enough." Stubbornly he refused to listen to her explanations. "Tell everybody they'll have to wait until next week for the paycheck. I don't care. Stephanie, I've got to see you. I want you to fly here.''

"It's impossible. I can't do what you're asking. If you'd think about it, you would understand why.'' Her voice was growing tight with a mixture of anger and hurt confusion. "You aren't being fair.''

"Fair? The way I'm feeling isn't fair,'' Brock argued. "I need you.''

"Please don't do this.'' She was close to tears. "I can't come.''

There was a long silence before his voice returned grimly to the line. "All right, if that's the way you feel about it.''

"That isn't the way I feel. It's just the way it is,'' she choked.

"Have it your way.'' Brock sounded disinterested and very distant. "Goodbye.''

Stephanie sobbed in a breath as the line went dead. She stared numbly at the telephone for a long time before she finally wiped the tears from her cheeks. She was sniffling when Perry entered the room a short while later. He handed her his handkerchief, but didn't ask what was wrong.

He didn't say a word when she stuffed the mistletoe in the bottom of the box of Christmas decorations and carried the ladder out to the back porch. Her brother hadn't had any desire to hang

147

it, and Stephanie thought it was highly unlikely that she would have a need for it.

IT WAS almost a week before she gathered the pride to write Brock a short note, saying only that she was sorry he hadn't understood her reason for turning down his invitation. But she subtly made it clear that she still believed she had made the right decision.

After writing that, she didn't write to him again. He had made it fairly plain that there wasn't any point. Perry had been a rock to her, never once reminding her that he had "told her so." Instead, he had tried to cheer her up each time her spirits sagged into the pits of despair—which was often.

They had weathered many depressing situations together. His support gave Stephanie the hope that she could do it again. Otherwise she wasn't certain what she would have done.

The week before Christmas their church had a Christmas caroling party. A skiing accident to one of the guests at the inn forced Perry to cancel at the last minute, but he encouraged Stephanie to go without him. Regarding it more as a religious festivity than a social party, she agreed.

He dropped her off at the church with instructions to call him when she was ready to go home and he would pick her up. It didn't prove necessary, however, since one of the first persons she met was Chris Berglund. His parents owned the farm a mile from theirs and the two had virtually grown up together—playmates becoming schoolmates. It had always seemed as though they were related, which they weren't.

Stephanie hadn't seen much of him since they had graduated from high school. Chris had gone on to college, coming back only for term breaks like this Christmas one.

When Chris learned she was without a lift home, he immediately volunteered to take her since it was right on his way to his parents. They gossiped, exchanged personal news and recalled funny incidents from their shared childhood days.

As he turned into the lane leading to the farmhouse, Stephanie leaned back in her seat and sighed. She couldn't remember when she had laughed like this and felt so lighthearted. She glanced at Chris, with his curly brown hair and dark-rimmed glasses, a thick parka adding bulk to his slim frame.

"I still can't believe you're going to be a doctor," she remarked. "I can remember when you used to squirm at the sight of blood."

"Thank heavens I outgrew that!" he laughed.

"Dr. Chris Berglund." Stephanie tried out the sound of the title with his name. "It has a very professional ring to it."

"It does, doesn't it?" he agreed with mock

smugness. "But I still have a few years of school left, plus my internship before that's a reality. I have to learn how to say 'Open your mouth and say, aah' with finesse!"

Stephanie laughed, as she was meant to do. "I'll bet your bedside manner will be impeccable."

"You know it." Chris slowed the car as he approached the house. "It looks like Perry is waiting up for you. Good grief, he even has the front light on for you. Is big brother playing the heavy-handed parent now?"

"That isn't his style. Perry is just Perry. I wouldn't trade him for the world," she replied, and meant it.

"He is a pretty special guy," Chris agreed, and stopped the car beside the shoveled sidewalk to the front door.

Stephanie climbed out of the car, joined by Chris as he walked around to see her to the door. "Why don't you come in for a drink?" she suggested. "Perry would love to see you."

"I'd better not." Chris turned down the invitation reluctantly. "I just got home this afternoon. With mom being in charge of the caroling party and all, I haven't got to visit much with the folks. The minister and his wife and a couple of mom and dad's friends are coming by the house tonight. I think they'd like to show me off."

"Naturally," Stephanie understood, stopping at the door and turning to him. "I'm glad you're home, Chris. It isn't the same when you aren't around."

"The next time I come, I'll bring a couple of guys from my fraternity. I'll fix you up with one of them," he winked. "I don't want my favorite girl turning into an old maid." He locked his hands behind her waist and pulled her closer. "You're much too pretty."

"Flatterer," she laughed, but there was a tight pain in her breast.

His kiss was a warm, friendly one, innocent and meaningless. It didn't occur to Stephanie to object—any more than it would have if a member of her family had kissed her. It was the same with Chris. Neither of them was hiding any secret passion for the other.

He was smiling when he drew away to leave. "Tell Perry I'll stop by the inn tomorrow. Maybe we can all have coffee together."

"Okay," she agreed, and added with a quick wave as he disappeared down the sidewalk, "Thanks for the ride!"

Her answer was a wave. Stephanie turned to enter the house as the car door slammed. Hurrying inside out of the cold, she paused to shut the front door and stomp the snow from her boots on the heavy mat inside.

"Hey, Perry!" she called to her brother as she turned and began unwinding the wool scarf from around her neck. "Guess who's home for Christmas?"

She had barely taken two steps into the living room when she saw a dark-coated figure standing beside the fireplace. She faltered in surprise before a searing joy ran through her veins.

"Brock!" she cried happily, and started forward with lighter steps.

"Surprise! Surprise!" Sarcasm dripped from his taunting voice, halting her as effectively as a barrier.

His left hand was thrust in the side pocket of his topcoat. In his right, he held a glass of whiskey. It had to be whiskey since that was the only kind of drink they kept in the house. His legs were slightly apart in a challenging stance. But it was the rawly bleak anger in his gray eyes that froze Stephanie. His masculine features might have been carved out of brown stone.

"When did you get here?" she managed finally. "Why didn't you let me know?"

"Fifteen minutes ago. What's the matter?" Brock jeered. "Are you wishing I'd come fifteen minutes from now so I wouldn't have witnessed that tender little scene out front?" His mouth thinned as he downed a swallow of whiskey. Angry disgust and contempt flared his nostrils.

"I'll bet you would have liked to know I was coming. You would have done a better job of juggling the men in your life so they wouldn't meet each other coming and going."

"Brock, that's not how it is," she protested in a pained voice.

"You mean that's not an example of how you wait for me?" he challenged with open scorn. "I saw you kiss him."

Stephanie half turned to glance at the glass pane on the top half of the front door, the outside light illuminating the entrance. If Chris had kissed her in the living room, they wouldn't have been more visible. Out of the corner of her eye she saw her brother appear in the kitchen opening, drawn by Brock's angry voice.

"It was Chris." She unconsciously appealed to her brother to make Brock understand how innocent the kiss had been.

"He's a neighbor—" Perry began, trying to come to her rescue.

"That's convenient," Brock snapped.

"You don't understand," Stephanie insisted helplessly.

"I understand all right." His voice was savagely low. "I understand that I was a fool to think you were different."

With unleashed fury he hurled the glass into the fireplace. Stephanie flinched at the crash of splintering glass and the subsequent small explosion of flames from the alcohol that splattered on the logs.

It all happened so quickly she didn't notice Brock was moving until he swept past her. By the time she turned, the front door was slamming in her face. She wrenched at the doorknob, the lock momentarily jamming from her haste.

She managed to jerk it open in time to see Brock striding around the station wagon to where his car was parked. The boxy bulk of that station wagon had previously hidden it from her view, but then she hadn't been looking for it, either.

As she ran down the sidewalk after Brock, she heard the car door slam and the motor start. Before she reached the driveway he had reversed onto the lane. Stephanie had a brief glimpse of his profile and the forbidding grimness of his expression before the car accelerated down the long drive.

"Stephanie?" Her brother was calling to her from the open front door.

She paused long enough to ask, "Are the keys in the wagon?"

"Yes. Where are you going?" he asked, already guessing.

"I've got to explain to him. I can't leave it like this." The answer was tossed over her shoulder as she ran to the car.

She lost sight of the Mercedes's taillights when she turned onto the main road. Judging by the direction Brock had taken, she took a chance that he was going to the inn.

His car was parked in the section reserved for employees, steam rising from the hood, when she arrived. She parked the station wagon beside it and hurried inside, slowing her steps to a fast walk through the lobby. Ignoring the questioning look she received from the night clerk, she didn't stop to explain what she was doing there at that hour of the night.

Her heart was pounding and she was out of breath when she reached the door to Brock's suite. Before she lost her nerve, she knocked rapidly three times. She felt a tense kind of relief when she heard hard strides approaching from the other side of the door. It was jerked open by an impatient hand. Brock's eyes narrowed on her with icy anger.

"I deserve the chance to explain what you saw," Stephanie rushed before he could order her to leave.

Minus his topcoat and suit jacket, he had on a white shirt, his tie askew from an attempt to loosen the knot. His hand returned to finish the job as he pivoted away from the door, not closing it. Stephanie moved hesitantly into the room, shutting the door behind her and watching the suppressed violence in the way he stripped the tie from around his neck and tossed it onto a seat cushion.

Without looking at her, he walked to the gold-leafed coromandel screen and opened it to reveal the bar. She watched him splash a couple of jiggers into a glass from a whiskey decanter. He took a quick swallow and moved away—not speaking, not looking at her.

"I . . . ." It was difficult to know how to begin when she was being so frigidly ignored. "Chris Berglund and I grew up together. We played as kids, we were in the same grade in school. He's studying to be a doctor and I haven't seen him in ages. He arrived home this afternoon for the Christmas break."

"You must have had a very joyous reunion," Brock remarked caustically.

"It was wonderful to see him again." Stephanie refused to deny that. "Chris and I are old friends. That's all we've ever been. It's more like we're brother and sister. I know how it might have looked—"

"Do you?" Brock spun around, withering her with the fiery blast of his anger. "Do you have any idea at all what it's like to break appointments, to tell important executives to go take a running jump into a lake, because there's this woman you can't get out of your head—and if you don't see her, you're likely to go crazy? So you take off, drop everything. Then you're there, in her home, waiting for her to come back from church— from *church*!'' he emphasized with biting contempt. "You hear a car drive up and voices. You're so anxious to see her that you nearly go flying out the door. But there she is—kissing someone else.''

"But it didn't mean anything.'' Her voice was hoarse, scraped by the rawness of the emotions he had displayed, his feeling of betrayal. "You've got to understand it was no different from kissing Perry.''

"Am I supposed to believe that you missed me?" he challenged, unconvinced. "That you wanted to see me again?''

"Yes.'' She was astounded that he could doubt it.

"Then why haven't you written me?" Brock demanded, setting his glass down with a thump to punctuate the question.

"Because I thought . . . . When you called me and I couldn't come to California . . . .'' Stephanie was so confused she couldn't finish one sentence before starting another. "You said goodbye . . . I thought it was final. You were angry because I refused,'' she reminded him.

"Yes.'' He began to cross the room. "I was furious—with you and with myself. When those letters stopped, I thought I'd lost you. I came all this way to apologize for being such a selfish, arrogant bastard.'' He stopped in front of her, reaching out to dig his fingers into the tender flesh of her shoulders. ''Then, to find you in that man's arms, I . . . .''

The male lines in his face were more deeply etched as he struggled to control his warring emotions. With a smothered curse he crushed her lips beneath his, grinding them against her teeth. The brutality of his kiss bruised and punished, shocking Stephanie into the stillness of silent endurance until the moment of wrath passed.

Lifting his head to view her swollen and throbbing lips, Brock permitted her to breathe for a minute. Then his hands were forcing their way inside her parka and crushing her into his tortured embrace. Rough kisses were scattered over her hair and temples as anguished sounds moaned from his throat.

''Do you blame me for going a little crazy?'' he groaned. ''For wondering . . . .'' He raised his head again, anger still smoldering in his eyes. ''How many many men are there? How many men would fly halfway across the world to be with you?''

''Brock, there's only you,'' Stephanie whispered, lifting a trembling hand to let her fingertips trace the iron line of his jaw.

"That's what you say." Rueful cynicism flashed across his expression. "But I don't know what you do when I'm not here. My God, I don't even know if you're still a virgin!"

She was stunned that his doubt ran that deep. "You don't mean that!"

"Prove it," Brock challenged with a new urgency in his voice. His hands tightened their hold to draw her closer to the hardening contours of his body, making her vividly aware of his need. "Stay with me tonight."

"You expect me to go to bed with you just to prove I'm still a virgin," she accused, her hands straining against his chest to keep some distance between them. "What kind of a reason is that?"

"It's a damned good one!" he flared. "Because you're going to have to convince me that I haven't been going through this hell for nothing!"

"No!" A sudden surge of strength enabled her to wrench free of his arms and she backed quickly toward the door. "I shouldn't have to prove anything to you. Do I ask you how many women you've slept with since you met me? Don't forget I know about Helen! What kind of things do you think I imagine when you're gone? You can't have lain awake as many nights as I have wondering who you were with. But I promise you, tonight it isn't going to be me! Not for a reason like yours!''

Pivoting, she raced out the door into the hallway, but her haste was unnecessary. Brock made no attempt to follow her. The demons that pursued her were from her own imagination. She slowed her flight to walk swiftly through the lobby and outside to the station wagon.

A sense of justifiable indignation and pride kept her eyes dry and her chin steady. It wasn't until she was at home and alone in her bedroom that she began to think about some of the things Brock had said and the implications that he cared for her—even loved her.

Her temper cooled quickly when she realized she might have rejected the very thing she wanted most of all. The next question was whether she could swallow her pride and admit that to Brock.

CHAPTER EIGHT

ALL NIGHT LONG Stephanie wrestled with her dilemma. She awakened on Saturday morning no nearer to a solution than she had been the night before. Perry noticed the faint circles under her eyes at the breakfast table.

"How did it go last night? Did Brock listen to you?" He pushed his empty plate back and leaned on the table to finish his last cup of coffee.

"He listened." But she didn't say whether he had believed her.

"And?" her brother prompted.

"We argued," Stephanie admitted and rose from the table. "Do you want anything else before you leave?"

"No." He shook his head and downed the coffee. "It's late, I'd better be going. Are you going to wash clothes this morning? My basket of laundry is still in my room," he remarked on her change of routine. Usually she brought the dirty clothes downstairs before she fixed his breakfast.

"Yes . . . I'm going to wash. I'll get them later." At the moment, the laundry was the furthest thing from her mind. "I'll see you tonight," she murmured absently.

After Perry had left, Stephanie decided to leave the laundry until later in the afternoon. Instead she chose to dust and clean the living room. Secretly she was hoping that Brock would make the first move to patch up their argument, so she didn't want to stay far from either the telephone or the front window.

The morning passed without a phone call, and she began to worry that Brock might have left. She couldn't stand the thought that they had parted on a bitter and angry note. Suddenly it seemed that she was being childishly stubborn by silently insisting that Brock had to be the first to say he was sorry they had argued.

She hurried to the phone and dialed the inn, asking to be connected to Brock's suite. Unconsciously she held her breath as she listened to his extension ring once, twice, three times, then—

"Yes?" It was Brock. She recognized his voice instantly.

"It's Stephanie," she said, and waited for some kind of favorable reaction.

His response was a long time coming. Then it was a disappointing and noncommittal, "Yes?"

The telephone became a very impersonal and inadequate means of communication. "I'd like to talk to you. May I come and see you?" she requested, trying to be calm and not as anxious as she felt.

Again there was a pulse beat of silence. "When?"

"Now." Before she got cold feet.

Brock's pause was several seconds long. "I have some overseas calls I'm expecting. Perhaps later . . . say, about five o'clock," he suggested in a completely emotionless tone.

"That will be fine," she answered, because there was nothing else she could say.

"Good. I'll expect you then," he replied, clipped and to the point. "Goodbye."

"Yes . . . goodbye," Stephanie responded, then there was a click and the line was buzzing its dead signal in her ear. She slowly replaced the receiver, wondering if she had made the right decision after all by contacting him first. Brock couldn't have sounded more indifferent.

The dirty laundry was forgotten. Stephanie spent the afternoon taking a bath, washing and setting her hair, and trying on a half a dozen outfits before finally deciding on the rust-colored dress she had worn when she and Perry had dined with Brock and his blond companion that first day she had met him.

Without transportation since Perry had the station wagon, she had to call the local cab. Precisely at five o'clock she was standing in front of the door to Brock's suite. Mentally she rehearsed the speech she was going to make, then knocked on the door.

Brock opened it within seconds. There was a moment of silence as their eyes met. Stephanie thought she saw a flicker of something in the gray depths, but it was too quickly veiled for her to identify it. Her senses reacted to the coral silk shirt he was wearing, half-unbuttoned to give her an inviting glimpse of sun-browned skin and his dark chest hairs.

"You're right on time. Come in." A smile curved his mouth, but it lacked warmth.

"Thanks," she murmured as he stepped to one side to admit her. She nervously fingered the metal clasp of her purse, ill at ease with him and not understanding why.

His sharp gaze noticed the way she was fiddling with her purse. "Would you like a drink?" he suggested.

"Please." She felt in need of some kind of fortification. At the questioning lift of a male eyebrow, Stephanie added, "A whiskey and soda will be fine."

As Brock walked to the concealing gold-leafed screen, her gaze made a nervous sweep of the room. The room was immaculate. Except for his briefcase sitting on the floor near the phone, there wasn't any evidence that the sitting room had been used. The door to the bedroom was shut, but Stephanie suspected the same would be true in there.

Yet the atmosphere in the living room was teeming with invisible and dangerous undercurrents. She could feel them tugging at her.

Her gaze ran back to Brock, so aloof and so compelling. He had fixed two drinks, one for her and one for himself. Carrying them both, he crossed the room to hand Stephanie hers. The drink was not accompanied by an invitation to sit down and make herself comfortable.

Realizing that, she held the glass in both her hands and stared at the ice cubes floating in the amber liquid. She was rapidly beginning to regret coming to see him. She heard the ice clink in Brock's glass as he took a drink, but she knew her hands would start shaking if she lifted her glass.

"You said you wanted to see me," he reminded her.

"Yes." Stephanie lifted her gaze. "Last night

I was offended by some of the things you suggested,'' she began and searched his expression, hoping for perhaps a hint of remorse.

But his face was an impassive mask. She realized he had no intention of making this easier for her. The speech she had so carefully rehearsed was suddenly and completely forgotten.

Everything was thrown out as she made one last attempt to reach him. "If you want me to, I'll stay with you tonight. I love you, Brock."

Her confession didn't seem to make any impression on him. There wasn't even a flicker of an eyelash. "You'll get over it," was his cool response.

Stephanie couldn't believe that he could shrug it aside with that much disinterest. She stared at him, too stunned to hear the connecting door to the bedroom open. It was only when a voluptuous blonde in a see-through peignoir waltzed into her vision that she realized she and Brock weren't alone. It was Helen, the same girl Brock had been with the first time he had come.

"Darling—" she linked her arms around Brock's and pouted very prettily "—you promised we'd be alone for the rest of the evening."

"Stephanie, you remember Helen, don't you?" Brock drawled. Her gaze was transfixed by his mockingly cold smile. No color remained in her face. She was as white as one of his white leather chairs. "Fortunately Helen was able to join me for the weekend, otherwise I might have had to endure a night of amateur entertainment."

His taunting words rolled out to strike her. The glass slipped out of her numbed fingers, but she didn't hear it crash to the floor. She reeled from the stinging blow, turning to rush blindly from the room. Hot tears rolled down her cheeks in an avalanche of pain.

Shame and humiliation consumed her with a burning heat. Conscious only of the desperate need to escape, she wasn't aware of the stares or turning heads as she ran through the lobby and out through the front door.

Not even the zero temperature cooled the scalding heat of her pain. Sobbing, she realized she had no place to run, except home. The station wagon was parked to one side in front of the entrance. Hurrying to it, she glanced inside and had to wipe the tears away before she could see the keys dangling out of the ignition.

Climbing behind the wheel, she started the engine and reversed out of the parking space. The tears refused to stop falling, now that the deluge had begun. As she turned onto the main road, she nearly sideswiped an incoming car, swinging the wheel to avoid it just in time.

Shrugging free of Helen's hold, Brock walked over and shut the door Stephanie had left open.

His shoes crunched on the broken glass around the liquor stain on the floor. He gulped a swig of his own drink, trying to wash down the bad taste in his mouth. His gaze flicked uninterestedly to the near-naked girl.

"The show is over. Put a robe on, Helen," he ordered in a flat voice.

Her gaze swept him with a disapproving look. With a swirl of gauzy nylon, she disappeared inside the bedroom. He finished the rest of his drink and waited for its deadening effect to begin. It didn't work with its usual swiftness and he walked to the bar to refill his glass.

He walked away, carrying the decanter of whiskey as well as his glass. Stretching his long frame in a chair, his legs spread in front of him, he stared broodingly out the window at the snow-covered mountains.

He barely glanced up when Helen returned, covered from neck to ankle in an ermine-trimmed robe of black. It was a perfect foil to her perfectly bleached platinum hair. Without waiting for him to suggest it, she walked to the bar and poured herself a gin and tonic.

"Do you want me to call a maid to clean up this mess?" she asked, gesturing toward the broken glass and the spreading pool of liquid.

"No." Brock shut his eyes. His lungs felt as if they were about to burst.

"Did you have to be so rough on her?" Helen complained. "Couldn't you have let her down with a little more class?"

"It was the best way I knew to be sure she got the message." He heard the weariness in his voice, the utter fatigue.

"There are times when I'm not sure that you have a heart, Brock Canfield," she retorted.

"There's such a thing as being cruel to be kind." He lifted his glass and studied its contents in the waning light of the winter afternoon. "I'm not the four-bedroom type."

A WALL OF tears blocked Stephanie's vision. She couldn't see where she was going or even if she was driving on the road. It had ceased to matter. When the station wagon began to skid on the slippery road, she stopped trying to control it and let it go wherever it wanted. It spun and bumped, coming to an abrupt halt. The suddenness of it catapulted her forward against the steering wheel.

It didn't occur to her that she had had an accident. She simply took advantage of the steering wheel's support, folding her arms to rest her forehead against them and cry. There was an ocean of pain dammed up behind her eyes. Tears seemed the only way to relieve the unbearable pressure.

"ARE YOU PLANNING to get drunk, Brock?" Helen questioned from her reclining position on the sofa. "Or is that whiskey decanter you're holding just a security blanket?"

Brock glanced at the crystal decanter with its glass stopper in place and his empty glass that hadn't been refilled. "I'm considering it."

But it didn't seem worth the effort. The stupor would eventually wear off and he'd be back to square one. A knock at the door tipped his head back as he lifted a hand to cover his eyes.

"Answer that," he told Helen. "Send whoever it is away. I don't want to see anyone."

With a soft rustle of material, the girl swung her legs off the sofa to rise and walk to the door in her satin mules. She opened the door with a secretive little flourish. "I'm sorry, but Mr. Canfield can't see anyone just now," she murmured coyly.

"He'll see me." Perry Hall pushed his way into the suite.

"Oh, dear, Brock, it's the brother," Helen declared in mock dismay.

Brock let his hand drop to the armrest. He could do without a confrontation with Stephanie's brother, but he had been expecting it. "What do you want, Perry?" he sighed.

"I want to know where Stephanie's gone." He stopped in front of Brock's chair, square jawed and stern.

"How should I know?" His gaze narrowed faintly. "She isn't here."

"But she was here. And I'm betting that *she*—" Perry gestured toward Helen "—is the reason Stephanie ran out of here crying."

"That's a question you'll have to put to Stephanie." Brock unstoppered the decanter and filled his glass.

"When I find her," Perry replied. "She drove off in my station wagon."

"Then she probably went home," Brock shrugged.

"She didn't. I've called and called, but there wasn't any answer. Finally I got hold of our neighbors. They went over to the house, but she wasn't there."

The announcement rolled Brock to his feet. "Are you saying that she's missing?" The demand came out as a smooth question.

"Yes. I don't know what happened here or what was said, but I do know the kind of state Stephanie was in when she ran out of the lobby," Perry retorted. "And she wasn't in any condition to be driving. Since you were responsible, you owe me the loan of your car so I can go and look for her.''

"I'll get the keys." Brock walked into the bedroom and came out wearing his parka. "I'm coming with you."

"I don't need you along," her brother rejected his offer.

"I'm not asking your permission." Brock moved toward the door. "Since, as you say, I'm responsible for your sister's overwrought condition, I'm going along to make certain she's all right."

"You should have thought about that before," Perry accused.

"I'm aware of my past mistakes," Brock countered. "What happened today will ultimately turn out for Stephanie's own good. You and I both know that, Perry."

"I warned her that you would hurt her, but she wouldn't listen," Perry sighed.

"I didn't hurt her as much as I could have."

STEPHANIE FELT DRAINED and empty, without the strength to even lift her head. Her throat was dry and aching, scraped raw by the last sobs. Her eyes burned with aridness. There wasn't even any relief when she closed them. She hurt; she hadn't realized it was possible to hurt so badly that being alive was agony.

There was a noise, then an influx of fresh, cold air, but she didn't welcome its reviving attempt. Something gripped her shoulders. A voice called her name. It sounded so much like Brock's that Stephanie was convinced she was dreaming. She moaned in protest when she was gently pulled away from the support of the steering wheel and forced to rest against the back of the seat.

"Are you hurt, Stephanie?" It still sounded like Brock. "Can you hear me?"

"Yes," she rasped thinly, but didn't bother to open her eyes. None of this was real, anyway.

The familiar and caressing gentleness of Brock's hands was exploring her face, smoothing the hair away from her forehead. The sensation was sweet torment.

"I can't find any sign of a cut or a bruise." It was Brock's voice again, low and concerned.

"Stephanie, do you remember what happened?"

The second voice made her frown. It belonged to her brother. "Perry?" Mustering her strength, she opened her eyes.

Again there was a sensation of being in a dream. Brock was half-sitting on the driver's seat and facing her. A deep furrow ran across his forehead, pulling his eyebrows together. She felt weepy again, but there weren't any tears left. Something

173

made her glance sideways. There was Perry, bending low and trying to crowd into the car.

"I'm here, Stephanie," her brother assured her. "Do you remember what happened? How long have you been here?"

"I don't . . . know." The last question she could answer, but the first meant pain. Stephanie looked back at Brock. None of it was a dream. She knew exactly where she was and why. She pushed his hand away from her face. "Why are you here? You should be back at the suite being entertained by your sexy friend," she accused in a breaking voice. "Go away and leave me alone!"

But he ignored her. "Did you hit your head when the car spun into this snowdrift?" His hand went back to her head, feeling for bumps on her scalp.

"No, no, I wasn't hurt at all," she insisted huskily, and pushed his hand away again. "I lost control of the car—on a patch of ice, I guess. Is that what stopped me—a snowbank?"

"You're lucky it wasn't a telephone pole," Brock muttered and reached for her arm. "Come on, let's get you out of the car."

"No!" Stephanie eluded his hand and turned to her brother. "I want to go home, Perry," she said tightly, edging along the seat to the passenger side.

She had a glimpse of her reflection in the rear view mirror. Her face was pale and colorless, her eyes swollen and red from the tears, and her cheeks stained with their flow. She looked like a washed-out mop. It wasn't fair that Brock had seen her this way.

She hadn't wanted to give him the satisfaction of knowing how his callousness had crushed her. That was why she had run. She stared at her hands, twisting white in her lap as Brock stepped away from the driver's side to let her brother slide behind the wheel.

After he had started the motor, he shifted the car into reverse. The tires spun, then found some traction and they were bouncing backward out of the hard-packed snow. Brock stood by the roadside, his hands in his pockets, watching them. For a moment he was outlined there, alone, his gaze lingering on her. Then the station wagon was moving forward.

"Why did you have to bring him along with you?" Stephanie choked painfully on the question, her eyes misting with tears again.

"It was his car. He insisted." His gaze left the road, swinging to her. "Are you okay?"

"No, I don't think so." She stared sightlessly out of the window at the bleak landscape of snow and barren trees. "All those lines always sounded so melodramatic before—but, Perry, I wish I could die.''

When they reached the house, Stephanie went directly to her room. Without changing clothes or turning on a light, she lay down on her bed, huddling in a tight ball atop the covers. It was nearly nine when Perry knocked on her door and entered the room carrying a tray with a bowl of hot soup and crackers.

''Go away, please,'' she requested in a flat voice.

Setting the tray on the bedside table, he switched on the lamp. ''You have to eat, Stephanie.''

''No.'' She rolled away into the shadows on the opposite side of the bed.

''Just a little, Stephanie,'' he insisted in that patient voice of his. She rolled back and he smiled gently. ''Sit up.'' He fixed the pillows to prop her up and set the tray on her lap. For his sake, she ate a few spoonfuls, but it had no taste for her. When she handed it back to him, Perry didn't attempt to coax her into eating more.

It was nearly midnight before she roused herself sufficiently out of her stupor to change into her nightdress and crawl beneath the covers. She didn't sleep, at least not the kind of sleep she normally knew.

With dull eyes, she watched the dawn creep into her bedroom through the east window. She heard the church bells ring their call to early service, but didn't leave her bed to respond to them. Perry came in with orange juice, coffee and toast. She sampled a little of each of them . . . for him.

All morning she stayed in her room. When Perry came to tell her he was going to the inn for an hour or so, Stephanie merely nodded. She heard him come home in the middle of the afternoon, but she didn't leave her bedroom.

At the supper hour, Perry came in. "The food's on the table."

"I'm not hungry." She sat in the center of her bed, hugging her pillow.

"Stephanie, you can't stay in this room forever," he pointed out. "It was rough. It hurt like hell, I know. But it's over. You've got to pick up the pieces and start again." She stared at him, hearing this truth that was so difficult to put into practice. "Come on." He offered his hand. "The longer you stay here, the harder it will be to leave."

Hesitantly, she placed her hand in his and let him help her off the bed. Together they went downstairs to the kitchen. She sat down at the table with its platter of Yankee pot roast, potatoes, onions and carrots. The irony of it stabbed her as she remembered Brock had said she was pot roast while he was Chateaubriand.

"Has . . . has Brock left?" she faltered on the question.

The carving knife was poised above the meat as Perry shot a quick glance at her. "Yes."

A violent shudder quaked through her, but she made no sound.

THE NEXT MORNING she was up before Perry. She discovered that routine was something solid to cling to in her shattered world. She made coffee, got their breakfast, dressed and drove to the inn with Perry. There was one difference. She closed her office door when she went to work. She was no longer interested in the comings and goings of the inn's guests.

There were questions, kindly meant, from her fellow workers, but she turned them aside. She knew they were making their own guesses about what might have transpired, but she didn't offer them any information that would fuel more gossip.

All around her were the festive decorations of Christmas, cheerful voices calling holiday greetings, and the merry songs of the season drifting through the halls. This time, no spirit of glad tidings lightened her heart.

Chris Berglund came over several times while he was home for the holidays. Stephanie suspected the frequency of his visits was at her brother's instigation. But mostly he talked to Perry while she made certain there was plenty of cocoa, coffee or beer for the two of them to drink. She appreciated that Perry was trying to keep the time from stretching so emptily. In a way his methods worked.

The coming of the new year brought changes. Stephanie's appetite was almost nonexistent. She ate meals because they were necessary, but she lost weight. She rarely slept the whole night through. In consequence, there was a haunting look to her blue eyes, mysterious and sad. She rarely smiled and laughed even less frequently. Her chestnut hair was worn pulled away from her face, secured in a neat coil. The style was very flattering and sophisticated, adding to her touch-me-not air.

Unless she was escorted by Perry, Stephanie didn't attend any social function. Even long-time friends saw little of her. Except to shop or go to the inn to work, she rarely left the farmhouse.

New Hampshire natives clucked their tongues when she walked down the streets, prophesying that she would surely become an old maid. With Perry seeing more and more of the young school-teacher, they wondered among themselves what she would do if her brother got married.

But Stephanie couldn't look ahead any further

than the next day. It was the way she had got through January, February and March. It hadn't been easy. She wondered if it ever would. But the worst was over . . . over.

CHAPTER NINE

PRECARIOUSLY BALANCED on a metal folding chair, Stephanie reached as far as she could, but she still couldn't reach the square of dust taunting her from the rear top of the filing cabinet. Sighing, she straightened to stand on the unsteady chair.

The door to her office opened and Perry entered. "Hi."

Affection warmed her eyes, although the curve to her lips was barely discernible. "Hi, yourself. Your timing is excellent." She carefully stepped down from the chair. "I need your long arm to dust the back of the cabinet."

"What's this? Spring-cleaning time?" Good-naturedly, he took the duster she handed him and stepped onto the chair, easily reaching the rear of the metal top.

"It's the right time of year," Stephanie pointed

out. The calendar on the wall was opened to April. "Besides, I didn't have anything else to do this afternoon."

"Mud season is always the slow time of year," he joked. "Want me to dust the top of the other cabinet?"

"As long as you're here, be my guest." Taking a spare duster, she started toward the metal storage cabinet where the extra stationery and forms were kept. The shelves looked as if someone had been finger painting in the dust.

"Brock's coming," said Perry.

She had lived in dread of those words. They hit her, spinning her around toward Perry. Accidentally she knocked the wooden cylinder filled with pens and pencils off her desk, scattering them on the foor.

"Damn!" She choked out the word and bent hurriedly to pick them up, grateful for a reason to hide the tears that sprang into her eyes.

She had forced the tears all inside by the time she had gathered all the pencils. Her hands were shaking when she returned the cylinder to the desk. Perry was feigning interest in the sharpness of her letter opener, giving her a chance to recover.

"When. . .?" She had to swallow the lump in her throat and try again. "When is he coming?"

"This weekend. On Friday," he tacked on to be more specific.

"Oh." The duster was twisted into a tight ball in her hands.

"Are you going to run and hide?" His question was really a challenge.

It made her feel like a first-class coward, because it was exactly what she wanted to do. "No." But it was a very small sound.

"Good girl," her brother praised. She lifted her head, letting him see the tortured anguish in her eyes. "Come on," he cajoled, "let's see some of that stiff New England backbone."

"Sure." She took a deep breath and turned away.

He clamped a hand on her shoulder in a firm display of affection. "There isn't much happening around here today. We'll leave early this afternoon, around four, okay?"

"Do you have a date tonight with Joyce?" she asked, trying to follow his change of subject.

"No, not tonight.. See you later." He moved toward the door.

Stephanie walked back to her desk and sat down. Brock was coming. It twisted her inside until she wanted to cry out, but she didn't. She had been bracing herself for this moment. Now it had come—her first true test. After nearly four months, surely she would survive it.

FRIDAY. FRIDAY. FRIDAY. Each beat of her pulse seemed to hammer out the word. When she arrived at the inn that morning she was a nervous wreck, despite her well-disciplined outward show of calm.

It took her twice as long as usual to get the payroll checks ready for Perry's signature. Especially the last few, because that was when Perry stuck his head in the door to tell her Brock had just driven up. After that, she mentally jumped at nearly every sound, expecting him to walk in.

She skipped lunch to finish payroll, finally getting it done at two o'clock. Gathering them into a folder, she walked down the hall to Perry's office. The door was standing open, but he wasn't there.

Probably with Brock, Stephanie surmised and walked in to leave the folder on his desk. Out of habit, she paused to straighten the leather desk set that had belonged to their father.

"Excuse me, miss." Brock's voice ran through her like a lightning bolt. "Could you tell me where I could find Mr. Hall?"

It gradually dawned on her that the question was being addressed to her. She turned slowly to see him framed by the doorway. Tall, dressed in a gray suit, he was every bit as compelling as she remembered him, if not more so. She watched the disbelief of recognition flash across his expression.

"Stephanie," he murmured her name and took a step into the office. "You've changed. I didn't recognize you."

His gray eyes seemed to examine every detail from her willowy figure to the new, sophisticated way she wore her hair. His inspection left the sensation that he had physically touched her. Inside, she was a quaking mass of nerves.

"Yes, I've changed," she admitted, but not where he was concerned. The love she felt was just as strong, if not tempered by the separation. She turned away, pretending to straighten some papers to keep from giving in to the impulse to throw herself into his arms. "I'm afraid I don't know where my brother is. Perhaps you should check at the desk."

"How are you?" Brock inquired, his voice coming from only a few feet behind.

"I'm fine." That was a lie. She was dying inside. But she turned to face him and lend strength to her assertion.

At closer quarters she could see the changes times had made on him. Still vital, still vigorously masculine, he looked leaner in the face. The hollows of his cheeks were almost gaunt. More lines were carved into his skin or else previous ones had grown deeper, especially around his eyes, where they fanned out. And he seemed harder.

"From all the reports I received, the inn did exceptionally good winter business," he remarked.

"Yes. It seems quite empty now, but spring is generally slow." Why was she letting this conversation continue? Why didn't she leave? Ste-

185

phanie was angry with herself for not possessing the willpower to walk out the door. With a defiant tilt of her chin, she flashed him a cold look. "But I'm sure that won't bother you, since you bring your entertainment with you." Then she was angry for referring even indirectly to his female companions. "Excuse me, I have work to do."

She brushed past him, hurrying from the room before she made a complete fool of herself. She met Perry in the hall.

"Brock's looking for you. He's in your office." Her voice was brittle with the force of her control.

Concern flashed quickly. "Are you okay?"

Her answer was a silent, affirmative nod. He touched her arm as he walked by her to his office. Stephanie slipped quickly into her own and leaned against the door, shaking in reaction. It was several minutes before her legs felt strong enough to carry her to the desk.

At five o'clock Perry came to take her home. As they drove away from the inn, he said, "You don't have to worry about getting dinner tonight."

"I suppose you're eating out tonight." *With Brock,* she added silently.

"You're half-right," he replied cheerfully, and she realized he had been in a good mood when he picked her up. "*We* are eating out tonight."

"Perry, I—" Stephanie started to refuse.

"It's in the way of a celebration," he inserted, and glanced at her. When he saw the look in her eyes, he smiled. "Brock isn't going to be there. At least, he isn't invited." Her brother actually laughed. "Just you, me and Joyce. She's meeting us at the inn."

Celebration. Joyce, the schoolteacher. "Are. . . ?" There was a quick rush of gladness at the implication. Stephanie turned in her seat, her eyes wide and shining. "Perry, are you and Joyce getting married? Are we celebrating your engagement?"

"That isn't exactly what we're celebrating, at least not yet," he hedged. "I haven't even asked her yet. Do you like her, Stephanie?"

"Yes, and I rather fancy the idea of having her for a sister-in-law," she admitted. "But let's get back to this dinner. What are we celebrating tonight if it isn't your engagement?"

"That's a surprise. I'm saving it for dinner," Perry declared with a secretive complacency. "And you haven't got all night to dress. I promised Joyce we'd meet her a little after six, so you have to hustle."

One other change her weight loss had made besides slenderizing her appearance was that her closet was filled with a whole new wardrobe. It wasn't nearly as difficult to chose what to wear since Stephanie liked them all. In view of Perry's insistence that tonight's dinner was a celebration, she picked an aquamarine dress of whipped silk.

Joyce Henderson was waiting for them when they returned to the inn. A petite and pert brunette, she was naturally outgoing and intelligent. Stephanie thought she was a perfect choice for her brother, who tended to be too serious at times.

"What's this all about, Perry?" Joyce questioned immediately. "You were so mysterious about it on the phone this afternoon."

"Just wait," he insisted, taking her arm and guiding her to the restaurant entrance.

"Has he told you, Stephanie?" She looked around Perry's bulk at Stephanie.

"He hasn't given me as much as a hint," she replied.

"You'll both find out soon," he promised. After they were seated at a table, he waved aside the dinner menus. "We'll order later. Bring us a bottle of champagne."

"Champagne?" Stephanie frowned. "You really meant it when you said this was going to be a celebration! How much longer are you going to keep us in suspense?"

"Wait for the champagne." Her brother was enjoying the secrecy.

The champagne arrived. Because the waiter was serving his boss, there was a little extra pomp and ceremony attached to popping the cork and pouring a sample for his approval. Finally the three glasses were filled with the sparkling wine.

"All right, the champagne is here. Now out with it," Joyce demanded.

Perry lifted his glass and started to speak, but his gaze focused on a point to the left of Stephanie, then ran swiftly to her. It was the only warning she received before Brock spoke.

"I find myself dining alone this evening. Do you mind if I join you?" he asked.

They were seated at a table for four, and the chair that was vacant was next to Stephanie. She wanted to cry out to Perry to refuse permission, but her voice failed her. Or perhaps she knew Perry wouldn't listen to her, anyway.

"Of course, Brock. Sit down," her brother invited with subdued enthusiasm and motioned to the waiter to bring another place setting.

Stephanie sat silently through Perry's introduction of Joyce to Brock, aware of the dark-suited shoulder and arm next to her. But she wouldn't look at him. She couldn't look at him.

It didn't seem to matter. Her senses were filled with his presence—the vigorously male smell of his cologne, the warm, rich sound of his voice and the sensation that she only had to reach out to touch him.

Another glass of champagne was poured for Brock. "Have you told them the news?" he asked Perry.

"Not yet," he admitted.

"You know what it is?" Stephanie sent Brock a surprised look and her gaze was caught by the enigmatical grayness of his.

He held it for an enchanted instant, then his gaze slid to Perry. "I know about it."

"Will one of you tell us?" Joyce suggested with faint exasperation.

Perry hesitated, bouncing a glance at Stephanie. "Brock is selling the inn."

"That doesn't come as a surprise." Although it was possibly a cause for celebration even if she didn't feel it at the moment. She fingered the stem of her wineglass, darting a look in Brock's direction. "The inn was really a nuisance to you, anyway. I'm sure you'll be glad to get it off your hands."

"I will, but not for your reason," Brock replied, but didn't explain what his reason was.

"Is this what we're celebrating?" Joyce was confused.

Perry glanced at her and smiled. "He's selling it to me. You're sitting with the future owner of the White Boar Inn."

"What? I don't believe it!" Joyce was incredulous and ecstatic at the same time. She was laughing while tears glittered in her eyes. "Perry, that's wonderful!"

"I think so," he agreed.

"I'm glad for you," Stephanie offered. For herself, she knew how much she would miss the previous owner.

But her brother didn't seem to notice her lukewarm congratulations as glasses were raised in a toast. Stephanie barely sipped at her champagne, not needing its heady effects when Brock was sitting beside her, disrupting her composure and destroying her calm.

"Perry didn't explain the proposal I offered him," said Brock, glancing at Stephanie over the rim of his glass. "Actually I gave him two choices."

"Yes, well, I made my choice," her brother shrugged. "It's what I really want. There isn't any question in my mind."

"What was the other choice?" Stephanie glanced from her brother to Brock. She sensed there was something significant here.

"I explained to him this afternoon that I'd decided to sell the inn," Brock began. "If he wanted to buy it, I agreed to personally finance it for him or . . ." he paused, "I offered to give him a full year's pay plus a bonus—more than enough to pay his tuition through law school."

"But . . . ." She stared at her brother. "I don't understand. . . ."

"Neither did I, until Brock offered me the choice." He shook his head, as if a little amazed by it himself. "But when it was there in front of me, I knew that what I really wanted was this place. All my life I thought I wanted to be a lawyer, but when it came right down to it, I couldn't give up this place."

"I know the feeling," said Brock. "The inn isn't the only thing I'm selling. Quite a few of my other companies are on the market. And I'm

191

consolidating the rest of my holdings.'' He set his wineglass down, watching the bubbles rise to the surface. ''As a matter of fact, I'm looking at some four-bedroom homes.''

Stephanie's heart stopped beating. She was afraid to breathe or move, terrified that she was reading something into that statement that Brock didn't mean. Her wide blue eyes stared at him. Slowly he lifted his gaze to look at her.

''Would you be interested in helping me pick one out, Stephanie?'' he asked huskily. ''I don't want there to be any question about my intentions, so I'm asking you in front of your brother—will you marry me?''

''Yes.'' Where was her pride? Quickly Stephanie retracted it. ''No.'' Then she wavered, ''I don't know.''

''You need a more private place than this to convince her, Brock,'' Perry suggested.

''Will you let me convince you?'' He studied her.

''Yes,'' she whispered.

''Excuse us.'' Brock rose from his chair and waited for her to join him.

She felt like a sleepwalker lost in a marvelous dream as Brock escorted her from the restaurant, his hand lightly resting on the small of her back, faintly possessive. She stiffened in mute resistance when she realized he was guiding her to his suite.

It was the scene of too many conflicting and

painful memories. Anywhere else and she might have melted right into his arms the minute they were alone. But when he closed the door, she put distance between them.

"Why, Brock? Why, after all this time?" she asked, remembering the days of hell she'd been through.

"Because I made the same discovery Perry did. I always thought I had the way of life I wanted, until I met you. Even then I didn't recognize what was happening. I didn't see the choice that was in front of me. In these last few months I've had my way of life, but I finally realized that it could all go down the drainpipe and I wouldn't care, if I had you."

"But—" Stephanie turned, searching his face, wanting desperately to believe him "—here . . . Helen . . . ." It was such a painful memory that she couldn't put it into words.

"I know how much I hurt you." A muscle flexed in his jaw as he clenched it. "I wanted you from the moment I met you. I fooled myself into believing we could have an affair—a long affair—even later I thought our marriage could survive my life-style," he said. "Then that night when I made a jealous idiot of myself over that neighbor of yours, and you pointed out the uncertainties and torment you felt when I was away, I knew that constant separations would ultimately kill what we had. I was being ripped apart by them already. I can only imagine what you were going through.''

''Why didn't you explain that?'' she questioned, aware that he was moving toward her.

''Because, my lovely Yankee, we might have convinced each other we could make it work. So when you called asking to see me, I knew you were coming with the intention of making up. I put you off and called Helen in Boston.'' His hands began to move in a series of restless caresses over her shoulders. ''I wanted you so much I couldn't trust myself alone with you—I couldn't trust myself to resist your possible arguments. So I staged that scene with Helen, arranged for her to walk in within minutes after you arrived.''

''How could you?'' It was a tautly whispered accusation, ripe with remembered pain.

''It was cruelly vicious, I admit it.'' His eyes glittered with profound regret. ''But I never for one minute thought that one of the first things you would say was that you loved me. The hardest thing I've ever done was reject you and your love. I thought it might be easier for you if I made you hate me.''

''You nearly succeeded!''

''Nearly?'' He cupped her chin in his hand and raised it to study her face. ''You mean you don't hate me.''

''No. Brock, I love you. I've never stopped loving you,'' Stephanie admitted.

His arm curved her slender form to the muscular hardness of his body as he bent his head to seek her lips, parting them hungrily, needing her as desperately and completely as she needed him. Love flamed wild and glorious, sweeping them up in its radiant heat. Breathing shakily, Brock lifted his head before the embrace turned into an inferno.

"Why did you wait so long?" Stephanie sighed.

"Because nobody was there to offer me a clear-cut choice—you or the Canfield legacy. I was too much of a fool to realize it was that simple. But you can believe this." He framed her face in his hands, gazing at it as if it was the loveliest work of art in the world. "I love you, Stephanie. And I don't care if I never have another glass of champagne, sleep in another hotel suite or eat Chateaubriand for the rest of my life."

"I never thought I'd be this happy again," she confessed, beaming with the joy filling her heart.

"Everything I said tonight—about selling and consolidating, you realize that it can't happen overnight," Brock cautioned. "It'll take at least a year. In the meantime I'll still have to travel a lot. After that, it will only be a few times a year. Then you can come with me."

"Whatever you say," Stephanie murmured.

"Just let me love you, let me make up for all the pain I've caused you." His mouth moved onto hers, gently at first, then with increasing ardor. Long minutes passed before either of them recovered sufficient control of their senses to come up for air. "How much time will your brother need to find a new bookkeeper so I can marry my bride?"

"This is the slack season." She smoothed her hand over his richly dark hair, enjoying the feel of its thickness against her fingers. "And I do have some influence with the boss. Maybe a week, two at the most."

"Where would you like to spend your honeymoon? The Caribbean? The Virgin Islands maybe?" he taunted affectionately. "What about Europe? Or maybe right here in the honeymoon suite where it all started?"

"Here." Stephanie didn't even hesitate over the choice.

"I think I'll arrange to have that king-sized bed replaced." His hands familiarly tested the slimness of her build. "I could lose you in that."

"Think so?" She brushed her lips across the corner of his mouth.

"I'm not going to take the chance," Brock murmured before he fastened his mouth onto her teasing lips in a kiss that branded her forever his.

BIG SKY COUNTRY

"WHY DON'T YOU TELL ME WHAT YOU THINK?"

Jill's voice was challenging. This man was far too perceptive.

"I imagine a girl of your beauty is accustomed to large quantities of masculine admiration. After a week here you might be in need of a man's company," Riordan suggested mockingly. "A casual flirtation to keep in practice."

"And I'm supposed to have tricked you into coming with me for that purpose?" Jill demanded.

"You've picked a romantic setting," he taunted. "A walk in the moonlight, just the two of us...alone."

Jill swallowed involuntarily. "If that's my intention, surely I'd have picked a man who at least was attracted to me? You've made your dislike very clear," she answered boldly.

"But I am attracted to you," he said. "I may think you're a scheming little witch—but that doesn't lessen the desire to make love to you!"

CHAPTER ONE

'KERRY?' Jill Randall tipped her head around the bathroom door, golden curls falling over one shoulder.

A faint smile touched the corners of her glossed lips at the sight of her room-mate. Kerry Adams was sitting in the middle of one single bed, a pillow clutched tightly in her arms as she stared dreamily into space. The blonde's smile became impish. Slipping a towel from the bathroom rack, Jill wadded it up and hurled it at her room-mate. It landed harmlessly on top of her head.

'Kerry, you're supposed to be getting ready!' Jill stood poised in the doorway, a hand resting on a slim but fully curved hip, her blue eyes laughing at the girl's dazed expression.

The towel was dragged away from its haphazard position on her head, drawing with it strands of straight brown hair, silky and shimmering like satin.

'Must I?' Kerry sighed. Then she pushed her petite frame from the bed and walked restlessly to the window, pushing aside the curtain to gaze outside. 'I wish Todd was coming over tonight.'

Jill shook her head and stepped back in front of the bathroom mirror. 'Unless you want to fail English Lit, you'd better hope Todd doesn't come over.'

'I know, but'—a fervent note crept into her room-mate's voice—'but I keep thinking I'm going to wake up and find it's all been a dream. That it never really happened.'

The teasing glint remained in Jill's eyes as she carefully used the sandy brown pencil to define her light brows more clearly. 'Kerry, it's only your *first* proposal.'

'And my last! Oh, Jill,' Kerry was in the doorway, a frightened happiness lighting a radiant glow in her otherwise undistinguished face, 'Todd asked me to marry him. To be his wife.'

'I know, love. You told me that before.' Jill's sensual mouth curved into a wide smile that laughed gently at Kerry. They had been room-mates for too long for Kerry to take offence.

'I have to keep repeating it or I'll stop believing that it actually happened. I'm not beautiful like you. I couldn't believe it when he asked me out that first time—or the second or the third or the fourth. But I never dreamt—— Oh, I did dream about it, but I never believed he could actually be serious about me! He never said so much as one word about the way he felt until the other night.'

'Didn't I tell you it would work?' Jill winked broadly.

Kerry draped the towel Jill had thrown over the rack, a regretful look stealing over her features. A heavy dose of guilty conscience dimmed the light in her brown eyes.

'I still don't know if I should have told him such an outright lie. I haven't got any intentions of leaving Montana to get a job, not even for the summer.'

200

'But Todd didn't know that,' Jill reminded her, switching the pencil to the other eyebrow. 'Besides, you didn't actually tell him you'd accepted a job out of state, did you?'

'No, I just said that your uncle in California said we could come and work at his resort this summer.'

'Then it wasn't a lie, was it? Uncle Peter did write to say we had jobs there if we wanted them.' There was an expressive shrug of her shoulders as she maintained her concentration on the image in the mirror. 'All you did was fib a little about whether you were accepting the offer or not.'

'I suppose so,' Kerry sighed, and leaned heavily against the door frame. Absently her hand reached up, separating a strand of dark hair from the others to twist it around her finger. 'It's just that when you love someone it doesn't seem fair to do all this manoeuvring to trick them into doing what you want.'

'Todd loves you. He probably would have eventually got around to popping the question. You simply adjusted the timetable in your favour. You'd made it so obvious that you were in love with him. It was only just that you find a way to make him declare his feelings.'

The first sentence was the only one Kerry heard. 'I'll never be able to understand why Todd Riordan would love me. He should marry someone like you who's beautiful and witty, not someone shy and average like me.'

Jill tipped her head to the side, her honey-gold hair curling about her shoulders. Her long hair was expensively clipped to achieve that studied style of tousled disarray that only the very beautiful can carry off.

'On the outside, Kerry, you may be the average All-American Girl, with your brown eyes and brown hair. Your face and figure might not be spectacular, but inside you're a very beautiful person. Opposites always attract, anyway. Todd Riordan has a very strong protective instinct and your innate shyness brings it to the fore. Plus I think he likes the way you worship him with those brown eyes of yours.'

There was more on the tip of her tongue that Jill didn't say, but she thought it to herself. Todd liked the idea that he was intellectually superior to Kerry. He needed someone he could dominate—never domineer, since he wasn't the type. Jill had always guessed that the woman he married would be a brown moth, not a butterfly.

He was a very ambitious young man. It wasn't that he would have objected to sharing the spotlight with a beautiful wife. He wasn't that self-centred. But Todd Riordan wanted to be certain in his own mind that his wife was sitting at home waiting for him without a gaggle of admirers ready and willing to amuse her in the event he was late coming home.

Kerry's ego was very fragile and Jill had spoken the truth when she had said that Kerry was a beautiful person inside. Not for anything would she intentionally hurt her friend by pointing out some of the more callous reasons why Todd Riordan wanted her for his wife.

'I wish you wouldn't talk like that, Jill,' Kerry

frowned, twisting the lock of hair tighter around her fingers. 'You sound so cynical when you do.'

'I prefer to think of it as being logical and realistic.' Her lashes were already long and curling, but they needed a coating of brown to better define them. Jill artfully stroked them with the mascara brush. 'Men are tall little boys. Oh, they each have their own personality, but inside they're still little boys. Once a female recognises that fact and treats men accordingly, she's already the winner. All you have to do, Kerry, is praise them when they're good; withhold their treats when they're bad; and play their games when there's something you want them to do for you.'

'That's easy for you to say. There isn't any man you can't have if you want him.' A faintly envious note crept into Kerry's voice as she studied the exquisitely feminine features of her room-mate. Features that could change from sensually alluring to innocently young with hardly a blink of an eye in between.

'That's true,' Jill agreed matter-of-factly. The mascara brush halted in midstroke, the rich azure colour of her eyes deepening when she glanced self-consciously at Kerry's reflection in the mirror. 'Lawdy, that sounded conceited, didn't it? I didn't mean it that way.'

'You're not conceited, just confident. If I looked like you, I probably would be, too. As it is, I'm just glad you don't want Todd.'

The strand of dark hair was released, Kerry's voice trailing away as she moved into the bedroom they shared. Automatically Jill resumed the application of mascara to her lashes.

'You are going to change into everyday clothes before going to the library, aren't you?' she inquired absently.

'Just a sweatshirt and jeans,' was the shrugging response.

With the mascara brush returned to the orderly row of cosmetics, Jill stared at her reflection for long moments. She was never startled by the beautiful girl that stared back at her. It was the same face she had always seen. She had been born a butterfly. From almost the beginning she had been the object of many little boys' attentions.

It was true—she could have any man she wanted. Some were more a challenge than others, but they all could be got. It was merely a matter of playing a game. Sometimes Jill thought of herself as more of a chameleon than a butterfly, changing into whatever personality the man she was snaring wanted her to be. Sexy, sporty, fragile, intellectual, it made no difference.

Jill never once doubted that she could take Todd away from Kerry if she wanted him. She could appear as helpless and naïve as Kerry actually was. With Todd, her beauty would be a handicap, but she could turn that around and show him what an advantage her looks would be to his career. She would never do it. Kerry was the best friend Jill had ever had, and Kerry loved Todd desperately.

Had she ever looked at a man with Kerry's love-starred eyes? The mist of pink hearts had never lasted beyond the initial infatuation that attracted her to a particular man. Once she had him in her grasp, her power so to speak, the infatuation disintegrated. The thrill of the chase always excited her, but the actual kill Jill found boring.

A long-sleeved white blouse was on the hanger on the back of the bathroom door. Jill slipped it on, buttoning it from the bottom up, watching the cotton material discreetly accent the thrust of her breasts.

A butterfly was an apt description of herself. A golden Monarch flitting from man to man, never dallying anywhere too long. Was this destined to be her life cycle, or would some man come along to clip her wings?

That was a fanciful thought. From birth she had known instinctively how to get around any man. There wasn't a one that she couldn't eventually get to do what she wanted. Once she had him dancing attendance on her, she simply spread her wings and flew away.

With a shrug that such thoughts were a waste of time, Jill tucked her blouse into the waistband of her powder blue denims. Fingers absently fluffed the burnished ends of her hair as she stepped from the bathroom to the bedroom.

'Ready?' Kerry tugged a yellow windbreaker over her faded grey sweatshirt. The overall effect was a tomboyish appearance that suited the bobbed hairstyle and average face, but wasn't at all complimentary of her true personality.

Jill noted all this with an absent, appraising eye,

but she had long ago given up trying to persuade her room-mate to dress differently. Kerry had achieved a marriage proposal from the man she loved, so Jill guessed that it didn't really make much difference.

'Who is ever ready to do research on a term paper?' Her fawn-coloured leather jacket was taken from the small closet, a twin to the one that held Kerry's clothes.

'Look at it this way,' Kerry laughed. 'A term paper deadline means the end of another term and summer vacation is around the corner.'

Jill swept up her notebooks and bag, walking to the door her room-mate held open for her. 'That's a cheerful thought,' she agreed with a wide smile.

'How soon are you going to be using the typewriter?'

The question by Kerry started a comparison of schedules between the two as they descended the stairs leading to the entrance hall. The used portable typewriter had been a joint investment, but their need to use it invariably occurred at the same time.

A girl appeared at the base of the stairs, took two quick steps, glanced up, then paused at the sight of the two girls coming down.

'There you are, Jill. I was just coming upstairs to get you. You have a phone call—sounds like Bob Jackson.'

The breathless announcement ended with a conspiratorial grin before the girl turned around to retrace her steps. Jill concealed a grimace. Bob Jackson was a recent conquest, one that she was now try-ing to fly away from. He couldn't seem to take the hint.

'Tell him I'll be right there,' Jill called after the retreating girl, and hurried her steps.

'He's persistent,' Kerry murmured.

'Don't I know it!' A brow was arched briefly in her direction. 'This shouldn't take long, though.'

The girl who had come to get her pointed to the telephone booth in the entrance hall. Jill walked quickly towards it while Kerry settled into the lumpy cushion of the sofa nearby. A hurried busy tone was easy to adopt.

'Hi, Jill. What are you doing?' The male voice belonging to Bob Jackson responded to her rushed greeting.

'Oh, Bob, it's you. I was just on my way to the library with Kerry trying to finish up the notes for my term paper. Talk about leaving things to the last minute! It's due on Monday, you know, and I've hardly begun.'

'Oh.' There was a hesitating pause and Jill knew her statement did not coincide with his plans for the weekend. 'All work and no play makes Jill a dull girl,' he offered in tentative jest. 'We're having a dance this Saturday, remember?'

'If this Jill doesn't get her term paper done, she's going to flunk.' It was a plausible excuse, although Jill was fully aware that it was not going to take her the entire weekend to complete the paper.

A night out would not hurt anything. She simply didn't want to spend it with Bob. Besides, Kerry had

207

mentioned that the three of them—Kerry, Todd and Jill—might go out to dinner this weekend, a miniature engagement party.

Her room-mate was sensitive about the fact that she had no family except for an aunt and uncle in Billings who had raised her when her parents died. Kerry never said anything specific, but Jill had sensed it had not been a mutually happy arrangement.

'What's one little evening going to hurt?' Bob wheedled. 'Come on, honey. We'll have a great time.'

The front door was slammed shut. Jill glanced automatically towards the noise. Absently she made some objection to Bob's statement as she stared curiously at the stranger who had made such a loud entrance.

Her gaze swept over his appearance, taking in the sheepskin-lined suede parka unbottoned to the coolness of the late spring night. Dark blue levis hugged slim hips and long legs, stopping on the arch of a pair of cowboy boots, dirty and worn with much use. Yet there was something about his erect bearing that said he wasn't an ordinary cowboy off the range.

Bob was saying something again and Jill let her gaze fall away from the stranger to concentrate on what was being said in her ear. Then the stranger's voice penetrated the glass walls of the booth.

'I was told I could find Kerry Adams here.'

The announcement was made to Connie Dickson, the same girl who had come to let Jill know about her telephone call. Jill's blue eyes darted swiftly back to the man, watching as Connie pointed to Kerry sitting on the sofa. Jill would have sworn she knew everyone that Kerry was even briefly acquainted with, but this man who had asked for her room-mate was a total stranger.

The harsh planes of his face were impassive as he passed the telephone booth where Jill stood. His long strides reminded Jill of the restless pacing of a caged jungle cat, impatient and angry. This man wasn't as calm as his expression indicated. The hard line of his mouth was too grim. The way his gaze narrowed on her unsuspecting room-mate gave Jill the uncomfortable feeling that he had just sighted his prey. There wasn't any way she could warn Kerry.

Jill didn't even pretend to pay attention to the male voice on the telephone. Her hearing was straining to catch what that man was saying to her friend.

'Kerry Adams?' He towered above her, his low voice clipped and abrupt as his earlier demand had been. Cold arrogance crackled through the tension that held him motionless. There was no flicker of recognition in Kerry's startled upward glance. 'I'm Todd's brother.'

Jill's eyes widened in surprise. Outside of both men being dark-complected the comparison ended there. Vaguely she had been aware that Todd had an older brother. Kerry had mentioned it at some time, or perhaps Todd had himself.

'Of course, how ... how do you d-do,' Kerry stammered uncertainly.

Her petite frame quickly straightened from the couch to stand in front of the man, momentarily forgetting the notebooks on her lap until they clattered to the floor, loose pages sliding across the linoleum.

Jill's mouth tightened as she watched Kerry's fumbling attempts to recover them, cheeks flaming in embarrassment and the man making no attempt to help in the recovery. He uttered not one diplomatic word to ease Kerry's discomfort or smiled to take away the humiliation of such awkwardness. He simply waited with thinning patience until Kerry had retrieved the papers and had them clutched defensively against her chest.

'T-Todd has talked about you often, Mr Riordan.' Kerry seemed unable to maintain the man's gaze, her look helplessly falling away.

Standing, the man dwarfed her petite frame, oddly dwarfing it more completely than when Kerry had been sitting on the sofa.

The tentative comment of friendship was ignored. 'Todd called me this morning. He said he'd asked you to marry him.'

The disbelief—— No, Jill recognised it was more than disbelief. It was cutting contempt that sliced through his words. Kerry swallowed convulsively.

'He did.' The admission was made in a tiny voice that was humbly apologetic. If possible, the man Riordan's expression became grimmer and more forbidding.

'When do you graduate, Miss Adams?' he challenged coldly.

'I—I have one more y-year.'

His voice became harshly soft. Jill held her breath in an effort to hear him. 'Todd has three, possibly four more years before he obtains his final law degree. Am I to support you as well as my brother for that period of time?'

Kerry seemed to shrink visibly away from him. Dominating bully! Jill swore angrily beneath her breath. He was domineering, she corrected her choice of words quickly. That man would use physical strength to impress his will on someone else if need be. Women were the weaker sex, an easy target. Shy, timid Kerry didn't have a chance against his slashing sarcasm.

'Bob, I have to go,' Jill spoke hurriedly into the phone, her temper seething as she uncaringly interrupted him. 'Call me tomorrow.'

As she hung up the receiver, her mind buzzed with the courses of action available to recue her best friend. Any attempt to argue on Kerry's behalf would be wasted. That man would never listen to a woman's logic, however right it might be. No doubt he considered a woman had only two places in life, in the kitchen and the bedroom. Beyond that, she should be seen and not heard.

Her eyes narrowed for a fleeting moment, a tiny smile of satisfaction edging the corners of her mouth. Very well, Jill thought, he believed women were silly, simpering creatures. She was about to give him a double dose!

Pushing open the folding door of the telephone booth, Jill stepped out, wrapping her arms around her notebooks and holding them to her chest. She paused, adopted her best 'dumb blonde' look and walked forward to engage her opponent.

'Hi, Kerry. I'm ready now,' she called brightly to her room-mate.

She was completely blind to the stricken look from Kerry. She couldn't allow one flicker of concern to cloud her blue eyes at the total lack of colour in her friend's face. Her deliberately innocent eyes swept to the man.

Although braced for his look of displeasure, she was jolted by his piercing gaze. Shards of silver-grey splintered over her face before he glanced away, dismissing her as being of little importance. Jill blinked for an instant to retain her poise. The jet blackness of his hair and brows had not prepared her to meet a pair of eyes of metallic grey.

A frightened, helpless confusion gripped Kerry. Her beseeching brown eyes riveted themselves to Jill's face. Jill tried to instil a warmth of reassurance in her smile that gently prodded for an introduction. It took an instant for the bewildered Kerry to understand.

'I ... I'd like you to meet m-my room-mate, m-my friend Jillian Randall.' Her shaking voice wavered traitorously. 'Thi—This is Todd's brother.' A wave of red engulfed Kerry's face. 'I'm so ... sorry, but I don't know your first name, Mr Riordan.'

'Riordan is sufficient.'

A cigarette was between his lips, a darkly tanned hand cupping a match to the end. The clipped indifference reinforced by the lack of a glance in Jill's direction.

'Mr Riordan, this is really a pleasure to meet you.' Jill wasn't about to offer him a hand in greeting. As rude as he was, he would ignore it, and she didn't intend to let herself to be cut like that. 'And please call me Jill. All my friends do.' The quicksilver sheen of his eyes passed over her face briefly and impatiently, openly wishing her gone. It only increased Jill's resolve to remain. 'I bet I know why you're here, Mr Riordan.' She smiled widely, darting a warm glance at Kerry, whose face was again drained of colour. 'You must have heard the news about Kerry and Todd. Isn't it wonderful?'

There was a speaking glance from Riordan that told her to shut up and get lost. Jill's assumed air of denseness naturally didn't understand.

'Everyone here is so envious of Kerry,' she rushed with false excitement. 'When you see Todd and Kerry together, it makes you feel all warm and wonderful inside. They're so very much in love it just shines like a golden light. And Todd is so protective of her. No one dares to say a word against Kerry in front of him. You'll really be proud of him, Mr Riordan, when you see the way he stands up for her.'

Put that in your pipe and smoke it, Jill thought silently. It might be his plan to break up the engagement, but she was confident that Todd would not be as easy to browbeat as Kerry was. His brother's gaze narrowed on Jill's guileless expression.

'Miss Randall!' Impatiently he snapped the words out, cigarette smoke swirling about his face, darkening his eyes to thunderclouds.

Jill spared a silent wish that he could be more aware of her blonde looks, but he seemed impervious to any attraction of her beauty.

'Jill,' she interrupted quickly before he could finish the statement that was undoubtedly intended to dismiss her. 'I think it's really terrific that you came all the way into town to meet your brother's fiancée. The two of you must be very close. How long are you going to stay?'

He dragged deeply on his cigarette, holding his temper in check with difficulty as he gazed through the smoke veil at Kerry.

'Until I've completed what I came to do,' he answered cryptically.

Namely break things up between Kerry and Todd? Jill wondered to herself. Indignation flashed through her that he should decide without meeting Kerry that he didn't want her as a sister-in-law.

She released the anger that rose in her throat through a soft laugh, letting the battling sparkle in her blue eyes be misinterpreted as happiness.

'That means you can go out to dinner with us tomorrow night,' she declared gaily. His glowering frown made her rush the explanation that was honey-sweet with satisfaction. 'Kerry, Todd and I are going out to dinner on Saturday to celebrate their engagement. Kerry doesn't have any family except an aunt and uncle. I feel as if she's my sister —we've more or less adopted each other. It's a pretend family celebration. You lost your parents, too, didn't you, Mr Riordan? So it's just you and Todd. Now all four of us can have dinner tomorrow and toast the newly engaged couple. Or did you bring your wife along, Mr Riordan?' Deliberately she blinked her long, curling lashes at his impassively hard expression.

'I don't have a wife, Miss Randall,' in a voice that plainly implied that it was truly none of her business.

Jill tipped her head back, swirling tawny gold hair about her shoulders, purring laughter rising in her throat. 'I'll bet you'll be an uncle, then, before you're even a father. And the name is Jill.'

His gaze trailed over her blankly happy expression to her throat. Jill was consumed by the sensation that he would like to shake her until her teeth fell out. Kerry moved uneasily beside her.

Jill let her blue gaze swing to her room-mate. Her knuckles were turning white with the death-grip she had on the notebooks, loose pages sticking out in crumpled disarray. Not even Jill's presence and monopolisation of the conversation was regaining Kerry's poise. She was on the verge of breaking, tears welling in her spaniel eyes.

Jill reached out, taking her room-mate's left wrist and twisting it to see the watch face. 'Look how late it is, Kerry!' she exclaimed, turning an innocently apologetic glance to Todd's brother. 'We have our term papers to finish by Monday and mounds of research notes to take. We aren't going to have much time before the library closes.' After releasing

Kerry's wrist, she dug her fingers into her roommate's shoulder, already turning her away towards the front door. 'You'll probably be getting together with Todd. He'll fill you in on what time we're all meeting for dinner tomorrow night. I'm really glad I had the chance to meet you. I know you're just as happy about these two as I am. Goodnight, Mr Riordan.'

Her cheery departing wave was returned by a look that was broodingly thoughtful. Jill could feel his wintry grey eyes following their path to the door. She kept up a steady, one-sided chatter until the door was safely closed behind them. Only then did she slacken their pace, drinking in deep gulps of the serene evening air.

The palms of her hands were wet. How strange! Jill thought, wiping the nervous perspiration on the hips of her light blue denims. She couldn't remember any time when she had been consciously or unconsciously intimidated by a man. This arrogant Riordan man had affected her more than she realised. Her gaze slid to Kerry, still visibly trembling from the encounter.

'So. That's Todd's older brother,' Jill breathed aloud.

Her statement released Kerry from the nameless fear that had held her speechless. Rounded eyes like dark saucers in a pale face swung around to stare at the blonde.

'Oh, Jill, he doesn't want me to marry Todd!' Hysteria strained at the edges of her voice. The dream of perfect love had turned into a nightmare.

'Before you got there he told me that if I truly loved Todd, I wouldn't hold him to the proposal. He said Todd still had to finish his education and begin his career and that I shouldn't saddle him with the burden of a wife.'

'That's a lot of garbage,' Jill responded calmly. Her shoulders lifted beneath the fawn leather jacket to indicate that he didn't know what he was talking about. 'There are a lot of women who put their husbands through college. It happens all the time. Todd isn't so extraordinary that you can't do it for him.'

'Todd is a Riordan,' Kerry whispered, 'and I could tell by the look in Riordan's eyes that he didn't think I was a suitable wife for Todd.' She paused for a fleeting second. 'Do you know, I've never heard Todd call him by his name. He either refers to him as his brother or simply as Riordan.'

Jill glanced over her shoulder and saw Riordan emerge from the building. 'Let's cut across the grass.' She tucked a hand quickly under Kerry's elbow and guided her off the sidewalk. 'And I certainly wouldn't worry whether Todd's brother thinks you'll make a suitable wife. It's only Todd's opinion that counts. He must think you will or he would never have proposed to you.'

'But I tricked him into that. I made him think I was leaving Montana for the entire summer and we wouldn't see each other until the term started. I shouldn't have done that.' Kerry's voice trailed off lamely, heavy with guilt and recrimination.

'What does it matter when Todd proposed to you

—now or next fall? Unless you think he might have waited three or four years until he had his degree safely in his hand and a job lined up? And if that Riordan man really does think you aren't suitable, I doubt if time would change his opinion.'

The wind tossed a burnished gold strand across Jill's face and she quickly smoothed it back. Her suggestion that Kerry fib about her summer plans might not have been exactly fair, but Jill wasn't going to waste time feeling guilty about it nor allow Kerry to either.

'Do you think Todd knows his brother is in town?' asked Jill in an afterthought.

As much as she disliked it, Jill thought she had to consider the possibility that Todd was having second thoughts about the marriage proposal and was using his brother as an excuse to break it off.

'I had the feeling that Riordan came straight to see me without talking to Todd except for this morning,' Kerry answered.

Jill whispered a silent prayer of relief. There might have been some things about Todd that didn't appeal to her personally, but she had always believed his affection for Kerry was honest and straightforward.

'When we get to the library,' Jill breathed in deeply, speaking aloud the battle plan that was forming in her mind, 'I think you should call Todd and let him know in a diplomatic way what happened tonight.'

'No.' Kerry shook her head, the dark brown bob of straight hair swirling vigorously across her cheeks.

'No?' Jill's blue eyes widened in stunned surprise as she stopped to stare at her room-mate. 'Why not, for heaven's sake? He is your fiancé.'

'But I'm not going to make trouble between Todd and his brother. We haven't been engaged for one whole day yet. I don't want to go running to him just because I might have misunderstood Riordan,' her room-mate argued.

Jill wondered if it was logic that made Kerry reluctant to go to Todd or an inner fear that Todd might be swayed by his brother's arguments.

'What about dinner tomorrow night?' Jill challenged softly.

'Todd ... Todd is going to call me in th-the morning. I'll find out what time he thinks the f-four of us should meet.' Her wavering voice indicated that her previous argument hadn't changed her apprehensions. She was unsure of Todd's reaction and wanted to postpone the moment when she would find out.

The desire was strong to insist that Kerry call Todd immediately, but Jill subdued it. Her room-mate was already subconsciously regretting her interference that had prompted the proposal. She had better sit back and be ready to pick up the pieces or with luck catch Kerry before she fell.

'In between now and tomorrow night,' Jill made her voice nonchalant, 'why don't you tell me everything you know about Todd's brother?'

CHAPTER TWO

THE sum total of Kerry's knowledge regarding Todd's brother could be numbered on the fingers of one hand, Jill discovered. He was Todd's elder by about eight years, which made him thirty-two or three. He had inherited the family ranch when their father passed away some five years ago. Kerry had forgotten where it was located except that it was somewhere near Dillon, Montana. Beyond that, Kerry couldn't fill in the blanks.

The eraser end of the pencil tapped the edge of her notebook with monotonous rhythm. Only half of Jill's mind was concentrating on the paragraph she was reading. The rest was thinking of Riordan.

Only a fraction of an inch might separate the heights of the two brothers. Again, the similarity stopped there. Todd was supply lean and his brother was muscled with broad shoulders tapering to a slim waist to give an impression of leanness.

Taken separately, their facial features were much alike. The clean cut of the cheekbones, the sharply defined jawline, the Roman boldness of the nose, the intelligent forehead. The mouths were different. Todd's was curved and mobile, ready to spring into a smile or a laugh. His brother's was hard and grim, nothing gentle about it at all.

The result was night and day. Warm sunshine

spilled over Todd to illuminate a smoothly handsome face. The dark shadows of night threw his
brother's features in sharp relief to make him strik-
ingly male but never handsome.

Jill leaned against the straight back of the chair,
giving up the pretence of interest in the book
opened before her. Tonight Riordan had been angry about the engagement of his brother, yet he had
seemed curiously detached at the same time. How
could a man confront his brother's fiancée with the
hope of breaking the engagement and remain aloof
at the same time? It was a contradiction of emotions.

A sideways glance at Kerry caught her gazing into
space, a hollow look of apprehension in her expression. Jill breathed in deeply and expelled the air
in a long sigh. Neither of them had accomplished
anything in the two hours they had spent at the
library.

The pages of her notebook were flipped shut with
an air of finality. 'Let's call it a night, Kerry,' she
murmured so as not to disturb the others studying
at the long table.

Without a whisper of protest, Kerry gathered her
papers trancelike into a stack and followed Jill out
of the library.

A round silver dollar moon hung above the
capital city of Montana, its silvery light touching
the crowning peaks of the mountains surrounding
the city. A cool night breeze ruffled the careless
wings of tawny hair at Jill's temples, the golden
colour paled by the moonlight. A crisscrossing
spider web of street lights illuminated the sidewalks

and the girls walking in tense silence.

The whisper of tyres on pavement went unnoticed until the car they belonged to rolled to a stop beside them, the passenger door opening to block their progress. Kerry was nearest to the street. It was on her the pair of steel grey eyes focused.

'Get in. I'll give you a ride,' was the curt command.

Riordan again! He must have been waiting outside the library for them to leave, Jill decided swiftly as Kerry remained frozen in her tracks. The invitation was meant for her room-mate alone and Jill knew it. Riordan intended to have his talk with Kerry, and Jill knew of only one way to circumvent it.

'Why, Mr Riordan! We didn't expect to see you out here waiting for us.' Jill stepped quickly forward, a bright smile curving her mouth. 'How thoughtful of you to offer us a ride. Studying can be so mentally exhausting that it just drains all your energy.' As she slipped into the passenger seat, she avoided the gaze that tried to impale her on the pair of steel sabres. 'A person can tell you're Todd's brother. He's always doing thoughtful things like this.'

Only when she was seated and about to make room for the bewildered Kerry did Jill allow her innocent blue eyes to be caught by his gaze. The line of his mouth was forbiddingly harsh. She let her eyes widen and the smile fade from her lips.

'Oh,' she murmured in a very tiny voice, 'you were only going to take Kerry, weren't you? You

222

didn't mean to give me a ride, too. I am sorry, Mr Riordan. I didn't mean to be so obtuse. You want to talk to Kerry alone, don't you?'

'If it wouldn't inconvenience you greatly, Miss Randall, I would,' he agreed with cynical tautness.

'It's all right.' Jill began sliding out of the car, making her shoulders give a falsely self-conscious shrug. 'It isn't all that far to walk. I've done it lots of times, although never at night and alone.'

As Jill stepped from the car, Kerry's gaze clung beseechingly to her face. Jill smiled faintly, not giving her room-mate the reassurance she wanted.

'You go ahead and ride with Mr Riordan,' she prompted gently. 'I'll see you back at our room.'

'Jill, no, not alone!' The frightened protest was to voice Kerry's apprehension at being alone with Todd's brother.

Jill deliberately misunderstood her. 'Don't be silly, Kerry. I'm not going to be molested. Except for that one block, it's all very well lighted. I'll be okay, really.'

As she expected, Kerry still didn't get into the car, hesitating while she silently pleaded for Jill to rescue her. From inside the car, Riordan swore under his breath.

'Both of you get in!' he snapped.

Her back was to the open door and Jill winked broadly at Kerry. It was difficult to conceal her smile of triumph, although she knew it was only a temporary one.

She urged Kerry to get in the car first while her mind raced for a way to rescue her friend once they arrived at their destination. There wasn't any chance that she would be able to sit in the car and take part in the discussion as she had done in the hallway.

As they pulled away from the curb, a silence settled in, threatening to become oppressive. An uncontrollable shiver quaked over Kerry's shoulders, signalling to Jill that she couldn't let Riordan's presence dominate them.

'I guess it's the romantic in me that always finds weddings so exciting.' Jill heard the sound of disgust that came from Riordan's throat and smiled securely in the darkness of the car. 'Kerry has already promised that I can be her maid of honour. I know Todd will ask you to be his best man. That's why I'm so glad I've had this chance to meet you before the wedding.' She rushed on, 'We've been talking about what colours Kerry should choose. She wants green and yellow. They are her favourites, but I was thinking it should be yellow and white or green and white. What's your opinion, Mr Riordan?' she asked, leaning forward as if she was really interested in his answer, then hurrying on before he could reply. 'I guess it really depends on when they decide to get married. Yellow and white would hardly be good winter colours, although I doubt if they could wait that long before tying the knot.'

The inanity of her chatter sickened Jill. She knew it reinforced Riordan's opinion that she was a silly dumb blonde. At the moment she was only interested in shielding Kerry for as long as she could.

All too soon the short distance was travelled from the library to their dormitory.

The car was stopped in front of the building. Unable to meet Kerry's pleading eyes, Jill glanced around her room-mate to the impassive profile of the driver.

'Thanks a lot for the ride, Mr Riordan,' she offered brightly, and received a curt nod of dismissal in reply.

A quick goodnight to Kerry and Jill was out of the car. She wanted to run to the front door, but she kept her steps unhurried. The instant the door was closed behind her, she raced for the telephone booth.

Excitement had her fingers shaking. Jill had to try twice before she dialled the number correctly. 'Todd Riordan, please, and hurry!' Her voice was oddly breathless. She curled her fingers in the coil of the telephone receiver as she waited impatiently.

'Todd Riordan here,' came his familiar male voice.

'Todd, this is Jill.'

'Jill?' His surprise was obvious. 'What's wrong? Is something the matter with Kerry?'

'Yes, in a way. I haven't much time to explain. Your brother is here.'

'Riordan? Damn him!' was the muttered response.

With a flash of insight Jill realised that Riordan had evidently made his opinion of Todd's engagement quite clear when Todd had made the telephone call to inform him of it. At least it didn't mean she had to make a lengthy explanation.

She took a deep breath. She might as well let Todd know that she was aware of his brother's displeasure.

'He and Kerry are outside the house now. I believe he's suggesting that your engagement is unwise. Kerry didn't want you to know about this, so when I go out there to tell her you're on the phone, I want you to pretend you're the one who called and not me.'

'I'll take care of it,' Todd answered grimly.

Setting the receiver on the small counter of the booth, Jill pivoted sharply out of the glass doors and retraced her path through the front door to the car. Her heart was pounding in her throat as she bent her head towards the window.

'Kerry, Todd's called. He wants to talk to you.' In spite of her attempt to relay the message calmly, there was a thread of victory. The sensation was increased by the look of utter relief on her room-mate's face.

Kerry nearly bolted out of the car, not offering one word of goodbye to the grim-faced man behind the wheel. Jill couldn't resist a glance to him. There were times when rubbing salt into wounds was very enjoyable.

'Maybe you would like to talk to Todd, Mr Riordan?' she suggested with saccharine sweetness.

His mouth tightened harshly. 'No, Miss Randall, I wouldn't.'

The key was turned in the ignition and the powerful engine purred to life. Jill closed the door that

Kerry had left open. Satisfaction glittered in her blue eyes as she watched the disappearing tail lights that declared her victor in this round.

At a more leisurely pace, she returned to the building. A glance at the tearfully happy smile on Kerry's face indicated that Todd was doing a very adequate job of reassuring her of his affection.

Riordan's first attempt had been thwarted and Todd was now aware of the attempt. Would Riordan try again? A light brown brow arched faintly in speculation. Yes, he probably would, she decided. Perhaps with Todd involved he wouldn't be nearly as blunt, but she doubted if his determination had lessened.

It wasn't part of Jill's nature to inquire later exactly what Todd had said to Kerry. She and Kerry exchanged a lot of confidences, but her room-mate was a very private person when it came to her inner emotions. There were personal aspects of her private life she was too shy to discuss and Jill wouldn't probe.

The only sour note in the evening's conclusion was that the dinner the following evening was no longer an uncertainty. Like it or not Jill had to attend. She couldn't plead the excuse that it was a family affair, not after she had bragged about the dinner to Riordan and invited him herself.

When the appointed hour arrived, Jill discovered that she was strangely looking forward to another encounter with Riordan. She attributed it to curiosity. It would be interesting to find out what his tactics would be now that he was presented with a united front. He had failed to divide Kerry from the rest and conquer her. Would he attempt to take on all three of them?

The hotel's wall mirror told Jill she had chosen her clothes well. The simple design of her dress gave her an air of innocent sophistication while the azure colour pointed up the purity of blue in her eyes.

Jill caught Todd's warm smile in the mirror and returned it. They were comrades in arms, united to protect the petite dark-haired girl walking between them.

'Where is he?' There was a tremor of nerves in Kerry's whispered question, her brown eyes sweeping the hotel lobby including its open staircase to locate the man they had come to meet.

Todd's arm tightened slightly around her waist. 'Riordan said he'd meet us in the lounge.'

'Doesn't your brother have a first name?' Jill focused her attention on the closed lounge door. She half expected him to appear with the striding suddenness of the first time.

'Yes, it's John, but I can't remember the last time anyone called him that. He's always been simply Riordan. And I wouldn't suggest that you call him John either, unless you fancy being turned into a frog. He despises the name.'

'John? But that's a good Christian name.' Her blue eyes widened in surprise.

'My mother named him after the man she admired most, her father,' Todd answered dryly as his hand slipped to Kerry's elbow. He reached around to open the lounge door.

Jill would have liked to pursue that curious statement, but there wasn't time for a discussion of the Riordan family history. They were inside the lounge and somewhere in the dim room Todd's brother was waiting for them.

Like Todd and Kerry, her eyes searched the scattered occupants of the room. She didn't recognise Riordan among the men sitting at the bar, nor was he sitting at any of the small round tables.

A light flickered in a corner booth, flaring brightly for an instant as a match would. The brief flame cast a golden light over onyx-black hair and the darkly tanned, rugged features of the man bending to its light.

Jill felt her senses sharpening immediately. Darting a glance at Todd, she saw by the arch of his brow that he too had seen his brother. Meeting her glance above Kerry's head, his hazel brown eyes said, let's get it over with. The arm at Kerry's waist turned her towards the booth and the three of them started forward at the same time.

An inner voice told Jill that Riordan had seen them the minute they had entered the lounge, although he didn't visibly acknowledge their presence until they were nearly at the booth. Then he slid with catlike grace to his feet to meet them.

The sheepskin-lined parka was gone. So were the denims and the cowboy boots. Jill realised, too late, that she had been partly taken in by his western garb in their previous meeting.

She had not anticipated the worldliness and sophistication that she saw now. A stranger viewing

229

this Riordan in grey slacks, black blazer and ribbed white turtleneck would see him as a business executive, not a man of the rugged outdoors as Jill had labelled him. She had underestimated him, and it was a mistake she didn't intend to repeat.

The metallic grey eyes ignored both Jill and Kerry as Riordan met the silent challenge of his brother's gaze. Todd resolutely forced him to acknowledge both of them by making formal introductions. The action brought a twisting smile of cynicism to the ruthlessly hard mouth, but the look directed briefly at Jill and Kerry in turn was smoothly without emotion.

'Shall we sit down?' Riordan suggested blandly.

With some misgivings, Jill noted that she was to sit on the booth seat next to Riordan. Naturally Todd wanted to be close to Kerry, although Jill wished that he would have chosen to sit beside his brother.

The desire to slide as close to the wall as possible was nearly irrepressible. The palms of her hands were beginning to become damp. Jill chided herself to relax and stop being intimidated by the man sitting beside her. She had manoeuvred him quite easily yesterday. There was no reason to think she couldn't do it again if the need arose.

To break the silence until the waitress arrived to take their drink order, Todd inquired about the ranch and received ambiguous replies from Riordan. In another second the weather is going to be discussed, Jill thought tensely, darting a quick look at the slightly pale face of her room-mate.

After the waitress had their order, Jill could see the impatience building in Todd's face. Riordan wasn't angry. There was none of the aloof black moodiness that had been evident yesterday in his expression. In fact, he seemed quite content with just making them uneasy.

'May I have a cigarette?' Jill broke in after another vague, uncommunicative response from Riordan to one of Todd's questions.

Todd was reaching into his jacket pocket when the hand of the man beside her shook a cigarette out of a pack and offered it to her. Was it amusement she saw glittering in the grey depths of Riordan's eyes? What had she done that he found so amusing? He couldn't possibly guess that her request for a cigarette had merely been a ploy to soften Todd's tight-lipped expression and distract his growing anger.

'No, thank you,' Jill refused with a demure smile. Todd's pack was in front of her and she took one from it. 'I prefer filter-tipped cigarettes,' she explained with studied lightness. 'The kind you smoke, Mr Riordan—well, the tobacco always clings to my lipstick.'

His gaze centred on the sensual curve of her lips, glistening with the moistness of gloss. 'I envy the tobacco,' he said dry-voiced.

A pulse throbbed in her throat as unwillingly Jill glanced at the firm line of his mouth, a hint of cruelty in its masculine hardness. It would be no gentle kiss that he gave a woman.

The scrape of a match head was followed by the

pungent scent of burning sulphur. Then his fingers were cupping the flame and offering it to Jill. Her gaze skittered away from the gleam of mockery in his eyes. He couldn't possibly read her thoughts, she scolded herself, bending her golden head to touch the tip of the cigarette to the flame.

The drinks arrived, causing a momentary distraction. The more time Jill had to think about Riordan's suggestive remark, the more she realised it had not been an attempt to flirt with her. He wasn't the type to flirt. He had been stating a fact. Men had often complimented her, so why should his casual reference to her beauty disturb her? It didn't make sense.

Her fingers closed around the cold glass in front of her. She smiled across the table at Kerry, who was glancing uncertainly at Todd. The electric current flowing from the man beside her needled Jill. She lifted her glass.

'I'd like to propose a toast,' Jill declared. From the corner of her eye she could see Riordan leaning back, almost physically detaching himself from the group. 'To the future Mr and Mrs Todd Riordan.'

A shy pink crept into Kerry's cheeks as she peered at Todd's smiling face through the veil of her dark lashes. The faint reflection of embarrassment made the sparkle of love in her brown eyes all the more radiant.

Three glasses met in the centre of the table, but it was the absence of the fourth that was most notable. The gentle smile that had been on Todd's face faded as his gaze clashed and locked with his brother's. Sooty lashes had narrowed to a black screen, throwing shadows to darken the watchful grey eyes.

Todd didn't carry the glass to his mouth. 'Riordan?' he prompted firmly.

Riordan appeared unmoved by the reprimand at his rudeness. In fact, he appeared very relaxed and in command.

'I've made my disapproval of your engagement quite obvious. Don't expect me to drink to it, Todd,' was the bland response.

'It happens to be my life. Surely it's my business what I do with it,' challenged Todd.

'Being your brother gives me the right to interfere or at the very least, voice my opinion.' The broad shoulders shrugged expressively. 'If you are intent on marrying this girl, I can't stop you. But I can and I will withhold my support.'

'That's not fair, Riordan, and you know it. That money is mine for my education,' Todd snapped.

'It's unfortunate that your father gave me sole control of the trust fund until you're thirty, then, isn't it?' The low voice was lazily calm as Riordan figuratively spread his cards on the table. He held a strong hand.

'It may come as a shock to you, but I think Kerry and I can make it without your support. It will mean sacrifices for both of us, holding down full time jobs and a full schedule of credits at college, but we can do it.' Todd's arm circled Kerry's shoulder, drawing her closer to him.

'And maintain the grade level you have?' Riordan mocked.

'Maybe not, but we would get our degrees.'

'I imagine it sounds all very noble to the two of you, struggling together, completely on your own. The harsh fact is that you'll be so busy struggling to survive that it will be four or five years before you realise you've made a mistake. The two of you simply aren't compatible. By that time there might be a child involved. You and I, Todd, know what it's like to grow up with parents that have separated.'

'Kerry and I are very compatible and very much in love,' Todd disagreed forcefully.

'That's what our parents claimed, too,' was the quiet and silencing reply.

Todd wasn't able to hold the level gaze of his brother, a certain indication to Jill that Riordan's remark had touched a vulnerable spot. He let the pregnant silence settle heavily over the table before he continued.

'I'm not trying to make things difficult. I'm trying to appeal to your reason, Todd,' he said calmly. 'This is not the time in your life to tie yourself down with a wife. Not because you're young—age matters little—but because the next few years you need to devote to your studies and your future career. You can't possibly give the attention your wife would be entitled to receive. Your timing is off, Todd. You're rushing into something with your eyes closed. Open them. Make certain you're not disguising lust with love. Take her to bed. Make her your lover or mistress. But don't be a fool and marry her!'

Kerry's ashen face flamed scarlet. Jill wondered angrily why she had thought Riordan would be any less blunt with the three of them. Todd had started to listen to his brother's arguments, but the disrespect in the last of his statements had fortunately wiped out the inroads Riordan had made. He had overplayed his hand.

'If,' Todd was angry and making no attempt to conceal it, 'you'd taken the trouble to get to know Kerry, you wouldn't be so quick to insult her!'

'I've never pretended to be the tactful one in this family.' Riordan's mouth twisted into a cold smile to match the glacial colour of his eyes. 'You'll be wasting energy to defend the girl's honour to me. If you feel the necessity for action, go arrange for a table in the dining room.'

There was a seething moment of silence before Todd rose to his feet, impatiently signalling to Kerry to accompany him. Jill was forgotten as the couple exited the lounge. She studied the building ashes on the end of her cigarette, murderous thoughts racing impotently through her mind.

'Well, Miss Randall?' Riordan's quietly challenging voice hadn't forgotten her.

Her eyes were round and blank when she turned to him. 'Yes?'

'You're quite obviously in favour of this engagement. Aren't you going to defend your girl-friend?' The deceptively soft tone sliced like toledo steel through silk.

'I wouldn't like to rudely contradict you, but I've seen Todd and Kerry together,' Jill murmured with innocent apology. 'I've noticed three things about them. There is a physical desire, as one would expect, but their feelings are essentially very strong and tender. And I think their personalities beautifully complement each other and fulfil basic needs.'

'Todd takes after our grandfather. His ambitions are political. Can you picture Kerry as a politician's wife? Her shyness, timidity will prove to be a problem in a few years.' Jill slowly brushed the ashes off the end of her cigarette, unable to meet the intense scrutiny for fear her eyes would reveal her partial agreement with Riordan's assessment. 'Todd should eventually marry someone like you who could be an asset to his chosen career,' he concluded.

'Like me?' A genuine frown of confusion puckered her brows, as she tucked a tawny gold strand of hair behind her ear.

'An attractive ... a beautiful woman to be his hostess and entertain the important people he will have to cultivate.'

'Really?' Jill tipped her head to one side as if considering his statement. 'It's strange how our opinions vary. Whenever I see a man in public office who has a beautiful wife, I always have the feeling that he's lost touch with the common people. Besides, I think Todd would rather have a wife waiting at home than working beside him.'

Again the sooty lashes narrowed, making an unreadable smoke-screen of his eyes. 'That's a very interesting opinion. You're convinced that a marriage between the two would work.'

'I think it would work very well,' she affirmed, trying to be offhand and not forceful with her statement despite her inner convictions.

'Are you in favour of couples marrying while they're still attending college, and, in Todd's case, of Kerry supporting them for a few years while he obtains all his degrees? That's quite a strain on a marriage, don't you agree?'

'Yes,' Jill nodded. A sparkle of battle glittered in her blue eyes so she forced a smile to hide the antagonism he aroused. 'Of course, if you were more kindly disposed in their favour, it wouldn't be quite as much of a struggle, would it?'

'That's what you think I should do?'

Riordan was leaning back, the ebony colour of his hair darkened further by the shadows of the booth, his striking powerful features fully illuminated by the dim light.

The unwavering study of his light-coloured eyes made Jill vividly aware of the primitive charm he possessed. Her heartbeat accelerated briefly under the potent spell of his virility.

Averting her head, Jill pretended a concentration in snubbing out the cigarette between her fingers. She had to break free of the magnetic pull of his gaze.

'I wouldn't presume to tell you what you should do.' She laughed softly, giving the impression that

237

the thought was ridiculous that a mere female could influence him one way or the other.

'Wouldn't you?'

The mocking words were said so softly that Jill wasn't sure whether she had heard them or only imagined them. There was no mistake the next time he spoke. His voice was clear and calm.

'But you wouldn't disagree if I said that it's your opinion I should get to know Kerry better before I make my decision irrevocable.'

'Of course, I wouldn't disagree with that. There's nothing worse than estrangement between two brothers and I know Kerry would be deeply hurt to be the cause of any more harsh words between you and Todd.' That was very definitely the truth. Kerry could be too sensitive. 'And I certainly wouldn't want the two of them to do something so foolish as to elope, not when there still might be a chance for your differences to be reconciled.'

The wide-eyed, dumb blonde look was firmly fixed on her face. Arguing with a man as arrogant as Riordan only made him more stubborn. It was better to let him believe that she spoke with the wisdom of the simple and was not trying to threaten him into changing his mind.

A measuring, thoughtful glance trailed over Jill's face. Then Riordan reached for his glass, downed the drink and replaced the empty glass on the table.

'Shall we go in search of Todd and your friend?' he suggested with a side look. 'They may have decided to eat without us.'

Jill gave a little nod of agreement and waited

until he was standing to slide out of the booth. His gaze swept appraisingly over her when she stood at his side, a silver glitter that was faintly mocking. Not a guiding hand touched her, but she was very much aware of him walking beside her as they left the lounge.

CHAPTER THREE

THE conversation at the dinner table was stilted. It would have taken only a few conciliatory comments from Riordan to ease the tension, but he didn't make them. Jill had thought her comments had made an impression on him. Looking back, she could see it hadn't made any difference in his stand against Kerry's engagement to Todd.

There hadn't been any further confrontations, if that was a consolation. There again Jill decided it was because Riordan believed he had pushed Todd as far as he dared. But if Riordan's aim had been to make Kerry unhappy, he had succeeded. Jill couldn't remember seeing her room-mate's face look so pinched and strained. Todd's look of concern and smiles of reassurance weren't as bolstering as they might have been if they were alone.

While Riordan was occupied paying the check, Jill made the decision that Todd and Kerry should be alone. The sooner, the better. She could easily catch a taxi.

'Todd,' she spoke quietly, not wanting to draw Riordan's attention, 'why don't you and Kerry go ahead and leave? I'll find my own way.'

'Are you sure you don't mind?' But the relief was in Todd's eyes.

'I suggested it, didn't I?' Jill smiled. Kerry

opened her mouth to protest, but Riordan was moving towards them, his deceptively lazy strides covering the distance swiftly.

The way Todd protectively nestled Kerry deeper in the crook of his arm lifted one corner of his brother's mouth in a mocking smile. It remained there to accept Kerry's frozen goodbye.

'I'll meet you here at seven in the morning for breakfast, Todd, before I leave for the ranch.' It wasn't a suggestion, it was a command. Jill's lips started to tighten at his autocratic action, but she relaxed them instantly into a smile when the grey eyes swung to her. 'Miss Randall.' There was an arrogant inclination of his dark head in goodbye.

'Goodnight, Mr Riordan.' She wasn't about to thank him for a miserable evening.

In the hotel lobby, they parted company, with Riordan disappearing almost immediately, presumably returning to his room. Todd hesitantly suggested that he and Kerry should give Jill a ride, but she airily waved it aside. The pair insisted on waiting until Jill had telephoned the taxi company and received assurances that a cab would be dispatched immediately.

Todd's car was pulling out of the hotel parking lot. Jill stared through the glass windows at the dark shape of Kerry's head resting on the driver's shoulder. The course of true love never did run smooth. Wasn't that the saying? It must be true love, because Todd and Kerry had actually had a bumpy start.

'Don't tell me they forgot to take you with them?'

241

Jill pivoted sharply about, her startled eyes focusing on Riordan. One arm held his jacket open, the hand negligently thrust in his trouser pocket. The other hand held a cigarette to his mouth, his eyes narrowed against the smoke curling from the burning tip.

'Or did you arrange to be left behind?' Riordan added in a mocking taunt.

For another full second, speech was denied her. A hand crept up to her convulsively working throat and she managed a jerky laugh.

'You startled me.' Her hair was caught in the collar of her light coat and she pushed it free. 'Kerry and Todd weren't going directly back, so I decided to take a taxi. I-I don't like being the gooseberry.'

Her voice was low and oddly breathless. He surely didn't think she had stayed behind on the offchance of seeing him again.

'I doubt that *you* would,' he agreed with biting emphasis on "you". 'But there's no need for you to take a cab. I was just going for a drive myself. I'll give you a ride.'

'You don't need to do that. There's already a cab on the way here.' Frantically Jill glanced out of the window, catching the headlight beam as a car swung up to the curb beneath the covered drive. 'In fact, it's here now. It was kind of you to offer, though.'

Before she could reach for the door handle, his arm was already in front of her to pull it open. Ducking under his arm, Jill unwillingly looked into his coolly appraising grey eyes, reflecting nothing but her own image. The cab driver was approach-

242

ing the door as she stepped on to the sidewalk with Riordan directly and disconcertingly behind her.

'Did you call for a cab?'

'Yes,' Jill responded quickly.

Riordan's hand closed over her elbow. 'But the lady won't be needing one.' He pressed a bill into the man's hand. 'For your trouble.'

The driver glanced at it, his face suddenly wreathing with a smile. 'Thank you, sir.' And the money was quickly shoved into his pocket as he turned away.

Her lips moved to protest, but it was useless to openly oppose this man. At this point, it was better to accept his offer calmly than to make a fuss.

'I hope I won't be taking you out of your way, Mr Riordan,' Jill said as his hand guided her towards the parking lot.

'Not at all, Miss Randall.' There was a suggestion of mockery in the deepening grooves around his mouth. 'I had no particular destination in mind. I have a tendency towards claustrophobia whenever I spend any time in town.'

The car door was held open for her. Jill didn't comment until he had slid behind the wheel beside her. 'You seem to fit in very well with the city environment.' Her gaze wandered over the perfectly tailored grey slacks and black blazer and the moulding knit of his turtleneck sweater.

His gaze flickered to her briefly before he looked over his shoulder to reverse out of the parking stall. 'Do you believe clothes make the man, Miss Randall?'

'Jill,' she corrected absently, then answered his question. 'You don't appear uncomfortable in them.'

'That's strange—Jill.' He hesitated deliberately over her christian name, making it come out husky and mocking. 'I would have thought you would realise that a wolf in sheep's clothing is still a wolf.'

'Are you a wolf, Mr Riordan?' Unwittingly her voice dropped the façade of innocence and became slightly baiting. 'Call me Riordan. I'm a lone wolf who prefers to travel without the supposed benefit of a pack or a mate.'

Jill leaned back in her seat. Was he warning her? Did he think she was making a play for him? Surely not. She had not flirted with him once or given him a single indication that she was interested in him as anything more than Todd's brother and Kerry's future brother-in-law.

Maybe he had become accustomed to women pursuing him. A lot of women would be attracted to that dangerous air he possessed. Catching him would be a challenge. Under different circumstances, she might have tried herself, just for the fun of it.

'You can travel faster that way,' she agreed. Directing her gaze out of the moving car window, she pretended an interest in the passing scenery. Silence seemed a way to end this vaguely personal conversation.

'Are you from Montana?' Riordan didn't let the silence last long.

'Yes. My parents live in West Yellowstone, where I was born and raised.'

'You must be accustomed to spectacular scenery.'

'Does anyone ever become accustomed to it? I hope not,' Jill smiled naturally.

'Do you have any brothers or sisters?'

'Four. Three brothers and one sister.'

'Older or younger than you?' Riordan asked, turning the wheel to guide the car around the corner.

'I have a brother who's two years older than me. The rest are younger.' She darted a quick glance at his averted profile, curious why he was interested in her family background. A germ of an idea took root. 'Andy, my older brother, is the only one of us who's married. He met his wife when he was stationed with the Marine Corps in California. He called my parents up one night and told them he was married. It was quite a shock for all of us, but once we had a chance to get to know his wife Sally, we all liked her.'

He turned his head slightly, running an eye over her face. 'Subtlety is not one of your accomplishments, is it?' he suggested dryly.

'But I've never failed to be persevering,' Jill returned with a malicious sparkle in her azure eyes.

'But your brother is your business and my brother is mine.' The line of his mouth was inflexible, the firm set of his features yielding not one fraction to her honey-coated attempt at persuasion.

A thundering discovery vibrated over Jill with

the suddenness of a summer storm. An intangible something had been troubling her ever since the first time she had seen Riordan, some little something that set him markedly apart from any man she had ever known. This very second she realised what it was.

Riordan didn't like her. Not because she was beautiful or because he believed she was dumb. It was because she was a woman. Jill held herself motionless, letting her mind register the discovery. Riordan was a woman-hater. No, hate wasn't the right word. He viewed them with contempt, mocking the sentimental yearnings of their soul and using them to satisfy physical needs. But why?

His childhood couldn't have been much different from Todd's, and Todd bore no emotional scars from the evident separation of their parents that Riordan had referred to briefly. Had he fallen in love with a woman at some time and been rejected?

It was possible, Jill conceded. He was a passionate man for all his impassive exterior. Not passionate in the erotic sense of the word, but in the depth of his convictions and feelings. He could carry a grudge for a very long time. Those grey eyes of his sliced through the fancy trappings of the modern world to leave only the basics. He wore the cloak of civilization when circumstances demanded, as now, but he was a man of the elements—primitive, ruthless, and strong.

So very opposite to Todd.

Jill brushed a hand in front of her eyes. Was this insight a blessing or a curse? She didn't want to know such things about Riordan. She didn't even want to think them.

Forcing her eyes to focus on the passing scenery, Jill willed her mind to concentrate on it. They had turned on to the main street of Helena called Last Chance Gulch.

Once it had been a gulch of the prickly pear and not a main paved street. That was in the beginning when four lucklesss prospectors had arrived to take their 'last chance' at striking it rich. That July of 1864, they found colour in their gold pans and by autumn, a hundred makeshift cabins comprised the goldrush settlement of Last Chance Gulch.

A town had been born. Last Chance Gulch was not a dignified name and survived only through the early months of the town's birth. Then the occupants changed it to Helena, naming the main street where twenty million dollars in gold was mined Last Chance Gulch.

The old, weathered buildings provided fertile colourful history for Jill to dwell on. The south end of Last Chance Gulch had been the site of Chinatown. The Chinese, who had provided much of the labour to build the railroads, also cultivated truck gardens and operated their own stores. They even had a long tunnel beneath their particular section that they used as a private opium den.

The architecture of the old buildings was predominantly Romanesque. Stone arches and columns combined with frieze and cornice and heavy timbers. The car was turning around another corner, leaving Last Chance Gulch to pass the Great Northern Depot, which once possessed a tall clock tower before the earthquake. Then Jill's attention was caught by the Moorish style of landmark of the former Shrine Temple, now the Helena Civic Center.

'What are you thinking about?' Riordan interrupted the silence again.

Jill could feel the cool touch of his eyes, but kept her gaze centred on the lighted street. 'The city, its history,' she shrugged.

A shiver danced over her skin as she wished she had never met him, or been momentarily entranced by his arrogant harshly handsome looks.

'Really?' was the aloofly disbelieving reply.

The car slowed to pull into the curb in front of the dormitory entrance. The motor was switched off and Riordan partially turned to face her. The metallic glitter of his gaze shimmered over the gold of Jill's hair burnished by the outside street light.

His arm stretched negligently on the back of the seat, his hand only spare inches from her head. Jill tensed slightly, reacting to a latent animal instinct that warned her to tread lightly.

'I thought you might be thinking of some new tactic to manoeuvre me into changing my mind.' His voice was low and cynical.

'Manoeuvre?' Jill swallowed. Her lashes fluttered, a gold-brown fringe above deepening blue eyes.

'Isn't that what you've been doing since we met?' The softly dangerous tone dared her to deny it.

'I don't know what you mean,' Jill protested

weakly. Her façade as an ingénue was being stripped away by his slicing gaze and she was helpless to stop it. 'If you mean, have I tried to convince you to give Kerry and Todd a chance? I have to admit that I have.'

'Do you honestly expect me to believe you're as innocent as you appear?' Riordan smiled coldly, his amusement secret and at her expense.

'You're talking in circles.' Jill fluttered her lashes in uncertain confusion, tossing her head to the side in bewilderment. 'I don't understand what you're saying.'

'Your act was very good, but intelligence has a way of letting itself be seen.'

'My act?' she repeated blankly.

Inside she knew she couldn't admit that there was any truth to his accusations. If she stopped playing the dumb blonde now, she would end up losing her temper and telling him exactly what she thought of his arrogant ways. That anger would not help Kerry at all, although it would certainly release some of her own frustration.

'Really, Mr Riordan, you aren't making any sense.' She reached for the door handle of the car. 'I'd better be going inside.'

It was locked. For a poised instant, her eyes searched frantically for the release before she realised that it was on the driver's side. Unwillingly she had to turn back to his mocking expression.

'Would you please unlock the door?'

Her request was met with silence and a complacent look. Jill nervously ran her tongue over her lower lip. The action focused his attention on her mouth.

'How do butterflies steal the nectar from so many flowers and remain looking untouched?' His own mouth twisted cynically, not requiring a reply.

Butterfly! The word shivered over her skin, goosebumps rising along the back of her neck. Only yesterday Jill had used that very word to describe herself. Riordan had chosen the same one. Coincidence? Or had some mysterious something passed between them, each giving the other insight about themselves?

'Why ... why did you say butterfly?' She had to ask the question, her voice breathless and at odds with the guileless expression.

'Because,' Riordan answered slowly and arrogantly, 'you are as beautiful, as fragile, and about as constant as a butterfly.' It was a condemnation, not a compliment. The back of a finger followed a strand of tawny gold hair brushed away from her face in its windblown style and down the back of her neck. Jill was pinned, like the butterfly he called her, by his steel-sharp gaze. 'I've always wondered if the honey tastes sweeter from the lips of a butterfly.'

His hand cupped the back of her neck, fingers twisting into her hair, adding further pressure to draw Jill towards him. Her hands spread across his chest in resistance.

A soft, surprised, 'No!' was offered in protest.

A tug of her hair turned her face up to meet his

250

descending mouth, a flash of cynical amusement in its hard line an instant before it captured her lips.

Brutally harsh, he ravaged her mouth. There was a buzzing in her ears, hot fires of humiliation raced through her veins. In another second, Jill felt, surely her neck would break under the force of his kiss.

It was not the way a man would kiss a woman but the way a man would take his pleasure of a tramp, without a thought or a care to her feelings. But his strength was overpowering. Her struggles were only the useless flutterings of butterfly wings against iron bars.

Beneath her doubled fists straining against his chest, she could feel the steady beating of his heart. Her own was hammering like a mad thing. The bruising kiss was sapping all her strength, taking it from her as if it was nectar from a flower. She had to dredge to the very depths of her reserves to keep from submitting weakly to his punishing embrace.

Riordan had attacked with the swiftness of an eagle swooping on its prey. With the same unexpectedness, he freed her mouth and relaxed the talon-hard grip on her neck, his fingers sliding to her fragile collarbone, capable of snapping it at the least provocation. Jill's head sank wearily in defeat, her tousled golden hair cascading forward over his hand to conceal the flaming humiliation in her cheeks.

But she wasn't allowed the precious seconds to regain her whirling equilibrium and take the calming breaths of air. Her chin was captured between

251

his thumb and forefinger and raised so Riordan could inspect the extent of his conquest. Mirrored in his silver eyes was her own flushed and resentful expression, nothing more.

'Which of us is stronger, Miss Randall?' His lip curled in a derisive smile.

'Physically you are!' she hissed, blue flames shooting from her eyes, but Riordan was made of steel, not wood, and the fire harmlessly ricocheted over its target.

The grooves around his mouth deepened. 'Don't make the mistake of thinking it's only physical,' he warned in a low voice.

Releasing her completely, he was once again sitting behind the wheel. A movement of his hand near the control panel was followed by the comforting click of the car door being unlocked.

'Goodnight, Miss Randall.'

Her knees trembled badly as she stepped from the car on to the curb. His assault on her—it could hardly be termed an embrace—had shaken her more than she realised, but it hadn't broken her spirit. With the security of distance between them, she turned, holding the door open as she leaned down to glare at him.

'Don't you make the mistake of thinking it's over, Riordan. I'm going to do everything I can to make certain Kerry and Todd are married as soon as possible!' She hurled the glove of challenge, slammed the door and pivoted sharply towards the building.

For a few quaking steps, Jill thought he might come after her. Unconsciously she held her breath,

252

expelling it in a long sigh when she heard the snarl of the car motor. Those were bold words she had spoken, but she was determined to make them fact.

Kerry returned some time past midnight. Jill was in her single bed, feigning sleep. Her mind was too filled with vindictive thoughts. She doubted if she could hold them back in the intimacy of a late night chat, and it was better if Kerry never found out about what had happened. Fortunately no attempt was made to waken her as her dark-haired room-mate changed into her nightclothes and slipped silently into the small bed opposite Jill's.

Morning brought the exhilarating knowledge that Riordan was on his way out of town if not already gone. Jill's sleep had been plagued by the lurking memory of his bruising kiss, but the rising sun seemed to burn away the humiliation she had suffered at his hands. Kerry, too, had seemed more relaxed and less haunted when she had dressed to meet Todd for church.

Arching her back, stretching cramping muscles, Jill couldn't help wondering what had taken place during Todd's meeting with Riordan that morning. Whatever had transpired, she could be sure of one thing—Riordan hadn't experienced a change of heart.

She blinked her eyes tiredly. Her mind was wandering from the task at hand again. If she had concentrated on what she was doing, the term paper would have been done an hour ago, she scolded her-self, and forced her gaze to focus on the bonded paper in the typewriter.

As she removed the error-free sheet, the hallway door opened. Jill glanced around to identify Kerry entering the room.

'Excellent timing, Kerry,' she greeted her room-mate with a smiling sigh. 'This is the last page. The typewriter is all yours.'

'I brought you a sandwich and a Coke. I thought you'd probably be hungry.' Kerry motioned towards the paper bag she had set on the bureau top.

'You're a life-saver!' Jill gathered up her papers and stacked them on the corduroy quilted cover of her bed. With the bag in hand, she returned to the bed, curling her long legs beneath her to sit cross-legged near the head of the bed. 'You and Todd must have gone out to dinner after church.'

Her comment was met with silence. A curious frown pulled Jill's arched brows together as she glanced up. Kerry was going through the motions of hanging her dusty rose coat in the closet, but her mind seemed far removed from the task.

'Kerry?' Jill snapped her fingers to prod her friend back to the present.

'What?' Kerry looked around blankly. 'I'm sorry. Did you say something?'

'Nothing important.' Jill set the Coke on the table between the two beds and took the wrapped sandwich from the bag. 'You were in a daze.'

'Was I?' The coat was carefully hung in the closet before Kerry walked slowly to her bed. She sat on the edge, staring thoughtfully at the hands she clasped in her lap. 'I suppose I was thinking,' she murmured.

'That's a safe guess,' Jill teased, but her expression was marked with concern. 'Of course, the next question is what were you thinking about?'

The hands twisted nervously in her lap. 'You remember that Todd met with Riordan this morning.'

'Yes.' Her blue gaze hardened warily. She unwrapped the sandwich, pretending an interest in it. 'What did the great man have to say?' She couldn't keep the sarcasm out of her voice.

'Todd's application for a transfer to Harvard has been accepted. Riordan received the notification at the ranch this last week,' Kerry told her.

So Riordan had another ace up his sleeve, Jill thought angrily. All he had to do was keep Todd and Kerry apart for the summer and the distance between Montana and the East Coast would take care of the year. He was probably counting on out of sight being out of mind.

'You and Todd will have to set the wedding date for some time in August, then, won't you?' Jill tossed her head back, letting the shaggy golden curls trail down her back. 'With your grade point you could easily transfer to a university out there.'

'I couldn't afford the out-of-state tuition, though,' Kerry sighed.

As Riordan had no doubt guessed, Jill added savagely to herself. 'And Todd wouldn't be able to help because Riordan is still holding the threat of shutting off the money supply over his head.' Her fingers tightened on the sandwich, smashing the bread and wishing it was Riordan's neck. 'The two of you can't allow him to blackmail you this way!'

'Todd doesn't think we should do anything too hasty yet.'

'He surely doesn't think Riordan is going to change his mind. This isn't the age of miracles.' At the pinched lines that appeared around Kerry's mouth, Jill wished that her reply hadn't been so completely negative. She should have left her friend with a little hope.

'Well,' Kerry breathed in deeply, 'Riordan did make a proposition to Todd this morning.'

'What kind?' Jill was sceptical of any proposition Riordan would offer.

'He ... he conceded that he might have been too harsh and quick in his judgment.'

'That's big of him,' Jill grumbled, biting into her sandwich.

'He admits he was prejudiced against me before we ever met and that he should at least get to know me better. He still doesn't approve of the engagement,' Kerry hastened to add.

'So what has he suggested?' Jill asked dryly. 'A trial period?'

Until the autumn term started and Todd was gone to Harvard, Jill completed the thought silently.

'Something like that,' her room-mate admitted, finally lifting her gaze from the twining fingers in her lap to look at Jill. 'Todd works at the ranch in the summer. Riordan has invited me to spend a month there so he and I can get better acquainted.'

Total disaster, was Jill's first thought. Kerry was already intimidated by the man. A month in his company would totally subdue her even with Todd's support. Jill did not underestimate Riordan. She knew his capabilities and the lengths he would go to achieve his ends.

She stared at her sandwich. 'There is an obstacle to his invitation, Kerry. How are you going to stay at his ranch and earn money to pay for your fall term as well?' Both she and Kerry were going to work for Jill's parents that summer in their motel-restaurant near the entrance to Yellowstone Park. 'Mom and Dad will have to hire someone to take your place. You won't even have a summer job after you've spent a month there.'

'Riordan has offered to compensate me for that.'

She should have guessed he would cover every contingency. Jill stuffed the partially eaten sandwich back in the sack. It had begun to taste like cotton.

'You can't seriously be considering the offer,' Jill protested desperately, pressing two fingers against her forehead, trying to rub away the throbbing ache that had started between her eyes. 'You know it wouldn't work. He'd make your life a total misery. You know what he can be like when Todd isn't around. How long do you think you could take it?'

'I couldn't, not alone. But'—brown eyes became round and pleading, engulfing the plainly petite features in a lost helpless look—'if you were with me——'

'I'll let you in on a little secret,' Jill interrupted quickly, drawing a deep breath and untangling her legs. 'Riordan doesn't like me and he isn't about to invite me to spend a month at his ranch. Besides, I too have to work this summer.'

'Jill.' Something in Kerry's voice put her instantly on guard. 'Riordan thought it might not look right for me to stay there at the house for a month with Todd and him. I mean, he does have a housekeeper, but—well, he invited you to come, too, as a kind of chaperone—with the same offer of compensation.'

'Oh, no!' Jill was on her feet, striding away from the bed to the solitary window. Sunlight glistened platinum gold over her hair dancing around her shoulders as she shook her head vigorously. Her hands rubbed the chilling gooseflesh on her upper arms. 'No!'

'Please.' There was a throbbing ache in the coaxing tone.

Jill spun round. 'It just wouldn't work, Kerry.'

Lord, but that man had a devious mind! He had considered every possible argument she could have made to prevent Kerry from going.

That he had invited Jill confirmed the magnitude of his arrogance. She had challenged him and now he was offering a front row seat for her to watch him tear the engagement apart. Riordan would have his revenge and be aware of any move Jill made to thwart his attempts. Jill had underestimated him again, and she didn't like the sensation of being bested.

Kerry's soulful eyes didn't see any of that. 'You must come.'

'Don't you see,' Jill protested in agitation, 'if I

258

come, I'll end up losing my temper and only make the situation worse for you and Todd. The wisest thing for you to do is refuse the invitation and take the chance that Riordan won't be able to influence Todd into breaking the engagement. That's the most logical thing, because Todd does love you.'

'I can't.'

The dark head was turned away, tears misting diamond-bright in her brown eyes. Jill wanted to take her by the shoulders and shake her hard.

'Why can't you? You can't go there alone!'

'Yes, I can,' Kerry nodded away a tear with her hand and letting her unreproachful gaze meet Jill's impatient look. 'I love Todd. I don't want to come between him and his brother. Not having a family I think I know how important they are. If there's only the slimmest chance that Riordan might approve of Todd marrying me after spending a month at the ranch, I'll take it. I'd feel better if you would come with me, but I'm going either way.'

'Kerry, this is a stupid time to turn heroic,' Jill sighed. Her mouth thinned in self-anger at the way Kerry winced from the unconsciously cutting remark against her natural timidity. 'Besides, there's my parents to consider. They're expecting me to work this summer, not have a vacation. I couldn't tell them at the last minute that they're going to have to find someone else to take my place.'

'You said yourself that they have more applications than jobs. They could easily hire someone else,' Kerry reminded her quietly.

'I suppose they could,' Jill conceded grudgingly,

'but they would never agree to this plan. Riordan has a housekeeper, You said so yourself, and chaperones went out of fashion with hoop skirts.'

'You could call them and see.'

Staring into the resigned yet pleading face of her room-mate, Jill knew she would have to make the telephone call. What kind of a friend would she be if she let this poor defenceless creature walk into Riordan's lion den without protection? The question was who was going to protect Jill. She hoped her parents.

They were infuriatingly understanding.

CHAPTER FOUR

THE Big Sky Country. The last of the big-time spenders. That's the way the brochures described Montana. The vast prairielands in the east rolled westward, gathering speed to swell into mountains towering like a tidal wave over the landscape.

Looking over the horizon where majestic mountain peaks tried to pierce the crystal blue bubble of sky, Jill felt the answering surge of her heartbeat. Their early summer coat of vivid green could only be rivalled by the bold splash of autumn or the stark white purity of winter.

Now it was green, a multitude of shades broken only by the dark brown of tree trunks driving upwards towards the sky, the rocky faces of the mountains catching the golden sun, and the gay pinks, yellows and white of wildflowers dotting the meadows and craggy slopes. Breathtaking and awesome, the scenery remained constant while ever-changing. The tremendous sensation of being released from an earthbound existence to soar to some magnificent plateau was overwhelming.

'I feel it every time,' Jill murmured.

'What did you say?' Kerry glanced at her curiously, not quite catching the softly spoken words.

'I was admiring the scenery.' Reluctantly she drew her gaze to the interior of the car. 'I never tire of looking at the mountains, especially when you can see them like this, unbroken by any man-made structure.'

'They make me feel small and insignificant,' Kerry inserted, 'but they are beautiful.'

Jill leaned forward to glance around her friend at their driver. 'I've lived in Montana all my life, but always in town. What's it like, Todd, to live in the mountains year round?'

He smiled faintly, sliding a brief look to her. 'I don't know.'

'What?' Her blonde head tilted to the side in surprise.

'When I was born my mother moved into town. I only spent the summers with my father on the ranch,' he explained. 'So I have no idea what it's like to be in the country during the last days of Indian summer or see the first winter storm clouds building on the mountain peaks. I've often wondered, too, what it would be like, but never enough to find out.'

'I didn't know. I mean, Kerry did mention that your parents didn't live together, but I guess I assumed they didn't separate until you were older.' Jill leaned back, staring thoughtfully ahead. It was difficult to imagine Riordan growing up in a town. The image of him being raised in the mountains under the domination of the elements was much easier to accept. 'Of course, Riordan was older than you. The adjustment must have been harder for him.'

'He wouldn't try to adjust,' Todd replied. 'My

mother told me that the minute he found out that she wasn't ever going back to the ranch, he ran away. He was nine years old and hitch-hiked all the way back to the ranch. That happened three of four times before my grandfather suggested that it might be better to let Riordan stay on the ranch with his father. She finally agreed. When I was older I remembered asking him one time how he'd had the courage to come all the way from Helena where Mom and I lived with her father to the ranch by himself.' The corners of his mouth were turned up in a wry smile. 'He said there wasn't any other way he could get home. The ranch has always been home to him. For me, it's just a place to spend the summer vacation.'

There was a twinge of envy that Riordan could rightfully call the mountains home. Then Jill considered the singleminded determination of the nine-year-old boy who had travelled the hundred and fifty-odd miles south-west of Helena.

That part of him hadn't changed. Now he was determined to prevent a marriage between Todd and Kerry. He wasn't going to let anything stand in his way. He had even invited Jill along to watch.

Drawing in a deep breath, Jill moved her head slightly in angry despair. There were three fools in this car. She wasn't sure which of them was the biggest. Probably herself, since the other two were blinded by their love for each other. The month promised to be a long and trying one, if she and Kerry survived.

'What was Riordan like as a boy?' It was better to

263

find out as much as she could about the enemy.

'I don't know,' Todd answered thoughtfully. 'When you're a kid yourself, you don't pay much attention to those things. He was always "big brother", teaching me to ride, taking me hunting, letting me tag along. He was just Riordan.'

Kerry shuddered involuntarily. Todd reached out and covered the small hand on her knee with his own. Out of the corner of her eye, Jill saw the reassuring squeeze.

'Don't start worrying,' he murmured softly. 'Once he gets to know you, he'll see what a great sister you'll make.'

Jill fell silent. Todd seemed unable to tell her much about Riordan and the mention of his name was only making Kerry more uneasy. A smile tugged at the corners of her mouth. She was concerned about making Kerry uneasy when she had been sitting on pins and needles for the last half hour herself. The points had grown sharper as they came closer to their destination. It couldn't be far now. They had turned off the main highway several miles back.

As if on cue Todd slowed the car and turned on to a dirt road leading further into the mountain wilderness. The fence opening had no gate as the tyres thumped over a cattle guard.

'This is it,' he announced, nodding his head at the window to indicate the land around them. 'The house is a few miles back.'

Glancing back, Jill couldn't see any sign identifying the ranch as Riordan's property. The only sign she had noticed was one saying: No Trespassing. A prophetic warning, perhaps?

A mid-afternoon sun glittered in her eyes as they topped a meadow rise and Jill caught her first glimpse of the ranch house. Large evergreens stood in a horseshoe guard on three sides of the house, protecting it from sweeping winter winds. The two-storey house itself was a tasteful example of turn-of-the century architecture, with its entrance porch a columned portico. Yet its wood and stone exterior was in keeping with its rustic setting.

'It's beautiful!' Kerry breathed, breaking the spell of immobility after the car had stopped in front.

'Just a little cabin in the mountains,' Todd jested, opening his door and stepping out.

It wasn't a mansion, but its graceful, old-world lines were impressive just the same, Jill decided. Curiosity burned to see the inside.

As she stepped out of the car, her gaze swept to the ranch buildings. There was no sign of any activity either there or in the house. She had expected Riordan to be on hand to greet them, subconsciously she was braced to meet his cynical, mocking grey eyes.

'I didn't expect it to be so nice,' Kerry whispered.

Jill glanced at the petite brunette now standing beside her. 'I for one can hardly wait to see if the inside lives up to the promise of the outside,' she replied quietly, turning to walk to the rear of the car where Todd was unloading their luggage.

With Todd carrying the heavier cases and the two

girls with the lighterweight ones, they mounted the steps to the heavy oak door.

The formal entry hall gleamed with hardwood wainscoting below bright upper walls of cream yellow. A carved oak staircase led to the upper floor at the end of the hall. On their left was a fireplace of native granite, the trophy head of a big sheep hanging above the mantel. The hardwood floor beneath their feet was inlaid geometric designs, known as parquetry.

Todd set the cases on to the floor. 'I wonder where Mary is,' he frowned.

Footsteps approached, unhurried and light. Jill's head turned in their direction, wondering what kind of a woman this Mary was. Anyone who kept house for Riordan would have to be a paragon of talents to satisfy him. From the polished entrance hall, Jill guessed that the housekeeper was.

If there had been a subconscious image of the housekeeper, Jill wasn't aware of it. Yet astonishment crackled through her at the sight of the young, almond-eyed woman who came into view.

Long chestnut hair flowed about her shoulders as the sensuously curved woman glided towards them. Her eyes were a tawny hazel shade like a cat's and there was a purring quality about her smile.

'Welcome home, Todd.' She ignored both girls to walk directly to Todd and press a less than motherly kiss on his cheek.

Jill doubted if the woman was Riordan's age, although her bone structure was deceiving and it was possible she was in her very early thirties. It wasn't difficult for Jill to believe that her talents went beyond housekeeping.

Todd laughed self-consciously and glanced at Kerry before returning his attention to the woman whose hand was still resting lightly on his arm. 'I didn't expect to see you here, Sheena.'

Sheena? This wasn't Mary, the housekeeper? Jill's eyebrows lifted fractionally in further surprise. The woman was certainly acting the hostess and not a guest.

The purring smile deepened although it didn't reach the woman's cat-gold eyes. 'I've been deputised as your official welcoming committee. Riordan had to be away from the ranchyard this afternoon. I'm sorry I didn't hear you drive in, but I was in the kitchen helping Mary with dinner tonight.'

'I—I hope you're joining us,' Todd offered politely but with little enthusiasm.

'I am.' Then the woman's gaze swung to Jill, indifferent in its appraisal of her blonde hair and blue eyes. 'I'm Sheena Benton, Riordan's closest neighbour. You must be Todd's girl-friend. Kerry, isn't it?'

Closest neighbour? Is that all? Jill thought cynically as she smoothly shook the artistically long and slender hand offered to her.

'No, I'm Jillian Randall, Kerry's friend,' she corrected lightly.

The tawny eyes narrowed fleetingly before they darted to the plain dark-haired girl at Jill's side. An

267

uncomfortable flush in Kerry's cheeks painfully aware of Jill's obvious beauty, her golden looks intensified by Kerry's mouse-soft colouring.

Jill wanted to cry out at the faint condemnation in the woman's eyes. Kerry's beauty was on the inside, but Jill doubted if this feline creature would understand.

Sheena Benton laughed throatily at her own mistake. There wasn't any amusement, however, when the tawny gaze refocused on Jill. There was a glitter of malevolence in the almond-shaped eyes. Instinctively Jill glanced at the woman's hands, half expecting to see them transformed into cat's claws to scratch her face.

'It's a pleasure to meet you, Jillian,' Sheena declared in a husky voice. Liar, Jill thought to herself. 'I must admit you hardly look like a chaperone.'

'I'm really here as Kerry's friend.'

Her hand was released as the woman turned to Kerry and inclined her head in a falsely apologetic fashion. 'I'm sorry about the mistake,' Sheena Benton said in a regal tone.

'It's quite all right,' Jill murmured self-consciously.

Kerry glanced through the corner of her lashes at Todd as though fearful he might suddenly be seeing how plain and unobtrusive she was. Warm hazel eyes affectionately returned her surreptitious look.

'You'll probably be very grateful for your friend's company after you've been here awhile,' Sheena continued. 'At the end of a week, the magnificent scenery around here begins to pale when you have

268

nothing else to do. That's when boredom sets in.'

'You don't look bored, Miss Benton,' Jill couldn't resist inserting.

'But then I live here. I've had a few town friends stay with me. Invariably they begin climbing the walls after a week.' A cold smile was directed at Jill. 'And it's Mrs Benton.'

'You're married?' she returned with some surprise.

'Widowed,' was the complacent reply. 'My husband was killed in a hunting accident four years ago.'

'It must have been a shock,' Jill suggested dryly.

'In the beginning I was kept much too busy trying to keep the ranch going, and by the time Riordan helped me find a competent manager, the worst of the shock had passed.' Feline shoulders shrugged as if to say the marriage was long ago and forgotten. 'As the owner, I still have enough responsibilities to keep me occupied. I don't have time to be bored.'

'Neither will Kerry,' Todd grinned, indifferent to the invisible sparks flying between Sheena and Jill. 'I intend to devote every spare moment to making sure she enjoys this month.'

'Spoken like a typical young lover,' Sheena laughed throatily, mocking their youth. 'You'll find life operates at a simpler level, Kerry. A night out will probably consist of a walk in the moonlight. Todd is a patient teacher, though. Maybe in a month you'll be a country girl like me.'

'Not too much of a country girl,' Todd qualified Sheena's statement. 'We're going to be living most of our life in cities. I want to keep Kerry mainly a townbird.'

The light shining in Kerry's eyes said she would be whatever Todd wanted her to be. In that silent second, Jill forgot the chestnut-haired woman with the tawny eyes and remembered the reason she was in this house. Her mission was to do everything in her power to make certain Kerry and Todd lived happily ever after, as the fairytales put it.

'Let me show you two girls to your room,' Sheena inserted smoothly, turning towards the staircase at the end of the entrance hall. 'I know you'll want to unpack and bathe and rest before dinner. Naturally you have your old room, Todd,' she tossed over her shoulder.

Jill led the way, following the woman gliding effortlessly over the flowered carpet covering the stairs. Sheena Benton seemed intent on impressing the idea that she was the hostess in the house, and not just for the afternoon.

'I hope you girls don't mind sharing a bathroom.' Sheena paused at the top of the stairs for them to catch up. 'You have adjoining rooms with a bathroom in between.'

'Sounds fine,' Jill nodded.

'Good.' With a brief smile, the woman walked familiarly down the wainscoted hallway, opened a door and stepped to the side. 'This is your room, Kerry.'

There was a fleeting impression of delicate shades of green before the petite brunette moved hesitantly into the doorway to block Jill's view. Sheena was already pivoting away, indicating for Jill to follow her.

'And your room, Jillian, is here,' she said.

The door swung open to a room dominated by white with a sprinkling of blue, contrasted by artistically carved woodwork of glistening walnut. A Persian rug in an intricate design of blue and white covered the floor. The skilfully styled furniture in the room was, if Jill didn't miss her guess, antique.

Her eyes sparkled with appreciation and admiration as she stepped further into the room. The large double bed had a white cover, hand-crocheted in a popcorn stitch, the perfect homey touch.

Setting her small suitcases on the floor, Jill turned to the woman standing in the doorway. 'It's lovely,' she murmured inadequately.

Any further attempt to express her delight with the room was checked by the look in Sheena's face. It forcibly said not to become too enamoured with a room she would only have for a month. Then Sheena's eyes seemed to change from an amber warning shade to an aloof tawny gold.

'The bathroom and your friend's room is through there,' she said, flicking a hand towards the door near the fireplace. 'Dinner is at seven.'

'Thank you.'

But Jill's polite words were spoken to a closing door. She pursed her lips thoughtfully. Something told her she had to not only watch out for Riordan but for Sheena as well. The woman didn't like her or want her here.

Shaking her head to rid her mind of its unwelcome thoughts, Jill walked to the connecting door. The bathroom was large and spacious, its fixtures old-fashioned but seemingly in working condition. The murmur of Todd's and Kerry's voices in the adjoining room made Jill tap discreetly on the door to her friend's bedroom.

'Come in,' Todd called.

A flushed Kerry was trying to squirm out of his arms when Jill walked into the room, but he wouldn't let her go, taking delight in her shyness.

'I did knock,' Jill pointed out with a teasing smile.

'Todd, please!'

'Oh, all right,' he laughed down at Kerry. Partially releasing her with one hand, he captured her chin and dropped a quick kiss on the button nose. Only then did he let Kerry go and turned to pick up the large blue suitcase belonging to Jill.

'I'll carry this into your room. By the way,' Todd paused after taking two steps, 'what did you think of Tiger-eyes, Jill?'

Grimacing wryly, she shrugged. 'I didn't realise it was possible to dislike someone on sight.'

'Sheena has staked a claim on Riordan. She doesn't like it when anyone gets too near, especially when they look like you.'

'Your warning is duly noted, but she hasn't got anything to worry about from me. I'm not interested in her claim,' Jill declared. 'She's welcome to Riordan. They would make a perfect pair.'

'Please, it's bad enough having her as a neighbour,' Todd's brow arched expressively. 'Don't wish her on me as a sister-in-law!'

'Todd, you shouldn't say things like that,' Kerry protested gently.

Love filled his face with a tender smile when he glanced at her. 'Why? Because I prefer my women feminine instead of feline?' he teased.

'Go and take Jill's suitcase into her room.' Despite the ordering tone, Jill could see the glow lighting Kerry's face at Todd's compliment. She very nearly looked beautiful.

'Whatever you say,' he winked, and this time made it out of the room.

Kerry stared after him for a moment. Wrapping her arms about her as if to ward off a sudden chill, she looked away from Jill's inquiring look.

'Well, we're here,' she sighed.

'It's a fabulous place, isn't it?' Jill replied to avoid any discussion of the reason why they were here.

Brown eyes swung admiringly around the room. 'Todd told me about it, but I didn't expect anything like this. His grandfather built the house for his wife. Can you imagine how difficult it was back then? All the furniture was shipped by rail to Bannack, then by waggon here.'

Jill wandered over to the fourposter bed with its canopy of spring green. Her hand trailed over the quilted cover on the bed. Varying shades of pale green material had been painstakingly stitched together in an intricate geometric pattern joined against a background of almost white green.

'This is beautiful. The one in my room is crocheted. Whoever did these had to have a lot of patience.'

'A lot of love,' Kerry corrected softly. 'It's these little touches that keep the place from seeming like a museum. It's a home because someone cared about the people in it. She took the time to make these because she cared and because she was proud of the home where she lived. Oh, Jill,' her voice trembled with emotion, 'I can hardly wait until I can have a home of my own. Some women are made to have careers, but I'm not. I want a husband and children and a place where I can do things like this for them.'

'You will,' Jill promised lightly. 'In the meantime, I suppose we should start getting unpacked. I want to take a bath and change clothes before dinner. Sheena said it was at seven.'

Kerry glanced at the slender watch on her wrist. 'It's later than I thought. We'll have just about enough time to make it.'

'That's probably just as well. I had the feeling Sheena didn't want us sticking our noses outside the door until then.' The edges of her mouth turned up in wry amusement as she moved away from the bed towards the connecting door. 'I'll leave you to unpack. Whoever gets done first takes the first bath.'

'It's a deal,' the other girl agreed.

Jill was the first to finish unpacking and lazed in the luxuriously deep tub until Kerry was done. In her bedroom, she slid a lace-trimmed slip over her undergarments and walked to the small vanity table.

274

Her tawny gold hair was piled on top of her head, held in place by a tortoiseshell clasp. Releasing the clasp, she shook her hair free with her fingers and reached for the hairbrush on the table.

Refreshed and stimulated by the relaxing bath, she wandered about the room. Her silken blonde hair crackled with electricity from the rhythmic and vigorous strokes of the brush. Pausing near the panelled drapes of Prussian blue, she gazed through the lace insets. The window looked out of the rear of the house, giving her a breathtaking view of the mountains rising above the valley meadow of the ranch.

The sun had begun its descent in the vividly blue sky. The jutting mountains caught the golden fire, transforming their rocky peaks into regal crowns. The strokes of the hairbrush slowed to a complete stop as Jill lifted aside the white lace curtains for an unobstructed view.

Deep green forests blanketed the mountain slopes in a velvet thick cape. She felt the witchery of the mountains reach out and capture her in its spell.

A movement in the long shadows of the guardian pines near the house caught the corner of her eye. Reluctantly, she let her gaze leave the majesty of the sun-bathed peaks. The outer ranch buildings were out of her sight beyond the stand of windbreak trees.

It was from that direction the tall figure had come, only now emerging from the shadows into the afternoon sunlight. Long reaching strides carried

Riordan swiftly towards the rear of the house.

He was dressed as she had first seen him, in snug-fitting faded demins, a white shirt, dusty now, accenting his muscular chest, and cowboy boots, the sunlight catching the shiny glint of a spur.

One leather glove was off and he was pulling impatiently at the other. It was nearly off when Riordan stopped, halting fluidly almost in mid-stride. The jet-dark head raised, tipped slightly to the side as his gaze focused unswervingly on the window where Jill stood.

Startled, she started to step back, then realised he couldn't possibly see her at that angle and distance. The glove was slowly removed and folded in the other hand with its mate. Riordan's mouth quirked at the corner as he continued to stare at the window.

A blush of self-anger at her own stupidity rouged her cheeks. He couldn't see her, but he could see the curtain lifted aside. This was his home. He knew which room the window looked out and he undoubtedly knew which room had been given to Jill.

Hastily she released the curtain and saw the amused upward curl of his mouth deepen. Then he was striding towards the house again, the leather gloves tapping the side of his leg in satisfaction.

Irritated by her own schoolgirlish reaction, Jill pivoted impatiently away from the window. She should have outstared him. She couldn't afford to let him have the slightest edge in any meeting. She wouldn't back down again.

'What are you wearing, Jill?' Kerry was standing in the open doorway of the bathroom, concentrating

276

on tying the sash of her robe, so she missed the look of anger on her friend's face.

'The—er—rose crêpe,' Jill replied, breathing in deeply to chase away any traces of temper. 'It's summerish but not too dressy.'

'I thought I'd wear my yellow flowered dress. What do you think?'

'It would be perfect.' Her smile was taut and unnatural, but Kerry didn't notice it.

'I'll go and get dressed. Come into my room whenever you're ready,' she announced, and turned towards her own room.

Jill walked to the walnut vanity mirror above the table. A few expert flicks of the brush achieved the windswept style of her hair, tousled like a wispy cloud trailing away from her face in shimmering waves of dusty amber. The pale tan of her complexion needed no make-up, a moisturing cream provided a subdued glow. A very light application of eye shadow gave a hint of blue to intensify the colour of her eyes.

'Applying warpaint,' her reflection teased wickedly. Yes, Jill smiled, reaching for the mascara.

At half past six, she was ready and helping Kerry with the stubborn zipper of her dress.

'Do you think we should go down now? It isn't seven yet,' Kerry asked, standing quietly while Jill hooked the fastener.

'I don't see why not. It'll give us time to see more of the house before dinner.'

Kerry hesitated as Jill walked to the hall door. 'Do I look all right?'

'Like a mountain flower,' she grinned in a light-hearted response to ease her friend's attack of nerves. 'Come on!'

There were three steps into the hallway leading to the stairs when Jill heard the approach of footsteps behind them, and her muscles stiffened automatically. It had to be Riordan. She hadn't heard him pass her room, but with his cat-soft way of walking, it was possible she wouldn't. Besides, it was only logical to assume he would shower and change after working all day.

The desire was there to pretend she didn't hear the firm strides of the man walking behind them. She might have ignored them if she hadn't seen Kerry glancing over her shoulder. There was no choice except for Jill to do the same.

No silver-grey eyes met the sparkling challenge of hers. Instead she saw the darker softness of Todd's gazing warmly at the now halted Kerry. Relief shuddered through her. It wasn't a welcome reaction. She wanted to be more poised and in command than this when she met Riordan face to face.

Todd's hands were reaching out for Kerry's. 'You look beautiful, honey.'

'Do you think so?' She gazed rapturously into his eyes. The radiant glow of love chased away all her plainness, making her as beautiful as Todd declared she was.

Feeling superfluous, Jill said, 'I'll see you two downstairs.'

Ostensibly her presence in the house was as a chaperone and companion to Kerry, but Jill didn't intend to turn into her friend's shadow. She and Todd were entitled to be alone once in a while, and Jill was going to make sure it was often.

At the base of the stairs, Jill hesitated. Glancing to the rear of the carved banister, she caught a glimpse of white-covered table through an open door. Guessing it was the dining room, she walked towards it.

The open door ahead of it led into the living room. She gave it a cursory glance of identification as she walked by, believing she was more likely to find her hostess in the dining room.

The oval table, covered by an intricately crocheted cloth, was set with fragile, flowered china and gleaming crystal. A chandelier hung from the cross-beamed ceiling to illuminate the table. A silken fabric covered the walls above the wainscoting, its white-on-white design alleviating the heavy darkness of the furniture and panelling. But the room was empty and Jill was not inclined to wait in there for the others.

Retracing her steps, she wandered into the living room. Her gaze was drawn immediately to the painting hanging above the mantel of the marble-faced fireplace.

It was a portrait of a woman, a very beautiful woman with copper hair and sparkling hazel eyes. The peach-tinted lips were curved in a breathless smile that embraced life. Yet, despite all the vitality flowing in every slender line, there was a definite air or fragility and innocence.

'My mother,' a male voice said.

Jill whirled away from the portrait, to face the corner of the room where Riordan's voice had come. Grey eyes mocked the wary look in her expression as he rose from a wing-backed chair, a glass in one hand.

He had changed from the dusty demins to tailored slacks of camel tan. The long-sleeved silk shirt, predominantly white with a design in green and tan, moulded the breadth of his shoulders and tapered to his comparatively slim waist. The top buttons were undone, revealing dark, curling hairs on his chest. The black thickness of his hair glistened as if still damp from a shower.

Her rapid noting of his dress was being echoed by Riordan, although his slow appraisal of her was more insolent as he inspected the way the clinging material of her loose-fitting dress revealed her full curves without being blatantly suggestive.

His aloof gaze was stripping. Jill felt the heat of betrayal warming her face. But she refused to look away even when his mocking eyes stopped at her mouth, as if reminding her of the time he had punishingly possessed her lips.

'I've heard of pink elephants, Miss Randall, but pink butterflies?' His mouth quirked with cynical amusement. Unwillingly Jill protectively touched the rose-coloured material of her dress. 'Would you like a drink?'

'No,' she snapped, and regretted her sharpness as a dark brow raised suggestively in her direction. She added more quietly, 'Thank you anyway.'

It wouldn't do to lose her temper so early in the

evening, and on her first night in his house, too.

'I must apologise for not being here to greet you and Miss Adams.' His low derisive voice was not the least bit apologetic. 'I hope you weren't at your window watching for me any extended length of time.'

'I wasn't watching for *you*,' Jill declared coldly. 'I was enjoying the view of the mountains from my window.'

Satisfaction glittered in his eyes. He had deliberately trapped her into admitting she had seen him and she had foolishly risen to the bait. She turned away, angry with herself for not being better prepared for this encounter.

An older woman was pausing in the doorway, wearing a dress of blue gingham with an apron in a matching blue tied around her large-boned frame. Short blue-black hair was dulled by a suggestion of grey, but nothing dimmed the alertness of her nearly black eyes shining out of a strongly structured face as she glanced from Jill to Riordan. This was obviously the housekeeper, Jill decided.

'Mrs Benton sent me in with this tray of nuts and olives,' the woman explained, walking into the room. 'She said you'd be having drinks in here before coming to the table.'

'Miss Randall, this is my housekeeper Mary Rivers,' Riordan confirmed Jill's deduction. 'She's a full-blooded Crow Indian, the granddaughter of a war chief. This is Jill Randall, a friend of the young lady Todd brought home.'

'I'm pleased to meet you.' Jill's smile came naturally, prompted by the friendliness in the woman's expression.

An answering smile crinkled the corners of the intelligent dark eyes. The lines had become ingrained from much use.

'I hope you enjoy your stay here, Miss Randall.' The words of welcome were spoken sincerely—the first Jill had heard. 'Despite my ancestry, I seldom go on the warpath! After thirty years in this house, it takes a lot to provoke me.'

Jill darted a swift glance to Riordan's impassive face. Mary Rivers had obviously overheard his needling remarks and had offered a discreet word of advice—a suggestion easier said than done

'May I help you with anything in the kitchen?' Jill offered.

'It's nearly all ready,' the woman refused, still maintaining her smile. 'Besides, too many cooks——'

Her voice trailed away, leaving Jill with the impression that the housekeeper believed Sheena Benton already made it one too many cooks. The thought brought a smile she was forced to hide as the chestnut-haired woman entered the room, bestowing a dazzling smile on Riordan.

'I'd best get back to the kitchen,' the housekeeper murmured, and withdrew.

The cat-flecked eyes of Sheena Benton weren't quite so warm as they blinked at Jill. 'Have you been down long, Miss Randall? I'm afraid I was in the kitchen.'

'Only a few minutes,' Jill acknowledged. Silently

and partly grudgingly, she admired the gold dress that matched the woman's eyes and sensuously hugged her curves.

Riordan's eyes were watching her above the rim of the glass he held to his mouth. He probably knew his tiger mistress did not like pink butterflies either and was waiting for an excuse to claw the fragile wings.

When his gaze slid to the doorway, Jill followed it, seeing Todd return a lipstick-stained handkerchief to his pocket as he ushered a flushed and radiant Kerry into the room.

CHAPTER FIVE

THE odd number of people had placed Jill alone on side of the oval table opposite Todd and Kerry with Riordan and Sheena as host and hostess at the ends of the table. Sheena had dominated the conversation with witty anecdotes of ranch life.

In the main, she had related stories that involved either Riordan or Todd, always subtly pointing out her closeness to the host and silently reminding Jill and Kerry that they were outsiders—Jill more so than Kerry.

Jill's ostracism hadn't ended in the dining room. She should have known Sheena couldn't have cut her out of the group without Riordan's approval. In the living room, Sheena as acting hostess naturally sat on the sofa in front of the silver coffee service and Riordan joined her.

Todd and Kerry took the two chairs opposite the sofa, which left Jill with only two choices. One was out of the question since it meant sitting on the sofa beside Riordan. Accepting the china cup and saucer from Sheena, Jill sat in the chair which placed her outside their circle.

Seething inwardly, Jill maintained an outward air of calm and composure. She was not going to try to force her way into the conversation or draw attention to herself in any way. It would be what

Riordan expected her to do. Instead she sat in apparent acceptance of her exile from the group and listened.

There was satisfaction in discovering that Kerry was no longer being excluded as Sheena offered a series of polite questions about her childhood, college life and studies. Kerry's replies were soft as they always were with strangers, but she answered without hesitation, a fact that Jill silently applauded, knowing the courage it required for her shy friend.

'Todd, you'll have to show Kerry the beaver pool,' Sheena declared, glancing to the brunette after she had given the command. 'It isn't far from the house, a nice walk and it's a perfect swimming pool. The water is a bit chilly since it's snow drainage from the mountains, but the setting is idyllic. It'll be something for you to do while Todd is working. You do swim, don't you?'

'Well, actually, I don't know how,' Kerry replied self-consciously. 'I never had the opportunity to learn while I was growing up.'

'What about horseback riding? I'm sure Riordan could find you a suitably gentle mount. You'll enjoy an afternoon canter over the open meadow—that is, if you ride?' A feline brow arched inquiringly.

A hand nervously crept to a dark curl as Kerry darted a sideways glance at Todd. 'I have ridden a couple of times, but I'm not very good.'

Sheena smiled faintly. At Jill's angle she couldn't tell if the smile was motivated by satisfaction or polite understanding. The latter seemed very unlikely. Riordan was leaning against the sofa back, apparently content to let Sheena suggest activities to occupy the free daylight hours.

'In any event,' Sheena shrugged away Kerry's lack of enthusiasm for horseback riding. 'I know there'll be times when you'll simply want to get away from the ranch. I want you to feel free to come to my home any time. I've extravagantly installed a tennis court in my backyard—it's a passion of mine. If I should happen to be gone, you're more than welcome to use it anyway.'

A reddening pink crept into Kerry's cheeks as she lowered her gaze to the china cup in her lap. 'It's very kind of you to offer, but I'm afraid I don't know how to play tennis. You see, I'm really not athletically inclined.'

Jill's lips parted slightly in dawning discovery. How could she have been so blind? Riordan hadn't really been interested in separating Jill from the group to make her feel unwelcome. He had wanted her away from Kerry while he subtly pointed out to Todd how little he and Kerry had in common.

'Good lord, Kerry!' Sheena exclaimed with cutting laughter. 'You don't know how to swim or play tennis. You don't like riding. What are you going to do here for a month? You'll go stark raving mad if you spend every day sitting around the house by yourself!'

'You've forgotten Kerry isn't alone.' The cup clattered noisily in its saucer as Jill set it on the small table near her chair. Her blue eyes clashed openly with Riordan's metal grey, letting him know she had seen through his ruse and did not intend to sit silently any longer. 'I'm sure we'll find plenty to do to occupy the daytime hours.'

'And I'm more than willing to entertain Kerry in the evenings,' Todd inserted, his previously uncertain expression changing into a smile. 'Tomorrw morning I'll show you around the ranch so you won't get disorientated if you go for a walk. I'll persuade Mary to fix a picnic basket for the afternoon. The beaver pool would be a perfect place to have it.'

'I'd like that,' Kerry murmured, hesitantly returning his warm smile.

Riordan leaned forward and took a cigarette from the pack on the table. 'I'm afraid it won't be possible,' he said calmly. His bland expression was directed at the match flame he carried to the cigarette. 'I'm shorthanded right now, so I won't be able to let you have a couple of days to unwind from the end of term, Todd. You'll have to be up and out bright and early in the morning.'

'What?' A startled frown crossed the youthfully handsome face. 'Why are you shorthanded? Who isn't here?'

'Tom Manson. I fired him last week for drinking.'

'Tom's been nipping at the bottle for years and we both know it.' Todd's hazel eyes darkened with suspicion. 'After turning a blind eye to it all this time, why did you suddenly fire him for it?'

'He was drunk last week and nearly set the barn on fire. I wasn't about to give him a second chance to succeed.' The level grey eyes dared Todd to challenge his decision. Except for a slight tightening of his mouth in resignation, Todd made no reply as he turned towards Kerry.

'I'm sorry, honey. I guess that takes care of that.'

'It's all right,' Kerry assured him, her hand finally stopping its nervous twisting of her hair. 'We'll do it another day.'

'Speaking of other days,' Sheena glanced at the slender gold watch on her wrist, 'it isn't too long until tomorrow and I still, unfortunately, have to drive home. I'll get my clothes and other things from the bedroom.'

Whose bedroom? Jill wondered cattily as the woman rose lazily to her feet. Accidentally her gaze met Riordan's. Something of her dislike of Sheena Benton must have been in her expression, because amusement twitched the corners of his hard mouth.

Todd unconsciously broke their vaguely challenging exchange of glances by asking what the agenda would be for the following day. The discussion between the two men stayed on ranch business until Sheena reappeared in the doorway.

'Goodnight, everybody.' Her purring smile swept over all the occupants of the room, stopping on Kerry. 'Remember, if you feel lonesome, be sure to call me or come over. It's been a pleasure meeting you. And you, too, Miss Randall.'

It was added as a deliberate afterthought. Jill's fingers curled. Sheena's catlike actions seemed to be contagious!

'It was kind of you to be here to welcome us, Mrs Benton,' she answered insincerely.

Sheena's gaze narrowed for a fleeting second. 'It was my pleasure. Riordan,' a winging brow arched towards him, 'will you walk me to my car?'

He didn't reply but rose to his feet. The suffocating tension that had enveloped Jill seemed to leave the room with him. She hadn't realised how stiffly she had been holding herself until she drew a free breath.

A certain aura of confinement remained, probably brought on by inactivity. Jill knew Todd and Kerry wouldn't object if she left them alone. In fact, they'd welcome it.

'I think I'll take the coffee service into the kitchen,' she announced without receiving any objections in response.

The kitchen was large and spacious with an old breakfast table and Windsor chairs in the centre. Despite the modern appliances, the room retained the old-fashioned charm of the rest of the house.

Mary Rivers waved aside Jill's offer to help clean up the few cups and saucers, insisting that it wouldn't require two pairs of hands. Jill stayed for a few minutes anyway. They talked without saying anything.

When she came away from the room, Jill knew her first impression of the matronly housekeeper had been correct. She was a warm, friendly woman and Jill liked her. She hoped it would be mutual.

As she neared the base of the stairs in the entrance hall, the front door opened and Riordan walked in. Nerve ends tensed instinctively. After a fractional pause in her steps, Jill continued forward, her gaze sweeping coolly over his aloof features.

At the base of the stairs, she made a split-second decision and turned to climb them, aware of the long smooth strides carrying Riordan towards her.

'Are you retreating so early?' he mocked softly.

Jill paused on the first step, her hand resting on the polished banister, but she didn't turn round.

'It's been a long day.' Silently she added that it promised to be a long month, especially if tonight was any example of what she was to expect.

'Is something wrong, Miss Randall?' Again, ridiculing amusement dominated his voice. Only this time he was at the stairs, stepping to the banister support, putting himself in her line of vision.

'Nothing,' she shrugged, her gaze striking blue sparks as it clashed with the flint-grey hardness of his. Pointedly she directed her attention to the quirking corner of his mouth and the faint smear of lipstick. 'You should suggest that Mrs Benton blot her lipstick. It isn't so likely to rub off.'

The grooves around his mouth deepened as Riordan made no move to wipe away the lipstick trace. 'The evening hasn't been very enjoyable for you, has it? You're used to a cluster of admirers, I'm sure, but gooseberries always are sour. Maybe after a month, you'll get used to the taste.'

It was one of those horrible moments when words deserted Jill. An hour from now she would be able to think of a suitably cutting retort that she could have made. Seething with impotent anger, she couldn't keep her voice from trembling.

'Please tell Kerry that I'm tired and have gone up to my room.'

'Of course.' Riordan inclined his head with patronising politeness, the sardonic smile laughing at her excuse.

Her legs were shaking, but they still managed to carry her swiftly up the stairs to her room. Although she wasn't tired, she changed into nightclothes and climbed into bed anyway.

Later she heard Kerry and Todd bidding each other goodnight in the hall and the closing of their respective bedroom doors. It seemed as if she lay awake a long time after that before drifting to sleep, but she never heard Riordan come up the stairs.

After a week, life at the ranch fell into a pattern. The daylight hours were the ones that brought the most pleasure to Jill. She and Kerry often took exploring walks in the morning, discovering the beaver pool and other places but wisely keeping the ranch buildings in sight at all times. In the afternoons they lazed in the sun or helped Mary when she would let them. It wasn't a demanding routine but a welcome change from the hectic college schedule of classes and study.

As Jill had expected, Sheena had stopped over. Both of her two visits coincided with times that Riordan was at the house, deliberately planned, Jill was sure. Neither visit had changed Jill's opinion of the woman.

Part of Jill's pleasure was derived from the fact

that Riordan was gone from the house with the rising of the sun. Todd, too, of course. Generally it was nearly dark before they returned. Only three days had they been close enough to the ranch house to return for lunch, an event that Kerry looked forward to and Jill dreaded.

The evenings were blessedly short. By the time Riordan and Todd returned, showered away the day's dirt and dinner was eaten, it was nearly time to go to bed. Still, it was more time in Riordan's company than Jill wanted to spend. He was constantly baiting her with a word or a look, guaranteed to set her teeth on edge. Kerry he virtually ignored, intimidating her into gaucherie merely with his presence.

Since the object of this visit was ostensibly for Riordan to get to know Kerry better, his indifference annoyed Jill, but she was helpless to do anything about it. She could hardly point out Kerry's good qualities as if her friend was a slave on an auction block.

The Tiffany glass pane in the living room window lacked its usual brilliant colour. The thunderheads concealing the mountain peaks had completely blocked out the sun. The fat drops that had been ricocheting off the windows had turned into a sheeting downpour of rain. Serrated bolts of lighting were followed by rolling explosions of thunder that rattled the window panes.

Todd had dashed into the house alone more than a quarter of an hour ago, drenched to the skin. Jill hadn't cared where Riordan was. She was curled in a corner of the living room sofa staring at the portrait above the fireplace, wondering how that beautiful woman could mother two so very different sons.

'Hi, where's Kerry?' Todd walked into the living room, tucking a clean shirt into his dry trousers.

His brown hair was still damp, gleaming almost as black as Riordan's. For an instant the resemblance between the two brothers was strong. It vanished when Jill met the friendly hazel eyes.

'In the kitchen, making you some hot chocolate,' she replied.

'That woman is going to make some man a great wife,' he sighed, sinking into the winged chair opposite the sofa. A crack of lightning was ominously close. 'Rain, rain, rain!' A smile of contentment turned up his mouth. 'I was beginning to think I was never going to have an afternoon off. What have you been doing this lovely rainy day, Jill?'

Her gaze swept to the portrait. 'Reading,' she answered absently, although the book had been discarded on the cushion beside her for some time. With a curious frown, she glanced to Todd. 'May I ask a nosy question?'

'Ask it and I'll decide whether I want to answer it,' he grinned, obviously refreshed and in a jesting mood.

'The portrait of your mother is still hanging above the fireplace. I guess I was wondering why.' She tipped her head to one side, watching Todd's teasing smile fade as he turned towards the portrait, a soft admiring affection in his gaze. 'She and your father were separated for nearly eighteen years, weren't they?'

'It's always hung there ever since I can remember. And separated isn't really the right word to use.' Todd leaned back in his chair, his expression thoughtful when he glanced at Jill. 'They lived separately, which isn't quite the same thing. For nine months of the year Mom and I lived with her father. In the summer, we came here.'

'Every year?'

'Every year,' he nodded. 'I'd wake up one morning in Helena and Mom would say we were going to the ranch. She never called ahead to say we were coming, but I can't remember a time that Dad wasn't there to meet her. It's very hard to explain how very much they loved each other, but they did, genuinely. And every summer it was like a honeymoon. They would laugh, talk in whispers, and Dad would steal a kiss every once in a while. I couldn't begin to count the number of times I saw them simply gazing into each other's eyes. Then on an August morning, Mom would say we were going back to my grandfather's.'

'But why?' Confusion clouded Jill's eyes. 'I mean if they loved each other so much, why did they live apart?'

He breathed in deeply and gazed at the portrait. 'Mother couldn't stand the isolation of the ranch. She needed people around her. She was gregarious, always wanting to meet new faces. I can remember her telling me how she used to pray for something to break down when she lived here. It didn't matter what it was so long as it required a repairman to fix it and she would have someone new to talk to if only for an hour. For eight years, she said that she kept thinking she would adjust. Finally she couldn't tolerate it any more.'

'It's a miracle they stayed in love all those years. Being separated nine months of every year would put a strain on any relationship,' she declared with an amazed shake of her blonde hair.

'Dad did come to Helena every year at Christmas time for a couple of days. Riordan came, too, until he was about sixteen. On our way up here the other day, you asked me about Riordan as a boy,' Todd frowned absently. 'I think in a way he believed that Mother deserted him and Dad, even though Riordan realised that she had wanted him to live with her. He never said anything to me, but I imagine he thought she had lovers. She never did, Jill. You can't hide something like that for eighteen years, not even from a small boy, and I lived with her all the time. There was only one man for her and that was my father. It was a very special and rare kind of love they had for each other, and one that was very strong.'

'It had to be,' Jill agreed, staring at the portrait.

'Do you know what Dad used to call her? His butterfly.'

Everything inside Jill seemed to freeze. The chilling that stopped her heartbeat halted the breathing of her lungs. A numbing paralysis spread through her limbs. A resentment that had mani-

295

fested in Riordan's childhood was responsible for his bitter dislike and contempt of her, another butterfly.

'There you are, Todd.' Kerry's happy voice came from the open doorway. 'I fixed you some hot chocolate. I thought you might like some after your drenching.'

'Remind me to marry you,' Todd winked, grabbing her hand as she set the cup on the walnut table between the two winged chairs.

'I will,' Kerry laughed but with a breathless catch.

Thunder clapped, vibrating the walls.

'Todd!' At the sound of Riordan's commanding voice, Jill nearly jumped off the sofa.

The thunder had evidently drowned out the opening and closing of the front door. He was standing in the doorway, his clothes comparatively dry. A telltale dampness around his shirtsleeves and collar indicated he had been wearing a rain slicker.

'Just because it's raining, it doesn't mean there isn't work to do,' he said curtly.

Jill kept her face averted from those disconcerning grey eyes. All of her senses were reacting to his presence with alarming intensity.

'I've just changed into dry clothes,' Todd grumbled in protest.

'If you'd taken your slicker, you wouldn't have got soaked,' was the unsympathetic response. 'Come on, we might as well sharpen the mower blades.'

'There goes my afternoon off!' Sighing, Todd rose from the chair, smiling apologetically at Kerry.

'Thanks for the cocoa, honey, but I'm afraid you'll have to drink it.'

When the front door closed behind the two men, a long resigned sigh broke from Kerry's lips. 'Here, Jill, you drink it. I don't want it.'

The cup was set on the table in front of the sofa. 'Hey!' Jill scolded, catching the look of utter depression on her friend's face. 'It's not the end of the world. Todd will be back.'

'In time for dinner.' Kerry stuffed her hands in the pockets of her slacks and walked dejectedly to the window.

'You knew he had to work when we came,' Jill reminded her.

'I knew.' The downcast chin was raised to stare unseeingly through the rain-sheeted glass.

'Don't let the weather get you down. Why don't we start a fire in the fireplace? That ought to chase away the gloom.'

'It's not that.' Kerry turned tiredly away from the window. 'Haven't you noticed?'

'Noticed what?'

'We've been here seven days and in all that time I've seen Todd alone about a total of one hour. He works from dawn to dusk, never has any free time, and at night his brother is always around.'

'And me, too,' Jill inserted gently.

She suddenly realised that she had been so anxious to insulate herself from Riordan, she hadn't considered that Todd and Kerry would want to be alone. And it had been one of her prime objectives on their arrival.

'I'm not blaming you,' Kerry assured her quickly.

'I know you're not, but maybe there's something I can do to arrange some time for you and Todd.'

'If only there was!' Kerry's brows lifted expressively.

Surprisingly, opportunity presented itself that evening. Jill had been deliberately pleasant to Riordan at the dinner table, not overly so in case he suspected some ulterior motive. Mostly she attempted to avoid exchanging innuendoes, asking questions without becoming too personal.

When the four of them left the table to have coffee in the living room, as had become the custom, Riordan glanced out through the night-darkened windows. "The rain has stopped. We'll have to get out and check the stock tomorrow.'

'It isn't raining?' Jill repeated, taking hold of the opportunity. 'If you three don't mind, I think I'll skip the coffee. After being in the house all day, a walk sounds very welcome.' Riordan was behind her, so he didn't see the wink she gave Kerry.

'Of course not,' Kerry answered, a secret sparkle of understanding in her brown eyes.

'I'll get my sweater.' Jill started for the stairs and paused. 'I'd better see if Mary has a flashlight I can borrow.' She laughed lightly. 'I don't want to stumble over something and break a leg in the dark.'

'I'll come with you,' Riordan said.

'There's no need,' she refused quickly. 'I'll be all right by myself, honestly.'

'I'm sure you would be, but I'll come with you just the same.' The chiselled features were aloofly set, a faintly sardonic quirk to the ruthless mouth.

Jill hesitated, deliberately giving the impression that she would like to argue the point. Riordan wasn't as easy to manipulate as some men she had known.

'All right,' she gave in after letting him hold her wavering gaze with his long measuring look. 'I'll get my sweater.'

A pulse was throbbing much too wildly in her throat when she descended the stairs, sweater in hand. She blamed it on the disturbing grey eyes watching every step. Her breathless smile was genuine. She had taken the time to run a brush through the wind-tossed style of her hair and add the shimmer of gloss to her lips.

With no false modesty, she knew she presented an alluringly innocent picture. This time, unlike the previous time she had tried to trick him, the emphasis was on the alluring rather than the innocent. He might despise butterflies, but Riordan was human—Sheena proved that.

Her feet carried her lightly across the hall and through the door he held open. She paused outside long enough for him to close the door and turn to join her. Then, leading the way, she moved down the few steps to the stone walk. As she turned on to the lane, she pretended to ignore the man walking a fraction of a pace behind her.

The course of the rutted lane across the meadow had been a deliberate choice. Here she would be walking directly in the moonlight, its silver gleam catching the sheen of her lips and accenting the blondeness of her hair.

Her eyes swept the panoramic landscape. It wasn't necessary to pretend an enchantment of the night's beauty. A lopsided moon was directly in front of them, dominating the starfire of the black sky. In the distance, Jill could see the bank of thunderclouds and the lightning that played hide and seek within.

'It's beautiful,' she murmured as if to herself, but she had not forgotten for one instant that Riordan was with her.

'Yes.'

The dry cynicism startled Jill. A glance at that strong profile told her that he was untouched by the beauty of the night or her. As unyielding as his expression was, the moonlight had softened the rugged lines, giving him a dangerous, ruthless kind of attraction.

Jill had forgotten how tall he was and the way his well-proportioned frame gave a deceptive impression of leanness. Strolling beside him the way she was, she was aware of the solid muscles in his arms, chest and legs.

'Don't you think it's beautiful?' she paused when he did, questioning the reason for his less than enthusiastic response.

A match flamed to the end of a cigarette and was shaken out. His silver gaze swung to her face, metallic and reflecting.

'Are you angling for a compliment?' Riordan taunted.

'A compliment?' she repeated blankly.

'Wasn't I supposed to be affected by the vision of your loveliness in the moonlight?' His mouth twisted into a jeering smile.

Anger sparkled in her eyes as she unflinchingly met his steady look. 'No.' Her voice was calm and completely indifferent.

Smoothly she started forward, feeling his doubting gaze on her profile and knowing that she had intended to prompt some measure of admiration. She'd cut off her arm before she would admit that now.

'Aren't we supposed to talk about Todd and Kerry?' The sarcastic inflection of his low voice whipped at the raw edges of her temper.

Jill kept walking, gazing about the mountain meadow without seeing anything. 'If you want to,' she shrugged carelessly.

'Isn't that why you invited me along?'

'I didn't invite you along, Riordan. You invited yourself,' she reminded him, sending him a complacent glance from the sweep of her lashes.

His mouth twitched with amusement. 'I know you wanted me to come with you. I just haven't figured why.' A gauzy cloud of smoke was blown ahead of them, the wispy trail waiting to ensnare Jill.

'My reason for taking this walk is nothing more complicated than a desire to be outdoors in the fresh air,' she defended airily. She tossed her head back to send him a glittering look. 'The evening is much too peaceful to start an argument with you.'

'You've been conciliatory all evening. Why, Jill?' The husky issuance of her name started a disturbing reaction in her stomach.

'I've already told you.'

'You've given a reason, but you haven't told the truth.'

The man was too perceptive by far. 'Why don't you tell me what the truth is?' she challenged lightly.

'I imagine a girl as beautiful as you has become accustomed to large quantities of admiration from the opposite sex. After a week here, you might be in need of a man's company,' Riordan suggested mockingly. 'A casual flirtation to keep in practice.'

'And I'm supposed to have tricked you into coming with me for that purpose?' Jill demanded, her head thrown back, the sheen of her blonde hair glistening palely in the moonlight.

'You've picked a romantic setting,' he taunted. 'A walk in the moonlight on a path that takes us some distance from the house, just the two of us alone.'

She swallowed involuntarily, glancing furtively around, not realising how far they had walked from the ranch house. They were very much alone, surrounded by meadow and moonlight.

'If that was my intention, I would surely have picked a man who at least was attracted to me. You've made your dislike of me very clear,' she reresponded boldly.

'On the contrary, I am attracted to you. I may think you're a scheming little witch,' his mouth curved into a humourless smile while he lazily inspected her upturned face, 'but it doesn't lessen the desire to make love to you. You're a very beautiful woman.'

The bluntness of his declaration sent shivers of ice down her spine. 'Save your compliments for Sheena. I'm sure she would appreciate them much more than I do,' Jill answered sharply, averting her face.

His thumb and finger caught her chin and turned her back. 'Jealous?' Riordan mocked huskily, his eyes glittering over the deepening colour in her cheeks that not even the dim light could hide.

Her eyes blazing, she wrenched away from his touch. 'You're conceited, arrogant——'

The sheen in his eyes turned to metallic steel as he clamped a hand over her mouth, shutting off the tirade with the swiftness of a slicing blade. Her hands came up to tear his fingers away and she was crushed against his chest.

'I wondered how long it would take before you lost your temper.' Slowly he removed his hand. 'You can scream all you want. There isn't anyone around to hear you.'

'Let me go!' Jill hissed.

Riordan smiled coldly, lacing his fingers through her hair to prevent her from twisting her face away. His mouth descended towards her and Jill was helpless to avoid it. A gasp of protest was torn from her throat as he nuzzled the throbbing pulse in her neck.

'Make your token resistance if you must,' he

jeered, raising havoc with her heartbeat as he nibbled at her ear, 'but you know you intended this to happen all along.'

'No,' she denied.

His mouth trailed over her cheek to tease the corner of her lips, the warmth of his breath caressing her skin.

'Why else did you want me to come with you?' Riordan smiled with arrogant conceit.

The tantalising closeness of his mouth, sensually touching without taking, was unnerving. A purely physical reaction started trembling through her limbs.

'Don't!' She spoke against his mouth, fire leaping somewhere inside her. 'I left the h-house because I wanted privacy——'

'Naturally,' he agreed.

'No. Privacy for Todd and Kerry,' Jill explained desperately. 'I—I thought they should have some time alone. That's why I wanted you to come with me.'

His head raised from hers, a brow arching in satisfaction. 'Now I know the truth,' he murmured, relaxing his hold so she could pull free.

Staring at him, Jill bit into her lip still burning from the nearness of his. 'You tricked me, didn't you?' she accused in a shallow breath. 'You never intended to try to seduce me.'

'Could I have?' The grooves around his mouth deepened.

'No!' She spun away.

Her flesh still tingled from the imprint of his male form and there was a funny empty ache in the pit of her stomach. Could he? a tiny voice inside asked.

'No!' The second vigorous denial was made to the voice.

'We'd better head back to the house,' Riordan said with silent laughter in his voice, 'while you're still trying to make up your mind. If you aren't convinced, then I may become curious enough to find out for myself.'

It sounded very much like a threat to Jill. Sometimes it was better to retreat and lose a battle than to lose a war. Right now Riordan was much too disturbing an influence for her to think straight.

As they entered the house with Jill a hurried step ahead of Riordan, Kerry walked out of the living room. There was no inner glow to her expression as Jill had come to expect. For a moment she forgot her own haste to reach the safety of the bedroom.

'Where's Todd?' Jill glanced curiously towards the living room. A frown puzzled her forehead, trying to guess if the two had quarrelled.

'He's in the living room,' Kerry answered tightly, her lips thinning in irritation. 'He was so tired he fell asleep twenty minutes ago.'

Jill's lashes fluttered shut in sighing disbelief. A low throaty chuckle sounded behind her, rolling into outright laughter. She darted an angry look at Riordan, catching the crinkling of his eyes at the corner, the merry glint of grey in the pupils and the broad, laughing smile. It was a Riordan that she had never seen before.

A wickedness entered the merry glint. 'Ah, the irony of it, Jill,' he concluded with a wry shake of his ebony dark head.

'What's so funny?' Kerry frowned after Riordan had strode away, still smiling, towards the rear of the house.

Jill put a hand to her mussed hair, a faint smile tugging the corners of her mouth. 'Don't ask, Kerry,' she answered with a short sighing laugh. 'From your viewpoint, I don't think it would be very funny.'

CHAPTER SIX

'WE'VE changed the bedding in all the rooms except Riordan's, Mary,' Jill announced, tucking an escaping wisp of hair under her old-fashioned blue bandanna. 'I'm afraid we couldn't figure out which room was his.'

Mary Rivers was on her hands and knees in the hallway cleaning and polishing the woodwork. She straightened stiffly upright, a hand pushing against the small of her back.

'I already took care of his room. He sleeps downstairs in the rear—I didn't think to mention it. Old age, I expect.'

'Would you want me to put the sheets in the washer?' Kerry asked, holding the armload in front of her.

'You girls have done enough. You're guests in this house, not daily help.' The housekeeper shook her head in refusal of the offer.

'We enjoy helping,' Jill insisted.

'It's much better than sitting around doing nothing. At least this way we can be useful,' Kerry added. 'Besides, what's involved in washing sheets? All I have to do is stick them in the washer, add detergent and push a button.'

'While she's doing that, I can help you with this woodwork.' Without allowing time for a protest,

Jill bent over to pick up the cloth and polish at Mary Rivers' feet.

'I can't let you girls do this.' The housekeeper tried to take the cleaning items from Jill's hand, but she held them out of reach.

'How are you going to stop us?' Kerry asked pertly, turning down the hall towards the kitchen and the utility room beyond it.

'Come on, Mary,' Jill coaxed. 'Let us help. You said yourself that by the time you do the cooking and regular cleaning, you're lucky to have the spring house-cleaning done by fall. We've been here over ten days. We can't keep doing nothing while you work.'

'You make the beds and straighten your own rooms. That's enough of a help to me.'

'Let us help you with other things. Not all the time but every once in a while, like now. We've little else to do with our time,' Jill pointed out.

'I give up!' Mary lifted her hands in the air in surrender. 'I'll get another polishing cloth and we'll both clean this entrance hall.'

'It's a deal,' Jill smiled. 'I'll do the woodwork near the floor so you won't be getting up and down so much. You can do that carving around the wainscoting.'

After two hours of scooting along the floor on her hands and knees, Jill's muscles in her back shoulders and arms started to protest. She hurt, but it was a good kind of hurt, if that was possible. The work was certainly an outlet for the restlessness that had been plaguing both girls.

The evenings had returned to their former pattern with Riordan dominating, by his presence, the other three. Jill didn't make any more attempt to manoeuvre Riordan away from Todd and Kerry.

Naturally Kerry had wheedled an account of Jill's only disastrous attempt bit by bit. Jill never admitted that she had actually thought Riordan intended to seduce her or that, for a few traitorous moments, her flesh had been tempted to respond to his teasing caresses.

Without these pertinent facts, Kerry had seen the ironic humour of the event. While Jill had been ineffectually trying to fend off Riordan's advances (as Kerry believed they were), she had been listening to Todd snore.

The end result of the episode for Jill had been an increasing awareness of her masculine host. She was certain that Riordan could, if he wanted to, arouse her physically as no other man had done. She had always been the one in control of all aspects of a relationship, and she didn't like the sensation of being so vulnerable. He didn't like butterflies. It was a possibility that he might some day decide to tarnish her wings.

A shiver danced over her skin as she remembered the tantalising warmth of his mouth just barely brushing hers. A dangerous curiosity kept wondering what it would be like to be kissed by him—not the degrading, punishing kiss he had subjected her to when they first met, but a kiss of passion.

And there was the silent challenge, too. Every man she had ever gone after, she had got. But what about Riordan? Was he the exception to the rule?

There was a jingling in the hallway behind her. Brushing a stray strand of hair away from her eyes, Jill started to turn around. What a silly time for Kerry to put on a bracelet, she thought. Then the jingling was accompanied by the sound of long, angry strides closing on her. There was a fleeting glimpse of Riordan's uncompromising and forbidding features.

In the next second, Jill's wrist was seized in a vice grip and she was yanked to her feet, unaware of the startled gasping cry that came from her throat. Her legs were momentarily too numb from the crawling position to support her. She sought to steady herself against his chest with her free hand.

'What the hell is going on here!' Riordan snapped. He pulled the hand from his chest to tear away the polishing cloth unconsciously still clutched in her fingers and hurl it to the far side of the hall. 'Mary!'

Jill stumbled heavily against him, her heart lurching as she came against the solid wall of muscle. His arm automatically released her wrist and circled her waist to catch her, taking her full weight as if it were no more than a child's.

The suddenness of her forced movement had thrown her head back, her stunned gaze staring into his narrowed eyes darkened like turbulent thunderclouds. She shuddered at the violence contained within.

'Mary, what's the meaning of this?' Thunder growled threateningly in his voice. 'And you'd better have a damned good explanation!'

His strong male scent was all around Jill, filling her senses to the exclusion of everything but his nearness. It seemed to take all her strength to look away from the compelling features so close to her own and focus on the housekeeper who was the recipient of his stormy gaze. Mary Rivers didn't appear intimidated by his anger. Instinctively Jill leaped to her defence anyway.

'I was helping,' she inserted breathlessly.

Riordan's gaze slashed to her for a paralysing second. 'Shut up, Jill. Mary is perfectly capable of answering for herself.' His attention was again riveted on the housekeeper. 'Well?'

'The girls offered to help,' she answered simply.

'You've been working, too?' An accusing glance was thrown over his shoulder. Jill could barely see Kerry hovering uncertainly near the stairs, her brown eyes rounded and stunned at the sight of Jill a captive of this snarling lion.

'I ... was doing the wash,' she murmured.

Riordan muttered an imprecation under his breath. 'I am only going to say this once, Mary.' A muscle worked convulsively in his strong jaw. 'They are my guests in my house and I will not have guests crawling around on their hands and knees cleaning woodwork or washing clothes!'

Mary Rivers stood calmly before him, straight and tall, her hands clasped in front of her. 'They're strong healthy girls, Riordan. You can't expect them to sit in this house day after day twiddling their thumbs.'

311

'I don't give a damn what they do. I will not have them working like hired help in this house. Is that clear?'

'How can you stop us?' Jill breathed in challenge. 'Mary tried and she couldn't. You weren't even here. I took the cloth and polish away from her and demanded to help.'

The arm around her waist tightened, crushing her more firmly against his rippling muscles. The hard glint in his eyes that commanded her silence gave Jill the impression that he would like to snap her in two.

'Stay out of this.' Narrowed slits of steel sliced across Jill's flushed face, then cut swiftly back to Mary. 'Have I made myself clear?'

'I'm not to blame for this.' The housekeeper held his gaze without flinching. 'As you pointed out, they're guests in this house. It's your responsibility and not mine to see that they're entertained. If you choose to neglect that, you have no right to lose your temper because they found their own way to amuse themselves and fill the empty time.'

'And you would do well, Mary,' Jill was cast away from him, sagging limply against the wall like a rag doll as Riordan turned to tower above the housekeeper, 'to remember that you are not a part of the family, but a paid employee!'

The spurs on his boots jingled noisily again as long strides carried him to the door. Jill flinched at the explosive slamming of the door, half expecting the rattling windows to shatter from the impact.

312

Her gaze shifted automatically to the housekeeper silently staring at the door.

'I'm sorry, Mary,' she offered sincerely, strength finally beginning to flow through her limbs. 'We never intended to get you into trouble.'

'He'll get over it,' Mary Rivers shrugged philosophically. A twinkle sparkled in her dark eyes. 'But in the meantime I think you'd better leave the housework to me until he cools down at least!'

The atmosphere in the house remained electrified. There wasn't any room that possessed an immunity to the invisible tension. Dinner that evening was an awkward affair.

Riordan's disposition hadn't improved. A black mood seemed to hover about the house during dinner. Not even his unexpected departure from the house after the meal put any of them at ease. It was those clouds that hovered in the house into the following day. Wanting to defy him, Jill was still hesitant to offer again to help Mary. She wasn't quite as convinced as Mary that Riordan was going to get over his anger.

Perhaps that was why his announcement the following night at the dinner table came as such a surprise. Her lips were slightly parted in disbelief as she continued to stare at him.

'A trail ride?' Todd echoed the words Riordan had just spoken.

Riordan appeared indifferent to the stunned reaction his suggestion had met. 'I thought we could leave first thing Monday morning. That will give

313

the girls some time to get accustomed to the horses. We can only be gone two days.'

'Horses?' Kerry swallowed.

A black brow arched briefly in cynical amusement. 'Yes, horses,' Riordan affirmed. 'Unless you want to walk to the top of the mountain?'

'No, of course not,' Kerry rushed nervously, glancing to Jill to see her reaction.

'You did say you could ride,' he reminded Kerry pointedly.

'She can ride well enough,' Todd answered for her, reaching out to cover Kerry's hand. 'I'll pick out a nice gentle mount for you.'

'And you, Jill?' Riordan drawled, his impassive grey eyes shifting to her. 'Can you ride, or will you require a nice gentle mount, too?'

Despite the casualness of his voice, there was a decided bite underlining the question. She tried to fathom his expression without success. She still couldn't believe that he sincerely meant to go through with it.

'I can ride.' Her reply was marred by uncertainty.

'You don't sound very enthusiastic,' he commented dryly.

'Maybe,' Jill breathed in deeply, drawing on her reserve of bold courage, 'because I don't think the invitation for this trail ride was offered willingly.'

'Jill!' whispered Kerry in a shocked plea for caution.

'You believe that Mary's little speech yesterday reminding me of my responsibilities as host blackmailed me into suggesting this?' Riordan challenged, leaning back in his chair and regarding Jill thoughtfully from his mask of aloofness.

'Yes, I do,' she nodded.

'Well, you're quite right in believing that.' The hard line of his mouth quirked briefly as he arrogantly inclined his head in acknowledgment. 'The question remains, do you want to go?'

Jill definitely wanted to go. Her brother had been the last one to take her on a trip into the high country around her home in Yellowstone. But this wasn't exactly Kerry's cup of tea. Of course, her friend would go to the moon if Todd asked.

Her chin raised thoughtfully, as she met Riordan's narrowed gaze of watchfulness. He was very well aware of Kerry's timidity towards animals, especially something as large as a horse, and her lack of an adventurous streak that made Kerry prefer the security of a house to the unknowns of the wilderness. Jill had been the one who had prompted the exploring walks around the ranch.

Kerry's only dissatisfaction in their stay here had been she hadn't seen as much of Todd as she wanted. She would have been content to potter about the house.

Jill didn't condemn Kerry for being unwilling to experience other worlds, but Riordan did. He considered it a fatal flaw for his brother's prospective bride to have. It was time he learned that Kerry had a lot of spunk, Jill decided. However much Kerry wanted the security of a house, she would go wherever Todd led her without a grumble. A lot of pioneer women had been like her because Kerry could make a home wherever her man was.

If Riordan expected to hear Kerry complain about the hardships of the long ride and camping out, or give way to fits of terror at crawling insects and the night cries of wild animals, he was going to be in for a surprise. A secret smile teased the corners of her mouth.

'Yes,' Jill finally responded to his question with a decisive nod of her head, 'I would like to go.'

'It's settled, then,' Riordan stated, a faint glitter of curiosity at the almost complacent look on Jill's face. 'I'll start making the necessary arrangements.'

Dawn was only splintering the sky when they pointed their horses away from the ranch buildings towards the shadowed mountain slopes three days later. Fresh and eager for the trail, Jill's horse snorted, sending vapour clouds into the brisk morning air. She glanced behind her at the wide path they had left in the dew-heavy grass of the meadow.

The silence seemed almost enchanted. Only it wasn't really silent. The grass swished beneath the horses' hooves, scattering diamond droplets of dew. All around was the chirping wake-up call of the birds. Loudest of all was the rhythmic creak of saddle leather.

'Having second thoughts?' Riordan asked in a low voice.

The roofs of the ranch buildings had almost disappeared behind the rise in the meadow as Jill faced the front again. There was a serene glow in her expression when she glanced at Riordan riding beside her, leading the packhorse carrying their supplies.

'None at all,' she assured the mocking grey eyes playing over her face.

The faint glow of pale yellow lasted only a few short minutes more before the sun popped above the craggy peaks to the east. The mountain seemed to catch the light of the rising sun, reflecting the golden hues. By the time they reached the foothills, it was well up in the sky, flooding the forested slopes with brilliant sunshine, piercing the foliage with golden streamers of light.

As they entered the forest of pines, their delicate scent dominated the air. Riordan led the way through the moderately dense growth with Jill behind him, followed by Kerry and Todd bringing up the rear. The narrow, weaving route through the trees was traversed single file which made conversation almost impossible. Jill didn't mind. She savoured the solitude of her own thoughts.

The private glimpses of wildlife were many. A jay followed them for some distance through the trees as if inspecting the invaders of his domain. Squirrels hid behind trunks waiting for them to pass before resuming their endless search for food.

At the edge of a small forest glade, Jill's horse stopped. She had been watching a squirrel peering warily around a trunk. Glancing forward, she saw that Riordan had reined in his horse and checked the packhorse's progress. Curious, she looked beyond him.

In the sun-drenched glade, two deer stared motionless in their direction. Then, with a flick of a white tail, they bounded away, gracefully leaping through the tall rippling grass dotted with brilliant reds and yellows of wildflowers.

Without a word or glance being exchanged with the others, Riordan nudged his bay horse into the open. Jill followed keeping single file and not attempting to draw level with him. For a moment, she ignored the scenery and concentrated on the wide shoulders ahead of her.

Riordan sat with casual ease, a part of the horse and environment, the untamed look about him more pronounced than before. The warmth of the sun had made itself felt and his suede jacket was swinging open. A wild tremor shook her senses as she caught a glimpse of his rugged profile. With the golden sun striking sparks off the chiselled features of his strong jaw and the faintly ruthless line of his mouth, his virile attraction pulled her like a powerful magnet.

Riordan was in his element in this wilderness country, Jill told herself, trying to shake away her purely physical reaction. Her blue eyes swung determinedly away from him to focus again on the landscape they rode through. But more and more often as the morning wore on, her gaze was drawn to the man riding in the lead.

Further on, the trees began to thin out, giving way to a grassy plateau studded with rocks and coloured with mountain wildflowers. It seemed as if their steady climb should have gained them great height, but craggy mountain peaks towered all around them. This was only an insignificant hill dwarfed by its bigger brothers, connected by a dipping ridge to their slopes.

Yet the crest of the hill beckoned Jill. Behind her, the valley floor was a twisting corridor through the fortress walls of the mountains. The vista at the top of the hill promised a look at it and the untouched wilderness beyond. She urged her horse even with Riordan, meeting his sideways glance of inquiry, a black brow lifting slightly.

'Are we riding to the top of the hill?' she asked.

The breathlessness in her question was merely from the exhilaration of the ride. It had nothing to do with the quicksilver glitter in his considering look, she told herself.

'We can.' He reined in his horse and turned sideways in the saddle towards the slower couple following them. 'We're going to the top, Todd.'

Todd waved them on. 'We'll meet you at the ridgeback.'

That wasn't what Jill had in mind. She had intended for the four of them to share the view, but she could hardly protest now. Riordan took a wrap on the packhorse's lead rope. Clicking to it, he touched a spur to his bay's flank, and the horse's striding walk obediently extended into a reaching trot. Jill followed.

The crest of the hill was farther and steeper than she had guessed. A lone pine growing out of an outcropping of jagged rock at the top seemed to be the point where Riordan was taking her. The last few yards she gave her horse his head to pick his way over the stony ground, always climbing.

'I didn't realise it was so far,' she said when her horse stopped beside Riordan's at the top. Her gaze was already sweeping the breathtaking panorama. 'But it was worth it.'

The ranch buildings far below were almost totally hidden by the windbreak of pines. The verdant meadow stretched like a curling green ribbon on the valley floor. The unexplored horizon on the opposite side of the hill was dominated by snow-capped peaks and virgin valleys, wild and unscarred by man, stunning in their casual grandeur.

Riordan dismounted, looping the rope to the packhorse around his saddle horn. 'We'll take a breather here and give the horses a rest.'

Her dismount was considerably less graceful than his, stiff muscles unaccustomed to extended periods of riding making their protest felt. All of that was forgotten as she spied a dark shape in the crystal blue sky.

'Riordan, look!' she whispered excitedly. He was loosening the cinch on his saddle and paused to follow her pointing finger. 'Is it an eagle or a hawk?'

'An eagle.' His sharp gaze remained fixed on the wide span of wings. Unconsciously Jill moved closer, her blood racing with excitement. 'I'd say it's a bald eagle. This is one of the few regions you can still find them where they haven't been driven out by civilisation.'

She was unable to take her eyes from the eagle soaring high on the wind currents above the mountains. 'I don't know how anyone can claim to be rich

320

if they haven't seen an eagle flying wild and free.'

'That's a profound statement.'

Something in his voice drew her gaze. Behind the lazily piercing quality of his eyes, she suspected she saw a glint of admiration. The sight of the eagle had made her spirits buoyantly light. It was like a heady wine, making her feel decidedly reckless.

'You mean coming from me,' she returned boldly, 'you don't expect such statements.'

Amusement glittered briefly before Riordan moved lazily around to her horse. A stirrup was laid over the saddle while he loosened the cinch. A breeze lifted the tousled wings of her hair, spinning wisps of burnished gold in the sunlight.

'Manoeuvring again, Jill?' he taunted softly.

Unbuttoning her medium-weight jacket of lined blue corduroy, she pushed it back so the refreshing breeze could reach her skin.

'I don't know what you mean,' she shrugged carelessly.

'You knew when you suggested we come to the top of this hill that Kerry wouldn't willingly make any side-trails on her horse.' Patting the horse's neck, he ducked beneath its head to stand beside Jill. 'Weren't you arranging for her to be alone with Todd?'

'If you say so.' With a contented sigh, she tilted her face to the sun, letting its warm rays spill over her, the hands on her hips holding the jacket open. 'I'm in much too good a mood to argue with you, Riordan.'

'I wasn't arguing,' he replied smoothly.

'Weren't you?' Amusement dimpled her cheeks.

Glancing through the gold tips of her lashes, she met his aloofly mocking eyes. They trailed slowly over her face down her neck to her blouse, dwelling on the material straining over the jutting roundness of her breasts. A silvery flame seemed to lick through the material, igniting a rush of warmth in her veins.

'I believe you're trying to flirt with me,' he drawled, stepping by her to remove a canteen from his saddle.

Studying the jet-black hair that curled around his collar and the wide shoulders, she tipped her head to one side, feeling playfully bold. 'And if I am?'

He unscrewed the lid of the canteen and handed it to her, his mouth quirking. 'I think you're out-classed.'

Her azure eyes sparkled brightly over the rim of the canteen as she took a swallow of the cool water. Her senses were vibrantly alert and ready to take up the challenge. Jill gave him back the canteen.

'I don't think you know me very well,' she retorted softly, almost in warning.

Had he not raised the canteen to his mouth at that moment, Riordan would have seen the mischief glittering in her eyes. At precisely the right second, she lifted her hand and tipped the canteen, spilling water over his face. Despite the dangerous glitter in the grey eyes, she couldn't keep from laughing.

'Why, you little minx!' Riordan growled, but without real anger. The lid was replaced on the canteen as he took a threatening step towards her.

The hasty, laughing step Jill took backwards sent her bumping into his horse, who moved only a protesting inch. She tried to elude his reaching hands and failed as they dug into the soft flesh of her upper arms.

'I'm sorry, Riordan, honestly.' But the bubbling amusement that remained in her voice belied the assertion. 'I couldn't help it.'

Her forearms were pressed against his chest as she laughingly tried to struggle free of his hold. Swinging her head back, she turned her mirthful eyes to his face.

The smouldering light in his eyes was not from anger and the smile slowly faded from her lips. Her gaze slid to his mouth, so hard, so masculine, and so close, and resistance ebbed with a rush.

In the next instant, her hands were curling around his neck and his mouth was closing over hers with savage insistence. Her lips parted voluntarily in response to his passionate demand. Hands slipped beneath her jacket, sliding smoothly to her back, arching and moulding her closer to his male outline.

Any sense of inhibition was forgotten as she yielded to his expert caresses. Primitive desire seared through her veins. Shivers of excitement danced over her skin as he minutely explored the hollow of her throat and the pulsing cord in her neck. Her breast seemed to swell as his hands cupped its roundness, arousing previously unknown longings for a more intimate caress. His mouth was hungry and possessive when it returned to hers.

The clatter of hoofs against stone shattered the erotic spell. 'Riordan, are you coming or not?' Todd called, still some distance away, the pine tree and the horse shielding them from his view.

As he lifted his head reluctantly, Riordan's hands slid to her waist, holding her against him. Jill nestled her head against his chest, a soft smile curving the lips that still throbbed from his ardent kiss.

'We'll be right there,' Riordan called in a voice that was husky and disturbed.

Excitement shivered over her skin. Beneath her head she could feel his ragged breathing and hear the uneven beat of his heart, very much in tempo with her own. She could have him.

In that exultant moment, she knew she could bring this man to his knees. It mattered little that he disliked her because now she knew he desired her. The knowledge provided an immense power she could use to gain her own ends.

Then Riordan was setting her away from him and walking to the horses to tighten the cinches. Outwardly he seemed completely unmoved by the charged embrace they had just shared. The grey eyes were cool and aloof, like impenetrable granite, when they met the brightness of hers. His control was remarkable. If she hadn't had those few seconds in his arms after he had broken off the kiss, she might not have guessed that she had so successfully aroused him.

'Mount up,' he said, swinging into his own saddle.

His eyes narrowed thoughtfully as Jill gave him a

bemused smile and complied with his order. This trail ride was going to be much more interesting and exciting than she had thought. She met his gaze with an alluring sweep of her long lashes, then moved her horse into the lead.

CHAPTER SEVEN

THE green meadow was nestled high in the mountains, a miniature valley where the mountain hesitated before soaring towards the sun. Cutting a path near the encroaching forest, a stream tumbled joyously over itself, crystal clear and cold from melting snow.

'I almost wish we never had to leave.' Jill turned regretfully away from the scene.

'Do you feel like going primitive?' The grey eyes slid to her briefly as Riordan pulled the saddle from Kerry's mount.

'Something like that,' she agreed, smiling at his amused mockery. 'What's wrong with returning to nature and the basics?'

'It's easy to do as long as you've bought supplies, but not quite so romantic when you have to forage for food like any other animal.' He set the saddle out of the way and tossed a short blanket to Jill. 'Rub the horse down and make sure he's dry.'

The horse stood docilely as she began to wipe dry the dark stain of perspiration where the saddle and pad had lain. 'So you don't think I would like the life in the rugged outdoors?'

As he glanced over the seat of Todd's saddle, his mouth twisted dryly. 'You tell me. After a month, your nails would be broken, your hands would be rough and calloused. That beautiful complexion of yours would probably be burned by the sun. And who would fix your shiny golden hair?'

Jill laughed. 'Why couldn't you have pointed out the hardships and dangers? You could have attacked something other than my vanity.' Inside she was secretly pleased that he had noticed so much about her.

'Want some help, Riordan?' Todd paused in front of the horse his brother was now rubbing down. 'The camp is all set up and Kerry is gathering more firewood from that deadfall.'

'No,' Riordan answered after glancing to the site that had been chosen for the night's camp. 'You might as well get those telescoping rods from the pack and start catching our supper. Jill and I will finish up here.'

'What will we eat if Todd doesn't catch any trout?' she challenged lightly when they were again alone with the horses.

'The contingency menu consists of the old western standby—beans.' His eyes crinkled at the corners.

It was only the second time Jill had seen him smile naturally. Her heart quickened at how devastingly attractive it made him.

Tapping the rump of Todd's horse to move it out of the way, Riordan walked around it to his own saddled mount. Jill finished her horse and walked to the bay's head, absently stroking its nose. It blew softly in her hand, the dark brown eyes almost curious in its inspection of her.

'What is your horse's name?' she asked, running her fingers through the horse's tangled black forelock.

Riordan shrugged indifferently. 'Boy. Fella.' Mockery gleamed silvery bright in the eyes that glanced to her face. 'At times, some other names a gentleman shouldn't repeat in front of a woman.'

'Doesn't he have a name?' Her head tilted to one side in surprise.

'No. He's only an animal. There are a few horses on the ranch that supposedly have names, the ones that happen to be registered stock.' He lifted the saddle off the horse's back, swinging it on to his shoulder and carrying it over to the others. He returned to start rubbing the horse down. 'This one is just a mountain-bred horse with no pedigree.'

'You honestly don't name your horses?' Jill persisted. 'Why?'

The brim of his hat was pulled low, throwing his face into shadow. She couldn't be certain, but she thought she saw his expression momentarily harden. For long seconds he didn't answer. She thought he was going to ignore her question altogether.

'I was about five when Dad gave me my first horse, a buckskin named Yellowstone Joe. I suppose like any boy I imagined he was the best horse in the world. When I was twelve, one Indian summer day I rode him into the mountains to go hunting. I didn't pay any attention to the time until I realised that it was afternoon. I was miles from the ranch with little chance of making it back before dark, unless I took a short cut. It meant going down a steep slide area, with a lot of loose rock. I'd taken Joe down it before, but I'd forgotten to consider that there'd been a storm recently. When we started down, the ground slid out from beneath us. I was thrown clear and rolled to the bottom. Joe was there, too, with both front legs broken.'

Her chest constricted sharply, her blue eyes darkening to mirror the unendurable pain she knew he must have felt. But for all the emotion in his voice, he could have been discussing the weather.

'I was miles from home and help, not that there was anything that could be done for Joe. I couldn't leave him like that, suffering and helpless. I knew he had to be put out of his misery and there wasn't anyone around but me. My marksmanship was off, and it took two shots to kill him. I started walking for home. Dad and a search party found me around nine o'clock that night.'

Jill could hardly distinguish his impassive features through the thick wall of tears, but she could tell his face was turned to her. She could just barely make out the cynical curl of his mouth.

'I don't put names on something I might have to destroy, not any more. Horses are only animals, like cattle you slaughter to eat. It was a lesson that had to be learned,' Riordan concluded unemotionally.

'Yes. Yes, I see.' Her voice was choked by the knot in her throat, hoarse and raw with commiseration for that twelve-year-old boy. She knew any minute the tears would spill from her eyes for Riordan to scorn. 'I—I think I'll go and help ... Kerry.'

'Go ahead,' he agreed blandly. 'I don't need you. I can finish up here.'

Jill wondered if he had stopped needing any-body that day when he was twelve. Two years before that, his mother left him for a reason he couldn't understand. Was it any wonder he had grown up so hard and cynical? She wanted desperately to reach out and gather that little boy in her arms and ease his hurt and grief. Only Riordan wasn't a little boy any more and he didn't allow himself to be hurt.

Try as she would, Jill couldn't forget the scene his indifferent voice had described. It haunted her, dulling the beauty of the meadow and marring the serenity of the mountain stream. That long-ago event didn't hurt him any more. She was a fool to let it hurt her.

It didn't change the fact that she had the power to bring him to his knees. She could still use the physical attraction he felt for her to manipulate him into approving of Todd and Kerry's marriage.

The cold, ruthless streak that had become em-bedded in him would not hesitate to use any means within his grasp. It wasn't as if she could hurt him again. He was beyond being hurt. He pitied no one, so why should she pity him?

Todd's catch of trout had been spitted and cooked slowly over the glowing embers of the campfire, then served with piping hot bannock biscuits Rior-dan had fried in an iron frying pan and canned tomatoes. It had been a delicious meal, only Jill's appetite had been dulled.

She stared at the speckled grey coffee pot suspended at the side of the fire. Kerry had enlisted Todd's aid in carrying the dishes to the stream to be washed. They had not camped close to the stream because Riordan had explained that animals came down at night to water and he didn't want their camp obstructing the animals' right of way to the stream. The explanation had not put Kerry at ease.

'More coffee?' Riordan stooped beside the fire and refilled his cup from the grey pot.

'No.' Jill shook her head absently, her hair catching and reflecting the amber flames of the fire.

From the stream, she heard a startled shriek from Kerry and Todd's laughing admonition that it was only a harmless raccoon. The corners of Riordan's mouth turned up crookedly.

'Your friend is a little jumpy.'

His faintly derogatory tone made blue diamond chips of her eyes, cold and cutting, her heart hardening against him. The time of indecision was thrust away. How dared he criticise Kerry's feelings of fear towards the unknown when he possessed no feelings himself.

'What can you expect, Riordan? Camping in the wilds is completely outside Kerry's experience.' Her voice was low and tautly controlled. 'It's not so difficult to understand that when you're in alien surroundings with alien creatures known to be wild, you feel apprehensive and not a little bit frightened.'

'You aren't frightened.'

'No.' She turned her head, sharply challenging his

331

hooded look. 'But my family camped a lot, back-packing into Yellowstone on weekends, so this isn't a totally new experience for me.'

'I see you're still intent on defending your friend.' Riordan was in the shadowy circle beyond the fire, the sardonic amusement in his voice mocking her.

'I see you're still intent on breaking them up,' Jill retorted smoothly, keeping the anger from her voice.

'I didn't realise butterflies could be so irritable. What's the matter, Jill?' he taunted.

Closing her eyes against the impulse to snap, she took a deep breath, releasing it in a shrugging sigh. 'Most butterflies probably never spend a day in the saddle riding up a mountain.'

'Stiff?'

'Brilliant deduction,' she responded dryly, un-consciously arching the protesting muscles in her back. She stared into the crackling flames of the campfire.

Pine needles rustled beside her, warning her a second too late of Riordan's approach. As she started to turn, a pair of hands closed firmly over her shoulders and began to knead the taut muscles in her back. A soft moan escaped her startled lips, a mixture of pain and enjoyment.

'If you weren't so prejudiced because Kerry is your friend, you would see that in the long run they aren't suited to each other and you would join forces with me in separating them before they make a big mistake.'

His fingers were working magic on her aching flesh. Jill almost wished there wasn't any need for conversation, but she shook her head determinedly.

'You don't know your brother very well, Riordan,' she murmured. 'I think you somehow believe that he survived the separation of your parents relatively untouched. But you're quite wrong. He's chosen a wife who he knows will be at his side through anything. If you thought this trail ride was going to point out their differences to Todd, you've failed. If it revealed anything to him, then it's the fact that Kerry joined in without one word of complaint, adjusting as best she could to the surrounings.'

'But will she continue to do that?' Riordan mocked softly with underlying sarcasm.

His strong fingers had sent a lethargy creeping through her bones, but at his question Jill stiffened, holding herself motionless as a light flashed in her eyes.

'It isn't Kerry you object to, is it, Riordan?' She answered the quiet demand herself. 'It's marriage. No matter who Todd chose, you wouldn't approve.'

'No,' was his simple and uncaring reply, laced with a touch of amusement.

A short breathy laugh slipped from her throat, not expecting that he should admit it so nonchalantly. Tilting her head to one side, she glanced over her shoulder at his lazily alert expression.

'Do you really despise women that much?' Her eyes searched the carved, imposing features, the enigmatic grey of his eyes.

The hard masculine mouth curved into a cold taunting smile. 'What do you think of men, Jill?

333

Do you admire them? Look up to them? View them as equals? Or do you enjoy twisting them around your pretty little finger and letting them fall when they no longer amuse you?'

His mocking accusation struck too close to the mark. She did tend to play with men, but not cruelly and callously as Riordan suggested. Deep down there was always the hope that the man she went after would be the one she loved. Only with Riordan did she want to be the unfeeling enchantress.

Her tongue nervously moistened her lower lip, unconsciously sensual until she saw the smouldering light darken his eyes. A wicked sparkle flashed in her eyes, enticing and challenging.

'And you, Riordan,' she murmured with husky suggestiveness, 'do you really despise everything about a woman? Or do you find that they have occasional uses?'

He smiled, recognising the invitation on her gleaming lips. A dark brow arched, the massaging hands on her back sliding near her ribcage.

'Occasionally,' he responded coolly.

Jill fixed her blue gaze on his mouth, feeling her heartbeat quicken. 'Like this morning on the hill-top?' Forgotten for the moment was her own naked response to his embrace. Only the memory of the way she had aroused him was considered.

His eyes narrowed thoughtfully as if measuring the strength of the trap she laid for him. The rakish thickness of his hair gleamed blacker in the fire-light, a faint arrogance hardening his impassive features. 'Did you enjoy it?'

'Did you?' Jill breathed.

The hands tightened on her ribs, lifting and turning her into his arms. The initial shock of having physical contact again with his hard-muscled chest made her mind spin. Her head rested against his arm, the tawny gold of her hair spinning over his shoulder while he inspected the perfection of her face with slow deliberation. Jill let herself relax pliantly. A hand slid across her stomach to curve over her hip.

Then the male mouth was closing over hers. That seductive searing fire that she had somehow forgotten consumed her again. There was no fierceness in his touch this time, only a series of long, drugging kisses calculated to undermine her sensibility to everything but his virility. A warning bell chimed that she was losing control. Riordan was seducing her, not the other way round. The insanity of it was that she didn't care. She wanted to go on drowning in the sensual oblivion of his caress.

From this admission came the strength to resist. With a tremulous gasp, she twisted away from his mouth using her arms to wedge a space between them. Her skin felt hot to the touch, the raging fire within refusing to be banked.

Strong fingers cupped her jaw, tilting her chin upwards. Not daring to meet his eyes for fear she would be captured by their silvery sheen, Jill stared at his mouth, so cool, so self-composed compared to the trembling softness of hers. The tanned fingers trailed down her neck until his hand rested lightly and deliberately on her breast.

'I want you,' Riordan said with soft arrogance.

Yes, he wanted her, Jill acknowledged, but not enough, not yet. Straightening towards him, she let her lips flutter submissively against his mouth as if in surrender to his dominant strength. Then, with a single fluid movement, she was out of his arms and on her feet standing in front of the fire. She could feel him watching the uneven rise and fall of her breasts and tried to stabilise her breathing. Her limbs were treacherously weak beneath her.

Riordan made no move to follow her, his long male length stretched in a half-sitting position, seemingly relaxed and undisturbed. She forced herself to play the rules of her game, the rules that would allow her to win.

'You'll have to forgive me, Riordan,' she sighed, tossing a faint smile over her shoulder. 'I'm afraid I got a bit carried away.'

'Why should I forgive you for that?' he returned evenly. 'I enjoyed it.'

'So did I—a little too much.' That was the absolute truth, but it served her purpose to say it. 'Todd and Kerry should be back soon. Would you care for another cup of coffee?'

'Since there's nothing stronger,' he agreed.

Forgetting that the pot had been sitting above the flames for a long time, she tried to pour the coffee without the aid of a pot-holder. Her fingers had barely closed around the handle before she released it.

'That's the way to get burned,' Riordan drawled, tossing her a towel.

Jill could have told him there was more than one way as she successfully filled his cup and one for herself as well. She had just sat down, a discreet distance from Riordan, when Kerry and Todd returned.

'Ah, coffee!' Todd kneeled beside the pot, wisely picking up the towel before he attempted to pour a cup. 'Was that a cougar I heard a while ago?' he directed his question at Riordan as he settled on to the ground near the fire, pulling Kerry down beside him and nestling her in the crook of his arm.

'Yes,' Riordan agreed. He caught Jill's startled glance, the glitter in his eyes mocking the fact that she had obviously been deaf to everything when she was in his arms.

'Aren't you going to organise a hunt to go after him?' Todd frowned. 'He could raise havoc with the spring calf crop.'

'So far he's restricted his prey to the deer. I certainly don't object if he keeps them to a manageable number. That way there aren't so many deer to compete with my cattle for graze. If he shows a taste for beef, I'll have to get rid of him,' Riordan shrugged.

Kerry shuddered. 'I hope he doesn't.'

'So do I,' Riordan responded dryly. 'As far as I'm concerned, the range is big enough for both of us. I respect the cougar's right to survive. If it's possible I'll drive him out of the area rather than destroy him. That isn't always possible.'

Unwillingly a tightness closed over Jill's throat that Riordan should feel compassion for wild

337

animals and none for humans. Was it his affinity for the land that made him that way?

Later, snuggled in her bedroll, the fire dying beside her, she stared at the stars, the question still unanswered. There was so much about Riordan she understood. His cynicism, his hardness, his aversion to any lasting relationship with a woman. Yet was there more? Was that little twelve-year-old boy still hiding somewhere inside, sensitive and alone?

The morning sun made Jill forget all her unanswered questions of the night before. The answers were really of little consequence anyway. She was still determined to go ahead with her plans. But she did recognise after last night that it was a dangerous game she was playing, luring Riordan with implied promises she had no intention of fulfilling. It served to make the game more exciting and the vivid colour of her eyes revealed it.

While Kerry poured water on the remains of the campfire, Jill stirred the coals to be certain no live ember remained. Todd was saddling the horses a few yards away and Riordan was loading the packhorse.

'It's all out,' Jill announced with a bright smile.

'Last night ... ' Kerry moved restively, drawing a curious glance from Jill. 'Last night, I saw you with Riordan. Jill, what are you doing?' Anxious brown eyes searched Jill's face, as if certain her friend had taken leave of her senses.

'Exactly what it looked like. I was letting Riordan chase me,' she replied. Her gaze moved thoughtfully to the broad shoulders of the man in question.

'You know the old saying, Kerry, "a boy chases a girl until she catches him." Well, I'm going to catch Riordan.'

'Do you mean you've fallen in love with him?' Kerry breathed incredulously.

'No, silly,' Jill laughed softly. 'I'm not that big a fool. But I think I can get him agree to your marriage before the month is up. It's impossible to reason with that man. That only leaves female trickery.'

'Oh, Jill, do you think you should?'

'Should has nothing to do with it. I'm doing it.'

'Come on, honey. We're ready to start back.' Todd stood holding the reins to Kerry's horse, effectively ending the conversation between the two.

The mountains in the east were reflecting the purpling pink glow of a setting western sun when the four rode into the ranchyard. During the ride down, Jill had not attempted to force a conversation with Riordan or even lightly flirt with him. This was the time to be slightly inaccessible, to be friendly if he made the move but never to imply an intimacy.

One of the ranch hands was there to take the horses. Jill smiled easily when Riordan helped her from the saddle, deliberately ignoring the fraction of a second his hands remained on her waist after she was on the ground.

'I hope Mary has fixed an enormous roast with potatoes and gravy and the works,' Todd declared. His arm was nonchalantly draped over Kerry's shoulders as they all started towards the house.

'I hope she's a mind-reader and has a hot bubbling tubful of water waiting for us,' Jill inserted. 'The food can wait.'

'You girls can laze in the tub if you want,' Todd grinned. 'I'll take a quick shower and eat.'

'Not all of it. I'm starved, too,' Kerry laughed.

'There's a car in the drive. Oh, oh!' Todd arched a brow expressively at his brother. 'It looks like you have a visitor.'

Jill recognised the gold and brown car. It belonged to none other than Sheena Benton. This was not exactly the way Jill had wanted to end the day. She slanted a glance at Riordan and caught the watchful glimmer of his grey eyes on her. He expected her to be disappointed.

'Maybe she can stay for dinner,' she suggested in a deliberately casual vein.

'I'll ask,' Riordan's mouth quirked.

Todd's eyes shifted from one to the other. He had seen what Kerry had seen the night before, and unless Kerry had enlightened him, which Jill doubted, he had put his own construction on it.

'It ought to be an interesting evening,' offered Todd dryly. His comment was followed by a sharp dig in his ribs by Kerry's elbow.

Entering the house through the rear door, they found the kitchen empty but with all sorts of delicious smells coming from the oven. In the entrance hall, they could hear Sheena's voice. Jill couldn't make out what she was saying, but it was obvious she was talking to Mary.

'Oh, Riordan, there you are,' Sheena declared

340

with purring delight when the foursome walked into the entrance hall.

'Hello, Sheena,' Riordan greeted her blandly. 'I didn't expect to see you here.'

'I was just leaving, actually. Mary told me you'd gone on a trail ride and, of course, I had no idea when you would be back. Did just the four of you go?' Her tiger eyes swerved to Jill, hostility sparkling in their almond shape.

'Just the four of us,' Jill answered with a challenging smile.

'It must have been a long ride back. You certainly look grimy and saddlesore,' Sheena replied.

Miaow! Jill thought, catching the snapping humour of Mary Rivers' black eyes and trying not to let an answering sparkle enter her own. It would simply not do for Sheena to discover that she and Mary were laughing at her, however silently.

'You're right on both counts,' Jill agreed. 'Although,' an impish demon made her glance at Riordan, 'it was certainly worth it!'

Amber fire flamed over her face and Jill knew she had thoroughly evoked Sheena's jealousy. So did Riordan. The grey eyes appeared complacently amused.

'What brings you here, Sheena?' he asked. 'Business or pleasure?'

'Business mainly.' The fires were banked as she swung her gaze to him, the light in her eyes adding that how much business depended on him. 'I was hoping I could persuade you to come over one evening and go over my accounts with me.'

341

'Will Friday night be soon enough?' He didn't seem surprised by the request, which led Jill to believe that it was a common one or a smokescreen for a more intimate rendezvous. Or both.

'Friday will be fine,' Sheena purred, sending a cool sweeping smile that bordered on triumph to the others in the room. 'I'll be going now to leave you all free to wash the traildust off.'

'Aren't you staying for dinner?' Clear blue eyes widened innocently. There was immense satisfacion in turning the tables on Sheena and pretending to be the hostess this time. 'I'm sure Mary can stretch the food.'

'You're welcome to stay if you like,' Riordan inserted, a faint twitch of amusement near one corner of his mouth as if he knew the intent of Jill's invitation.

'Thank you, darling,' Sheena purred. 'But I know you're all on the verge of collapse. I'll see you Friday.'

CHAPTER EIGHT

A BEE made a downward swoop towards her head and Jill ducked quickly away from his buzzing path. Raising a hand to shield her eyes from the sun, she looked again to the truck parked beside the fence, its tailgate down. Beyond it and partially hidden by it was Riordan's dark head. Her fingers tightened their grip on the unopened bottle of cold beer.

Since the trail ride, she had seen next to nothing of Riordan. A myriad small obstacles had been littered in her path, ranging from sick animals to mechanical breakdowns of ranch equipment. Her plans were threatening to stagnate unless she took them in hand. Today was Friday and it was imperative that she make an impression on Riordan before he visited Sheena tonight.

Jill wasn't concerned that given enough time she could overcome the competition presented by the older woman. The problem was she didn't have much time. In a little more than a week, she and Kerry were due to leave.

It had become a case of if the mountain wouldn't come to Mohammed, Mohammed had to go to the mountain. Luckily Riordan was fixing a fence close to the house today, so Mohammed didn't have far to go.

As Jill drew nearer the truck, she ran a hand

along the edges of the blouse she had tied around her midriff. There was a light golden quality to the bareness of her waist, courtesy of the hours she and Kerry had lain in the sun. On the surface, the tied blouse was concession to the blazing hot sun overhead, but actually it was intended to draw attention to the slenderness of her waist and suggestive curves of her hips and breasts.

'Hello!' Jill called, hooking a thumb in the loops of her slacks as she rounded the rear of the truck. 'Are you working hard?'

Straightening from the fence, Riordan glanced over his shoulder, an odd light flickering briefly in his grey eyes. Jill halted beside the truck, the world spinning crazily for an instant. A naked expanse of bronzed torso glowing with the sheen of perspiration met her eye. Riordan's shirt lay discarded on the fence post.

'Out for a walk?' There was a substantial degree of cynical mockery in his question.

Leather gloves were pulled off with slow deliberation to join a pair of pliers in one hand as he moved lazily towards the truck and Jill. His gaze slid to the brown-tinted bottle in her hand.

There was a roaring in her ears that she couldn't explain. She gladly shifted her attention to the bottle and away from the hypnotic sight of the tightly curling black hairs on his chest. Good heavens, she'd seen her brothers dressed considerably less decently than that. Why on earth was she letting it disturb her?

'Yes, I was feeling a bit restless and thought I'd

walk it off,' she admitted, tossing her head back with air of careless indifference. 'Since I had nowhere in particular to go, I thought I'd bring you something cold. The sun is hot today.'

'That was thoughtful of you.' He leaned against the side of the truck near Jill, laying his gloves and pliers near a roll of barb wire in the back of the truck before taking the bottle of beer she offered.

'I try to be useful,' she smiled, attempting to penetrate the smoky veil of his eyes for some reason behind his dry-voiced response. Riordan could be positively impenetrable at times. This was one.

She watched him unscrew the lid and toss it in back, then lift the bottle to his mouth. As he tilted his head back to drink, she studied the tanned column of his throat, the cords rippling sinewy strong.

Wiping the mouth of the bottle, Riordan offered it to her. 'Have a drink. You must be thirsty after your walk.'

Her throat did feel a bit dry and tight. Accepting the bottle and raising it to her lips, she could almost feel the warmth of his mouth imprinted on the glass as she took a drink of the malty cold liquid.

'Where's Kerry?' Riordan asked, his fingers accidentally or on purpose touching Jill's as he took the bottle from her hand.

'At the house.' Still insisting that Jill was out of her mind for attempting such a thing, Jill added to herself.

An uneasiness settled over her. She glanced away from Riordan, pretending an interest in the distant

345

mountains sculptured against a wide blue sky. The grey eyes watched silently, leaving her with the unshakeable feeling that it had been a mistake to come out here.

'I suppose I ought to let you get back to your work,' she offered, for want of anything better to say.

'Not yet,' Riordan drawled complacently.

Jill glanced in surprise at the wrist that was suddenly a firm captive of his hand. 'I ... only came to bring you something to drink. Mary thought you might like a cold beer.'

'Mary thought?' A brow arched quizzically, a dark glitter laughing at her in his eyes. 'She must be getting forgetful, otherwise she would have remembered the cooler of beer she sent with me at noon.'

Damn! Why had she allowed herself to be tripped up in her own lie? That was a teenager's mistake.

'Maybe that's what she said and I misunderstood her,' she bluffed. 'In either case, I'm keeping you from your work.'

'I'm not objecting.'

The bottle was set half-full inside the truck box. Applying pressure to her wrist, Riordan drew her towards him. Short of struggling Jill couldn't resist.

The initiative of any embrace was supposed to have been at her invitation and not this soon. She let her legs carry her reluctantly towards him, almost sighing in relief when he let her stop a scant foot from him. At the moment her senses were clamouring too loudly at his nearness. She needed a few seconds to regain her sense of objectivity before coming in physical contact with him.

His superior height forced her to tilt her head back to meet his hooded arrogant gaze. 'Riordan, I——'

A hand touched her cheek, halting her words as effectively as if it had covered her mouth. 'How many men have told you that your eyes are the colour of the sky?' he mused cynically. 'A Montana sky, vivid blue and pulling a man into the promise of heaven beyond.'

No sooner was Jill aware of her wrist being released then she felt his hand on the bare flesh of her waist. The strong male scent of him was an erotic stimulus she didn't want to feel.

'Please!' Her effort to appear indifferent was thwarted by the involuntary catch in her voice.

'Didn't you wander into this meadow with the intention of bestowing some of the honey from your lips on me, butterfly?' Riordan taunted.

A tiny gasp parted her lips. His hand curved around the back of her neck, drawing her upwards to his mouth. The naked chest was satiny smooth and sensual beneath her fingers, hard muscles flexing as he moulded her against him. Her lips moved in response to his to deepen the kiss until a wild, glorious song burst in her heart.

The melody raced through her veins. Jill was only half aware of Riordan pressing her backwards. Spiky blades of grass scratched her bare back as his weight pinned her to the ground. The caress of his hands was arousing, exhorting her to give and to plead with her body to receive more in return.

The tails of her blouse were untied and the buttons undone with careless ease. Her nipple hardened under his touch and she moaned in surrender. The reason she had come was completely lost under the spell of ecstasy flaming through her.

When his head raised from hers, she locked her arms around his neck to draw him back. His fingers closed over her wrists and firmly pulled her hands away, his mouth twisting harshly.

'Sorry, butterfly. I'm not satisfied either, but we are about to have company,' Riordan mocked the glaze of desire in her eyes.

Rolling to his feet, he stood above her. Dominated as she was by raging primitive emotions, it took a full second for Jill to realise the significance of what he had said. The sound of a car motor could be heard crossing the meadow and drawing nearer. She scrambled to her feet, cheeks flaming at her complete lack of control, and turned away from his taunting gaze to hastily button her blouse.

The task was barely completed by her shaking hands when the car stopped beside the truck. Self-consciously brushing golden hair away from her face, Jill turned. She wanted to scream in frustration at the sight of Sheena Benton.

'Am I interrupting something, Riordan?' Sheena drawled archly, leaning against the steering wheel of her car, fingers curling like unsheathed claws over the wheel.

'It'll keep,' Riordan shrugged, slanting a mocking glance at Jill's still flushed cheeks. 'What can I do for you?'

'I wanted to remind you about tonight.' Her statement was directed at Riordan, but the hatred in her eyes was solely for Jill.

'I hadn't forgotten,' Riordan assured her smoothly, an intimate dark light entering his eyes.

'If you can get away, why not come early?' Sheena suggested. A purring entered her voice at his look. 'You can check the accounts over dinner.'

'I should be able to arrange that,' he agreed aloofly, and was rewarded with a dazzling smile. Nausea churned Jill's stomach.

'I won't keep you,' Sheena murmured, shifting the car into gear and glancing with feline archness to Jill. 'Can I give you a lift to the house, Jill?'

'No, thank you,' she retorted coldly. 'I prefer to walk.'

The coral red mouth tightened with displeasure. 'Suit yourself,' Sheena clipped with a toss of her chestnut mane. Blowing a kiss to Riordan, she reversed to turn back the way she had come.

'Are you going back now?' Riordan asked with insinuating softness.

'Yes,' Jill answered decisively, wishing the heat in her cheeks would ease. 'Right away.'

'I would suggest before you get back to the house to fix your blouse,' he jeered. 'You've buttoned it crooked.'

A mortified glance at the front of her blouse confirmed his statement. There was not the slightest chance that the sharp-eyed Sheena had not noticed it.

'Thanks, I'll do that,' Jill retorted defiantly, refusing to show any guilt about her action.

But guilt hounded her steps all the way back to the house. She had intended to entrap Riordan with his physical attraction for her. Despite the way he had aroused her in previous encounters with his lovemaking, she had never expected he would awaken her inner desires and the extent of her womanhood. In all honesty, her confidence was badly shaken.

Riordan wasn't at the dinner table when she entered the dining room with Kerry and Todd. She left it to Mary Rivers to explain where he was. There was a noticeable lack of desire to mention her meeting with Riordan that afternoon and she avoided the questing look from Mary.

The perfectly prepared meal was utterly tasteless, but Jill forced down nearly everything on her plate. She didn't want to parry any questions about a lack of appetite. After the meal, she retreated to a corner of the living room with a book, ostensibly affording Kerry and Todd some privacy.

Her thoughts were as jumbled and confused as they had been earlier. The printed lines on the book page blurred. She simply couldn't concentrate —on anything. The only thing that seemed to register was the portrait of the copper-haired woman with sparkling hazel eyes that hung above the mantelpiece. A butterfly like herself.

Suddenly restless, Jill snapped the book in her lap shut, drawing startled glances from Todd and Kerry. 'I think I'll go and see if Mary needs some help in the kitchen,' she said in explanation.

But the kitchen was sparkling clean and the housekeeper was nowhere to be seen. With the half-formed idea to take a walk outside, Jill wandered down the back hall towards the rear entrance.

A closed door drew her hypnotically. She knew it was Riordan's room. Mary had mentioned it one day in passing, but Jill had never been inside. Curiosity surged to the forefront, a sudden need filling her to see his room.

Cautiously she opened the door and walked into the room, touching the light switch. The small light overhead left the corners of the room in shadow. Jill stared silently about her, taking in the single bed against one side of a wall with a small table beside it and the chest of drawers against another wall. A rigid, straight-backed chair occupied another corner.

Compared to the quiet elegance of the rest of the house, the stark simplicity of this room was unexpected. It was almost monastic. Very quietly Jill closed the door behind her, aware that she was trespassing but unable to leave.

Riordan was a man of basics. She had always guessed that. Yet, walking to the single bed, she couldn't stop wondering why he had chosen to shun the more luxurious creature comforts offered by the rest of the house for this. Did he need to sleep here to remain hard and cynical? Was he avoiding the gentle, feminine touches she had noticed in the rest of the house?

Fingering the agricultural book on the bedside table, Jill smiled at herself. She was crazy to come in here. The room revealed no more about Riordan than he did himself. She was being overly imaginative to believe otherwise.

A striped Hudson Bay blanket covered the bed. Without being consciously aware of what she was doing, Jill sat down on the edge of the bed. The mattress was firm without being rock-hard, a fact she noticed absently as she gazed about the room.

A movement caught her eye, and freezing with cold dread, she saw the doorknob turning. She couldn't breathe as the door opened, offering a hurried prayer that it would be Mary Rivers she saw. It was much too early for Riordan to come back.

But it was his broad-shouldered, lean-hipped frame that filled the opening. Grey eyes met the startled roundness of her blue ones. Jill's heart was in her throat. She couldn't think of one legitimate reason she could offer as an excuse for her presence in his room. With a speculative glitter, his gaze swept over her.

'This is an unexpected invitation,' Riordan murmured dryly, stepping into the room and closing the door.

Heat flamed through her cheeks as Jill suddenly realised she was sitting on his bed. She rose hurriedly to her feet.

The hard line of his mouth quirked mockingly. 'There's no need to get up. I would have joined you.'

'I ... I was just going,' Jill stammered.

'You don't need to slip into something more comfortable.' His steel-grey eyes studied her with lazy intensity, lingering on the trembling parting of her mouth, the pulsing vein in her neck and finally the vee of her blouse.

Her hand protectively covered the vee. 'You don't understand,' she protested nervously. 'I didn't expect you back so soon. I thought you ... I mean, Sheena ...' There simply wasn't any way she could put into words exactly what she thought he and Sheena would be doing.

'After this afternoon, did you honestly think I would prefer the scratchings of a jealous cat when I could have the fluttering softness of a butterfly?' Teeth flashed white with his wolfish smile as he took a step towards her.

'No!' Her breath was fast and uneven. 'I know what you must be thinking, finding me in your room and all,' she rushed wildly. 'I only came in because I was curious.' The grooves around his mouth deepened. 'It's not at all what you're thinking, I swear.'

'Don't bother to bat those innocent blue eyes at me,' he taunted. 'Or deny that your visit this afternoon was designed to implant your image in my mind when I went to see Sheena tonight. You were manoeuvring again, Jill. We both know it.'

She opened her mouth to try to protest the truth of his statement. It would be futile. There were too many disturbing emotions stirring inside of her for her to lie convincingly.

353

'Excuse me, but I really must go,' she murmured unsteadily, keeping her eyes downcast as she started towards the door.

'Now what's the game?' Riordan was in her way, blocking the path to the door. 'Are you playing hard to get?'

'I'm not playing anything. Please let me by.' There was room to pass him, but Jill didn't trust him.

'I see.' He was laughing at her, silently, but the cynical amusement was in his eyes. 'You simply flitted into my room by accident, drawn only by curiosity. Now you want to fly away, is that it, leaving me with the teasing picture of you waiting on my bed.'

'Riordan, please!' Jill swallowed tightly.

Trading words with him was useless. She had to escape before she became enmeshed in the backlash of her plans. At this moment she was too unprepared to cope with Riordan or her wayward reactions to him.

On legs quaking like aspen leaves, she started for the door. As she drew level with him, she held her breath, flinching when his hand moved. But it didn't reach out for her. Instead it snapped off the overhead light, throwing the room into darkness.

Stopped by the unexpectedness of his action and her own momentary blindness, Jill wasn't able to move. The suggestive intimacy of the bedroom, isolated from the living area of the house, washed over her like shockwaves.

'Once you trap a butterfly,' his low voice was

354

closer, a soft and seductive weapon, and she gasped as his hands gripped her shoulders, 'you must take it by the wings.'

'Let me go!' she cried breathlessly, frightened by her sudden desire to lean submissively against his chest. She tried to wrench free of his grip, but Riordan used her twisting motion to pivot her around, easily drawing her unbalanced body against him.

His dark head bent and he brushed his mouth against the sensitive skin below her right ear. Jill couldn't control the shudder of delight. The heady male scent of him enveloped her, earthy and clean. Tilting her head to one side, she tried to elude his provocative caress, but only succeeded in exposing more of her neck to his exploring mouth.

'No,' she pleaded, shaking back the feathery length of her gold hair and increasing the pressure of her hands that strained against his chest.

Riordan laughed softly, a deep delicious sound that shivered down her spine. His mouth lifted to the averted line of her jaw.

'Isn't this the way you planned it, Jill?' he taunted. His warm breath fanned across the already hot skin of her cheek.

'I didn't plan this,' she protested in a desperate whisper. Her eyes were beginning to adjust to the softness of the starlight streaming through the windows.

'You didn't *plan* to make me want you?' Riordan jeered. Jill breathed in sharply. 'I know you did. The idea has been in the back of your mind since the first time we met. Everything you've done has been calculated to blind me with desire for you so you could twist me around your finger, take what you wanted and fly away.'

'No,' Jill gulped.

She bent her head backwards, trying again to escape the disturbing nearness of his mouth. Strong fingers spread across the small of her back, moulding her arching body more fully against the male vigour of his. A dizzying weakness spread through her limbs. Her tightly closed lashes fluttered open, focusing her gaze on his rugged features. Half-closed eyes studied her upturned face with a silvery fire that stole her breath.

'You look like some pagan goddess,' Riordan murmured deeply, 'with that passionate mouth and those eyes sparkling with starfire.'

'Please!' she begged to be released.

A hand curled its fingers in the long silken hair at the back of her neck. Jill knew his mouth would tantalise her lips no longer and she started to struggle against the inevitable. But the hand on her neck wouldn't allow her to avoid his kiss. Her hammering fists glanced harmlessly off his chest and shoulders.

At last his conquering mouth had her fingers curling into the thin material of his shirt, clinging to him weakly in surrender. Riordan wasn't content with submission as he parted her lips with persuasive mastery, exploring her mouth until Jill responded with demanding hunger.

Reason was banished completely under the moulding caress of his hands. There was only the whirling, mindless ecstasy of his embrace urging her to new heights of sensual awareness. She was achingly conscious of her need for physical gratification, and the hard maleness of Riordan made her aware of his.

The trailing fire of his lips burned over her eyes, cheek and throat, branding her as his possession, and she didn't deny it. Her hands were around his neck, fingers winding into the thick blackness of his hair. His hard mouth closed again over hers, uniting their flames into a roaring fire of passion that sang in her ears.

Like a drowning person, Jill made one last attempt to be saved when his mouth blazed a path to the hollow of her throat.

'I can't——'

Her thoughts were too chaotic. What couldn't she do? She couldn't stop. She couldn't think. She couldn't breathe. She couldn't exist without the wildfire of his touch.

'I'm insane,' she ended with a sighing groan.

His head lifted briefly, fingers sliding to her throat. 'That's the way I want you to be,' Riordan muttered harshly. 'Driven to madness until you can think of nothing else but me.' He spoke against her lips, his mouth moving mobilely over them in a caress that was designed to make her ache for his kiss. 'I want your wings to be singed so you can't fly away until sunrise.'

Jill breathed in sharply, knowing she didn't ever want to fly away yet realising how dangerous it would be to give in to her emotions so completely.

'Kerry ... Todd,' she offered in protest.

Riordan's mouth shut off her words until she stopped caring about Kerry and Todd. Only then did he answer.

'They'll be enjoying the privacy you've been so keen for them to have. They won't miss you. I doubt if Todd even expects me back tonight.'

Weakly Jill shook her head, but unable to deny the truth of what he said. Lowering her head, she felt his lips against her hair, their moistness tangling in the silken gold.

'Riordan, I——'

The support of his hard masculine body was taken away from her and she swayed towards him. Her movement was checked as an arm slid under her knees and she was lifted into the air, cradled against his chest. Automatically her hands circled his neck.

As he turned towards the small bed, a shaft of starlight glittered over his face. The strength of purpose stamped in the forceful, handsome lines caught at Jill's throat. Nothing could stop him. The same primitive mood had her in its spell and she knew she didn't want to try to prevent what seemed so inevitable and paradoxically so right.

Sitting on the side of the bed, Riordan held her on his lap. His face was in shadows, but she knew the grey eyes were studying her. This was her last chance to protest. Instead her fingers began exploring the blunt angles of his features, feather-soft and caressing.

He seemed to be prolonging the moment when he claimed her as if to make the possession sweeter. Feeling wantonly bold, Jill leaned forward and pressed her lips against his mouth. It curved briefly under her touch into a complacent smile.

'The bed isn't made for two,' Riordan murmured huskily, the grooves around his mouth deepening in satisfaction, 'but tonight I don't think either one of us will care.'

An almost inaudible moan of complete surrender slipped from her throat as Riordan bent her backwards on to the mattress. His hand slid intimately from her thigh to her hip and along to the curve of her breast. The pressing weight of his male body followed her down, his mouth unerringly and possessively finding hers. Jill was lost in an erotic dream world of sensations that she never wanted to end. She succumbed with rapturous delight to each new touch.

'Jill?' A familiar voice was trying to enter her dream. Jill's head moved in protest to its call. 'Jill? Where are you?'

'No!' she gave a muffled cry to forbid the entry.

'Sssh.' Riordan's strong fingers lightly covered her mouth. His indirect acknowledgment of the voice that called her made the dream world begin to fade into reality.

'Jill?' Now she could recognise the voice as Kerry's, still distant but moving closer. 'Where could she be?'

'She did say she was going to the kitchen, didn't she?' Todd was with Kerry.

'Yes, but she isn't here,' came the muffled reply of concern.

Reason and sanity came back with shocking swiftness as Jill tried to twist from beneath Riordan's weight. He checked the movement easily.

'No,' his low voice commanded near her ear. 'You know you don't really want to leave.'

'Yes ... No.' The conflicting answers were crazily the truth as Jill was torn in two by her emotions.

'Maybe she went outside for a walk,' Todd suggested.

'It isn't like her not to tell me. Oh, Todd, let's check,' Kerry rushed, and footsteps started down the hall that led past Riordan's room to the rear door of the house.

Jill's hands pushed frantically against the stone wall of his chest. 'They'll find us,' she whispered desperately.

His warm breath moved over her cheek in silent laughter. 'They won't look for you in here,' he mocked, his mouth following the curve of her throat to the tantalising hollow between her breasts.

'N—n—no!' Her protest was shaken by the violent surge of desire brought on by his intimate touch.

'She could have gone up to her room, too,' Todd said as the two sets of footsteps walked by the bedroom door.

'Let's check outside first,' Kerry replied anxiously.

'She's a grown woman. She can take care of——' The 'herself' was lost as the closing back door cut off the rest of Todd's statement.

'I told you they wouldn't find us,' Riordan murmured against her skin.

'B—but they'll keep on looking,' Jill moaned softly, her hands still straining against him. 'Please let me go.'

'No.' His fingers closed over her chin, holding it motionless as his mouth closed over hers in a drugging kiss that sent her floating nearly all the way back into her dream world.

The click of the bedroom doorknob splintered through her. The alert tensing of Riordan's muscles told her he had heard it too, but he didn't lift his mouth from hers nor allow her protesting lips to twist away.

'Riordan, they're looking for her.' Mary Rivers spoke from the doorway.

His hold relaxed slightly as he raised his head, his gaze glittering, holding Jill's pleading blue eyes. Hot waves of shame licked through her veins.

'Get out of here, Mary,' Riordan ordered smoothly.

Tearing her eyes from his face, Jill twisted her head towards the housekeeper, her tall stocky build outlined by the light streaming into the room from the hallway. Her throat worked convulsively, but nothing came out. Part of her didn't want to be rescued.

'You can't do it, Riordan,' Mary sighed, but with firm conviction.

'Can't I?' he jeered arrogantly. 'The lady is more than willing,' he added with sarcastic emphasis.

'Let her go.'

He smiled coolly down at Jill. 'She's free to leave,' he rolled away from her, only a hand remaining spread on her stomach as a wicked grey light held her gaze captive, '*if* she really wants to leave.'

Perhaps if he hadn't been so confident she would stay or if he had asked her not to leave him, Jill would have remained where she was. Instead, with a frightened sob at what a fool she had nearly made of herself, she scrambled to her feet.

Two wavering steps towards the door were all she had taken before the soft flesh of her upper arms was seized in a biting grip. Weakly she allowed herself to be pulled back against his chest, her head lolling against his shoulder, unable to deny the disturbance his touch caused.

'Riordan,' Mary warned swiftly.

'No, she can go,' he interrupted in an ominously low voice laced with contempt. 'She and I both know that I wasn't seducing her. She was letting me seduce her. Almost since the day she came, she's been inviting me to make love to her, deliberately holding back so she could twist me around her finger. She knew I found her as physically attractive as any man would and she intended to use that attraction to get what she wanted. Isn't that right, Jill?' he demanded savagely.

She didn't have the strength to disagree even if he was wrong, but he wasn't wrong and she didn't argue. 'Yes, yes, that's right,' she admitted in a breathy whisper.

'But I'm not twisted around your finger.' The derisive jeer slashed at her pride. 'I take what I want

362

and when I'm through with it, I throw it away.' He released her with a slight push towards the door and Mary. 'You can go. But I'm not quite through with you yet.'

With that half-threat and half-promise ringing in the air, Jill stumbled forward. Mary wrapped a supporting arm around her shoulders and led her from the room. Drained of all emotion except the cold feeling of dread, Jill was barely aware of the housekeeper's presence.

'I'll take you upstairs to your room,' said Mary.

Jill was suddenly conscious of how dishevelled she must look. Her clothes were in a revealing state of disarray and her lips had to be swollen from his passionate kisses. She knew she had the look of woman who had been made love to. A sob strangled her throat. She very nearly had!

She cast a surreptitious glance at the housekeeper, wondering what this proud woman thought of her. The only part of Riordan's accusation that had been a lie was when he had suggested that she intended for him to seduce her. Jill had never contemplated going that far, but she had set out to twist him around her finger. She had planned to make Riordan want her so badly he would do anything.

When they reached her bedroom, Jill caught the look of gentle compassion in Mary's dark eyes. In shame and humiliation, she knew guiltily that she didn't deserve the woman's understanding.

'I'm all right,' Jill asserted forcefully, averting her face from the housekeeper's concerned gaze. Her legs now strong enough to deny the need for a supporting arm. Jill stepped forward. 'Would you tell Kerry that you saw me and that ... that I have a headache and have gone to my room?'

'I'll see that you're not disturbed,' Mary nodded perceptively, 'by anyone.'

By anyone, Jill knew she meant Riordan, too. And she didn't doubt that the woman would figuratively stand guard at her door. When Mary left, Jill buried her face in her hands, but she didn't cry.

Hysterical laughter sobbed in her throat. She barely smothered it with her hand. The irony of the situation struck her forcibly. All along she had believed Riordan was chasing her. Instead, she had been chasing him and he had caught her. She was the one who had been brought to her knees.

Never once in all her planning had she ever seriously considered the possibility that she might fall in love with Riordan. Yet that was exactly what she had done. She knew it as clearly and as certainly as she knew her own name.

Tonight had not been the result of a sudden desire for physical experience or the arousing attention of an experienc' ' lover. They were a potent combination but not an explanation for her complete abandonment of reason. Love was the answer, no matter how foolish and painful the emotion might be.

CHAPTER NINE

JILL stared at the rising golden globe on the eastern horizon. Blue eyes were glazed with pain, faint etchings of red at the corners. Not from tears. She hadn't cried. Not a single tear had come forward to ease the ache in her heart.

The redness was from exhaustion. She had not slept. She had not even attempted to sleep nor made the pretence that she would. Still dressed in the same clothes, she had alternately paced the room and stared sightlessly out the window. Sometimes she thought of nothing except what it had been like in Riordan's arms. At other times, her mind raced wildly to come up with a scheme to make Riordan love her. All were rejected eventually. He would see through them just as he had seen through all of her other manoeuvres.

There was a subdued knock at her door, and she spun from the window. It couldn't be Kerry. She would use the connecting door. Todd was out of the question. Mary?

'W—who is it?' she called shakily.

'Riordan,' was the low response.

A shaft of pure joy pierced her heart. She wanted to race to the door, fling it open and throw herself into his arms. She jammed a fist in her mouth.

'Go away,' she said tightly, biting into her knuckles.

The doorknob turned, but for some unknown reason Jill had locked it last night. Now she bowed her head in thankfulness.

'A locked door isn't going to stop me, Jill. Open it!'

It wasn't an idle threat. Still, she hesitated before walking over and turning the key in the lock. Control was the key, she told herself as she walked quickly away. She had to remain calm and controlled. She mustn't let her emotions surface, nor the love she felt for him.

Again at the window, she halted. He was in the room, the door closed behind him. Jill stared sightlessly out of the window.

'What do you want?' she demanded.

'If you had trouble sleeping last night, why didn't you come downstairs?'

Jill glanced sharply over her shoulder just as Riordan turned away from the bed that bore not the slightest imprint of having been slept in. Aloof grey eyes caught her look and held it, a cynical quirk to his hard mouth.

'Leave me alone, Riordan,' she snapped harshly at his arrogant expression, then breathed in deeply to regain the control she needed so desperately. Yet it seemed that the only way she had of concealing her love for him was to lash out with anger.

'Not yet,' he answered with cold mockery. 'I've come to tell you that you can move your things down to my room this morning. I'll have a larger bed and another chest of drawers moved in.'

Slowly Jill turned from the window, her head

366

tipped to one side in disbelief. 'What?' she breathed incredulously.

A brow arched higher. 'I thought I'd made it clear. I'm not the type to go sneaking around and taking part in midnight rendezvous.'

'So you're simply arranging for me to sleep with you?' Her hands moved to a challenging position on her hips.

'Spare me the pretence of indignation.' His mouth moved into a crooked, jeering line. 'I'm sure your friend Kerry is aware of the facts of life. No doubt she'll find it romantic and excitingly risqué. If you prefer, I'll explain to her and Todd.'

'And what will you explain? That I'm your new sleeping partner, your lover, your mistress?' Jill demanded coldly. 'I would be curious to know exactly what position you're offering me.'

The dark head was tipped arrogantly back, the grey eyes clear and piercing like an eagle's. 'Whatever label suits you,' replied Riordan.

'What is the duration of this position?' A cold sarcasm filled her heart and, momentarily at least, eased the pain. 'Until you're through with me?'

'I'm not setting any time limit, butterfly.' There was faint contempt in his tone. 'Whichever one of us tires of the other first can call it quits.'

'I see,' she said tautly. 'And you expect me to fall all over myself accepting this arrangement?'

Riordan moved slowly to stand in front of her and it was all Jill could do to hold her ground and not retreat. He towered over her for a long moment.

His hand reached out to touch the petal softness

of her cheek. Something melted inside her at his caress and she had to steel herself not to visibly react.

'You were eager enough for me to make love to you last night,' Riordan reminded her softly.

The peculiar light in his eyes made her heart skip a beat. Yet the indecision of what to do that had plagued her all night was gone. Under these circumstances, there was only one thing she could do.

'Yes,' she admitted calmly, 'I did want you to make love to me last night.'

There was a satisfied movement of his mouth. 'Do you want me to send Mary up to help you pack your things?'

Jill moved away from the hand that was still resting on her cheek and walked to the centre of the room. She clasped her hands in front of her, staring at her twining fingers for an instant before she tossed her head back and met his alert gaze.

'Please do send Mary.' A chilling calm spread over her. 'I would like to pack and get out of this house as soon as possible.'

The room crackled with a stunned silence. His gaze narrowed fractionally, followed by a short sardonically amused sigh.

'Are you flying away already, butterfly?' There was an indifferent movement of his mouth. 'Even that was too much of a commitment for you to make?'

His aloof comment stung. If he had indicated in any way that he cared for her, Jill would have willingly committed her life to him. She felt the moistness of tears on her lashes.

'There is one more thing,' she squeezed the words out through the lump in her throat, 'before I ask you to leave my room. I want you to give your approval of Todd's marriage to Kerry.'

Again he walked to stand in front of her, not touching her this time, as his gaze focused on a crystal drop threatening to fall from a dark gold lash.

'Tears?' Riordan jeered. 'That must be the oldest female manoeuvre in the book. You must be digging deep in your bag of tricks to come up with that one!'

Jill stared at her hands, unable to meet his satirical look. 'I don't doubt that you find them amusing. I don't think you're capable of feeling anything but your own primitive needs.' She took a deep breath, not raising her eyes. 'You don't know your brother very well either, because if you did, you would know he's capable of very deep feelings. He cares about you, but he'll only allow you to stand in the way of his happiness for a short while. You can threaten him with money or any other thing you want, but in the end he will marry Kerry and hate you. Maybe you don't care. Family probably means nothing to you. If it doesn't, then it can't matter what Todd does with his life.'

'Are you finished interfering?' Riordan snapped.

'Yes.' Jill turned away, her shoulders slightly hunched forward, a terrible coldness in her heart.

'Will you go now? And ... And I would prefer not to see you again before I leave.'

'That makes two of us,' he agreed mockingly.

The bedroom door slammed and another tear slipped from her lashes. Jill wiped it determinedly away. She wasn't going to cry, not when she knew she was doing the only thing possible. She walked to the closet and started yanking out her clothes. A few minutes later Mary was there, silently helping her, not needing the reason for Jill's sudden departure explained.

The last suitcase had been snapped shut when there was a knock on her door. Jill couldn't move, terrified that it might be Riordan and her resolve to leave would crumble if she had to be near him again. But when Mary opened the door, it was Todd who stood in the hallway.

'Riordan said that as soon as you were ready I'm supposed to take you home,' he said quietly. 'He said you had an argument.' But his hazel eyes said he knew it was more complicated than that.

'Yes—well,' she ran a shaking hand over her forehead, 'I'm ready.' She glanced hesitantly towards the connecting door to Kerry's room.

'I'll explain to Kerry if you'd like to leave now,' Todd offered.

She darted him a grateful look. 'Thank you, Todd. And you, too, Mary.' She gave the housekeeper a quick hug before picking up one of the smaller cases and hurrying towards the door.

With the rest of her luggage under his arm, Todd

370

started to follow, then glanced back at Mary. 'When Kerry wakes up——'

The housekeeper smiled gently. 'I'll tell her you'll explain everything when you get back.'

Butterflies could fly away and never look back. Jill didn't feel very much like a butterfly. She doubted if she ever would again.

Taking her foot off the accelerator, she gently applied the brakes to ease the car around the curve in the snow-packed road. The Christmas-wrapped packages on the seat started to slip and she put out a hand to stop them. She didn't feel in the holiday spirit either. She just hoped that once she was home with her parents and brothers and sisters, she would catch the festive mood.

After the way she had moped around the house this past summer when she had left the ranch, her parents were entitled to expect some improvement in her disposition. They had been wonderfully understanding, although they couldn't really believe there was a man who wouldn't love their daughter. Of course, Jill hadn't told them the whole story. Kerry was the only one who came close to knowing all of it.

The car she was driving had been a consoling gesture from her parents. They had shrugged it off by saying that they were tired of making double trips back and forth to Helena to pick her up on the holiday vacations. They would not be too pleased, though, when they discovered she had made this trip without Kerry's company.

Her engagement to Todd was still on, even though Todd had transferred to Harvard and Kerry had remained in Helena. They had made the decision not to marry until Kerry had finished college, even though it meant a separation. Jill had never had the courage to inquire whether the waiting period had been Riordan's idea, although she had guessed that it was. His name was never mentioned unless by Jill.

Todd had flown back from Harvard to spend Christmas with Kerry. Jill had invited both of them to come home with her, but Todd had declined. He wanted to be certain to catch his flight back. With the unpredictability of winter storms, he didn't object to being snowbound at the airport so long as he wasn't stranded two hundred miles away from it. Naturally Kerry preferred to stay in Helena with him, especially after he had given her his mother's engagement ring.

Jill touched the beige tan cameo suspended by a delicate gold chain around her neck, Todd's Christmas present to her. It, too, had belonged to his mother – she remembered how startled she had been when he told her that. She had held it for long minutes, unwilling to put it around her neck.

'Does Riordan know you gave me this?' she had asked finally. A cold hand had closed over her heart to keep it from beating.

Shortly after Todd had arrived in Helena, he had driven to the ranch to see his brother and to select Kerry's engagement ring from his mother's jewellery.

'Yes, he knows,' Todd had answered quietly. His eyes had examined Jill's frozen expression. 'After I'd taken Kerry's ring from the box, I mentioned that I wanted to buy you a gift, so Riordan told me to pick out something I thought you might like from Mother's jewellery.'

Jill had forced a bright smile on to her taut lips. 'It's very lovely, and I do like it,' she said, fastening the cameo necklace around her neck. 'Are you and Kerry driving out to the ranch for Christmas day?'

'No, Jill, Kerry and I want a peaceful Christmas,' he had said with decided emphasis.

'I'm sure Sheena will keep him company,' Jill had shrugged, but a shaft of jealousy had drilled deep.

'She's gone to Palm Springs for the holidays. She came to see Riordan while I was there,' Todd had explained.

Later Jill had summoned the courage to ask if Riordan had given his approval of their engagement. It had seemed likely since Riordan had evidently permitted Todd to give Kerry their mother's ring.

Todd had breathed in deeply, a slightly closed look stealing into his expression. 'Let's just say that he's reconciled to the fact that he can't change my mind.'

Sighing heavily, Jill couldn't help wondering if Riordan hadn't relaxed his opposition to their engagement just a little bit. He might not have given his wholehearted approval, but at least he was not taking such a hard line against it.

And the necklace she wore, did it have any special significance? Was it an indirect and private way of apologising? Whoever said that hope sprang eternal certainly was right, Jill thought wryly. Here she was hoping for a miracle. Of course, Christmas is a miracle time, she reminded herself, so maybe it was only natural.

Christmas. It was a time for family gatherings and enormous dinners. Jill could visualise her own home with holly strung on evergreen branches all through the living room, dining room and hall. Her father would have mistletoe hung in every archway and from every light fixture. And her mother would have the socks they had used as children hung over the fireplace, waiting for Santa.

The tree would be gigantic, covered with tinsel, angel hair, and the ornaments that had become old friends over the years. Plates of Christmas candy and bowls of coloured popcorn balls would be all over the house, promising an extra five pounds of weight to anyone who dared to touch them. Logs would be in readiness in the fireplace, but a fire wouldn't be started until Christmas morning, after Santa Claus had safely made his visit.

That was Christmas to Jill.

Unbidden the question came—what was Christmas to Riordan? Todd had told her Riordan was in his teens when he had stopped accompanying his father to Helena to spend Christmas with his mother. How many lonely Christmasses had he spent in that big house without family and only Mara Rivers? No family and probably no decorations

Men didn't take the time to do such things on their own, and what would there have been to celebrate?

And what about that little twelve-year-old boy who had been forced to shoot his horse when it had broken its legs? That little boy who had grown into a man, a man who wouldn't give horses names in case he had to destroy one again. That same man was spending Christmas alone again this year. His own brother had chosen the company of the woman he loved over Riordan, just as their father had done.

Suddenly it didn't matter whether Todd's decision was warranted or not. It just seemed so totally unfair that Riordan was going to be alone again.

Jill turned into the first ploughed side-road she found and reversed her direction back the way she had come. A couple of miles back she had passed the crossroads intersection and the highway that would take her to the Riordan ranch. One of the packages on the seat contained a sweater for her father. With luck, it would fit Riordan. Another contained a handcrafted shawl she could give Mary.

His present would be a conciliatory gesture on her part. He might just meet her halfway. There was that eternal hope again! she smiled sadly. More than likely, Riordan would think it was another trick she was playing, a manoeuvre of some sort. But she didn't care. She simply had to see him.

The lane leading from the cleared county road to the ranch house had not been ploughed. Several sets of tracks ran over each other in the general direction of the buildings located on the other side of the meadow, presently out of sight behind the rise. Jill offered a silent prayer that she wouldn't get stuck as the car crunched over the tyre-packed snow.

The winter sun set early in the north country. It was barely past mid-afternoon and already there was a purpling pink cast to the snow-covered mountains. Jill refused to think about the rest of her drive home in the dark.

Stopping in front of the house nestled in the protective stand of snow-draped evergreens, it looked somehow bigger and emptier than she remembered. A tense excitement gripped her as she selected the packages from the rest and stepped out of the car.

At the front door, she hesitated, gathering her courage before she opened the door. Maybe it was a subconscious wish to catch Riordan unawares that had prompted her to enter without knocking, or maybe she had become accustomed to simply walking in after spending those fateful weeks in the house that summer.

The house was silently empty. A fire crackling in the entryway hearth would have made the house seem warm, but there was none. Slipping off her snowboots, Jill listened attentively for some sound of human occupation.

It suddenly occurred to her that Riordan might not even be here. He could be at one of the barns or at another section of the ranch altogether. That would only leave Mary Rivers. She would undoubtedly be in the kitchen. Jill slowly exhaled the breath she had been unconsciously holding. It was probably just as well that she hadn't seen Riordan, she decided, but she would speak to Mary.

The awesome silence of the house had her tip-toeing on the hardwood floor of the hall leading to the kitchen in the rear. As she drew closer, she caught the aroma of cooking and smiled. Mary was there.

Her hand was on the kitchen doorknob ready to turn it to open the door when she heard Riordan's voice come from inside the kitchen.

'I don't care what you're fixing. I told you I'm not hungry,' he snapped.

'Then have some coffee and stop grouching about like a grizzly,' Mary replied evenly.

'I am not grouching,' Riordan answered tightly.

'Snapping my head off every five minutes is not grouching?' the housekeeper inquired dryly. 'You either have a severe case of cabin fever or you're thinking about that girl. Which is it?'

Jill held her breath, unable to move until Riordan had answered. There was a heavy silence before he spoke in a cuttingly indifferent voice.

'What girl?'

'Jill, of course, as if you didn't know.'

'I wasn't thinking of her,' Riordan replied.

'Weren't you?' Mary countered. 'When are you going to give up and ask the girl to marry you?'

Jill's heart exploded against her ribcage, pounding so fiercely it seemed impossible they couldn't hear it.

There was a sudden scrape of a chair leg. 'That would be the height of absurdity!' he jeered. The pounding of her heart stopped almost abruptly.

'Why?'

'You know why, Mary,' Riordan sighed angrily. His cryptic statement was followed by a long pause as though he was waiting for the housekeeper to comment. Bitterness and contempt coated his next words. 'I remember one August when Mother made one of her unexpected departures. I was thirteen or fourteen at the time. Dad came in the house after saying goodbye to her, looking all hollow and beaten. I demanded that he go and get her and make her stay with us, but he said he couldn't use force to keep her or beg or bribe her to stay. The only thing he could do, he said, was to simply love her.'

'He was right, Riordan,' Mary agreed quietly.

'Right!' he returned with a scoffing laugh. 'In all the times she left him, I never saw Dad cry once—only when she died. Then he became half a man. When she was alive, you know how many winter evenings he sat in front of her portrait and how impossible it was to get him to leave that room when she died. No woman has a right to bring a man down like that. He was strong and intelligent, a giant, and she had no right to make a fool of him.'

'She loved him,' Mary said.

'She used him,' Riordan corrected grimly. 'If she'd loved him, she would have stayed here where she belonged.'

'But she never belonged here—I think that's something you were never able to understand. No matter much she loved your father, your mother would never have been happy on this ranch. It wasn't her environment. As much as your father loved her, didn't you ever wonder why he didn't move to the city to be with her?' Mary answered her own question. 'He would have been miserable because he didn't belong there. Their love for each other was the bridge between the two worlds, and it was a very strong one.'

'Like a migrating butterfly, Mother flew over that bridge every spring and left every fall.' His voice was savagely harsh. 'I will not be plunged into darkness for nine months of the year the way Dad was. I may have inherited his curse for falling in love with butterflies, but I will never marry one!'

The fragile hope that had been building inside Jill began to crumble. It was just as she had told herself last summer. Although Riordan was attracted to her, he also despised her violently.

'Butterflies,' Mary murmured with amused disbelief. 'You believe Jill is a butterfly?'

'Picture her in your mind, Mary,' he sighed bitterly. 'Her hair is as golden as the sun and her eyes are as big and as blue as the sky. She's so fragile, I could snap her in two with one hand. Men are drawn to her just like they were drawn to my mother.'

'Riordan, you're blind!'

'Oh, no,' he declared. 'I kept my eyes open all the time so I could see all the traps she laid for me.'

'Since when do butterflies have to lay traps?' Jill had to strain to hear the housekeeper's soft voice. 'Jill is very beautiful, but she isn't a butterfly. Look at the way she fought for her friend and stood up

379

to you. She's slender and supple like a willow, but not fragile.'

In the silence that followed, Jill's mind raced to assimilate Mary's words. Finally she came up with the same verdict. She was not a butterfly. She not only loved Riordan but she loved his home and life as well. She had never needed to feed on the admiration of others to survive as his mother had. Wild elation swept over her.

The silence was shattered by Riordan's snarl. 'You don't know what you're talking about!'

Long striding steps were carrying him to the hallway door where Jill stood. Suddenly she didn't want him to discover she had been there listening. She stepped hurriedly away from the door, intending to retreat to the front of the house, but it was too late as the door was yanked open.

Riordan stopped short.

The harsh lines of anger on his face changed to stunned surprise, but his features were nonetheless forbidding. Jill blinked at him uncertainly. This couldn't be the same man whose voice she had heard state that he loved her. There was not even a flicker of gladness in the wintry silver eyes at the sight of her.

'What are you doing here?' he demanded coldly.

Her fingers tightened convulsively on the packages in her arms. 'It's Christmas,' she offered in hesitant explanation.

His gaze slid to the gaily wrapped presents. 'Get out, Jill,' he said with the same freezing calm. 'I don't want anything from you.'

380

Chilled by his cold command, Jill swayed to carry out his order. Then a voice warned that this was her last chance. If she left him now, there would never be another.

'Did you——' She halted to chase the quiver from her voice. 'Did you mean it when you said you loved me?'

'You were listening?' A dark brow arched, arrogantly aloof. Jill nodded numbly. 'Yes, I meant it,' Riordan acknowledged, 'but it doesn't change anything.'

'It must,' she breathed fervently, taking a step towards him, then another, all the while anxiously searching his face for some indication of his love. 'I did try to trick you and manoeuvre you and do all those things you accused me of, but I never intended to let my own emotions become involved. Riordan, you must believe me. I mean, whoever heard of a butterfly coming back in the dead of winter?' She made a feeble attempt at a joke, but it failed miserably as he remained withdrawn. 'I never meant to fall in love with you. It just happened. I love you.'

He reached out and took the packages from her arms, flipped them on to a table in the hall, then gathered her to him, saying not a word and letting the blazing light in his eyes do all the talking. Covering her mouth with a hungry kiss, he lifted her off the floor and carried her into the living room.

It was much later before anything other than incoherent love words could be spoken. Jill was nestled against his shoulder, the long length of him stretched in a half-sitting position on the sofa. The thudding beat of his heart was beneath her head, the most blissful sound she had ever heard.

'Do you think she really loved him?' Riordan murmured.

Peering through the top of her lashes, Jill could see he was gazing at the portrait. 'I think she did. She gave him all the love she had.'

His arms tightened around her. 'And you, darling? Will you promise to give me all the love you have?'

'Yes,' she whispered achingly. Her fingers crept to his face, caressing the rugged features she loved so much. 'Oh, Riordan, that will be the easiest promise in the world to keep.'

'I'll probably be very jealous and possessive and you'll start to hate me,' he smiled wryly.

'Not any more than I shall be.' She outlined his hard, passionate mouth with her fingertip and sighed. 'I wish I didn't have to leave. Darling, please come home with me. We'll drive together and you can meet my family.'

He moved her hand away, tucking a hand under her chin and lifting her head so he could plant a hard kiss on her lips. 'I don't intend to let you out of my sight.' His low voice vibrated with emotion, delicious shivers ran over Jill's skin at its intensity. 'We'll get married while we're at your parents' and be husband and wife before the New Year comes.'

Jill glowed. 'Are you sure you want to marry me?'

'Sure?' His grey eyes, warm and vibrantly alive,

caressed her face. 'Did you think I intended to make another cheap proposition? I admit it was cheap, darling. But that morning I came to your room I knew I had to have you. What I didn't realise was how completely I wanted you—for ever. That was something I learned in the last six months—painfully, I might add. Besides, I have to marry you to exorcise your ghost from this house. You don't know what it's like to have you haunting my bedroom every night.'

'I think I might have an idea,' she murmured, snuggling deeper in his arms, unbelievably content. 'I can hardly wait to tell Kerry that we're getting married.'

'I never expected to beat Todd to the altar,' Riordan chuckled.

Her eyes had been half-closed, savouring the dreamlike sensation of being in his arms and loved by him. Her lashes sprang open suddenly, tension darkening the blue shade of her eyes.

'Riordan, what about college?' she breathed uncertainly. 'I only have a half a year to go to get my diploma.'

He stiffened for an instant, then untangled her from his arms and rolled to his feet, walking to the fireplace. His hand rubbed the back of his neck, ruffling the jet black hair curling near his collar.

'You don't want me to go back, do you?' she said, sitting up and gazing at his broad shoulders sadly.

'No, I don't want you to go back!' Riordan snapped savagely. 'I've just found you. How could I possibly want to let you go!'

Jill swallowed tightly. She knew the torment he was going through. A knife was twisting in her own heart. She could guess how much deeper the pain went for him.

'It's all right.' She lowered her head, her tawny gold hair swinging forward to hide a selfish disappointment. 'I'll quit. I don't mind, really.'

'Like hell you will!' He pivoted sharply towards her. 'You'll finish college. I'm not going to let you quit.'

'You don't know what you're saying.' Her head jerked up to stare unbelievingly into his unrelenting gaze.

'It's only for a few months. I'll ... I'll move into town.'

'You'd hate it,' Jill shook her head.

'I could stand it.' He walked back to the sofa, his hands digging into her shoulders as she pulled her to her feet. 'But I couldn't stand being without you, not for a day.'

'Nor I you.' She cupped his face in her hands. 'But I won't let you leave this ranch. I love you too much to ask that of you, Riordan.' She breathed in sharply, a compromise suddenly offering itself. 'I know what I'll do. I'll transfer my credits to the university in Dillon and drive back and forth every day from the ranch.'

His mouth tightened grimly. 'And drive me insane with worry about you out alone on the roads!'

Jill slipped her arm around his neck, lifting her face invitingly towards his. 'But I'll be home every night, darling.'